WASHOE COUNTY LIBRARY
3 1235 01806 8028

I0046857

the WAKING

the WAKING

mike NICHOLS

wm

william MORROW

An Imprint of HarperCollins*Publishers*

This is a work of fiction. The characters, incidents, and dialogues are products of the author's imagination and are not to be construed as real. Any resemblance to actual persons, living or dead, is entirely coincidental.

Grateful acknowledgment is made to reprint an excerpt from "Tulips" from *Ariel* by Sylvia Plath. Copyright © 1962 by Ted Hughes. Copyright renewed. Reprinted by permission of HarperCollins Publishers Inc.

HarperCollins books may be purchased for educational, business, or sales promotional use. For information please write: Special Markets Department, HarperCollins Publishers Inc., 10 East 53rd Street, New York, NY 10022.

FIRST EDITION

Printed on acid-free paper

Library of Congress Cataloging-in-Publication Data
Nichols, Michael, 1963–
The waking / Michael Nichols.—1st ed.
p. cm.
ISBN 0-06-273423-7 (alk. paper)
I. Title.
PS3614.I35 W35 2002
813'.6—dc21 2001051742

02 03 04 05 06 JTC/RRD 10 9 8 7 6 5 4 3 2 1

for JANE

I didn't want any flowers, I only wanted
To lie with my hands turned up and be utterly empty.
How free it is, you have no idea how free—
The peacefulness is so big it dazes you.
And it asks nothing, a name tag, a few trinkets.
It is what the dead close on finally; I imagine them
Shutting their mouths on it, like a Communion tablet.

—SYLVIA PLATH, "TULIPS"

part ONE

1.

It was ten degrees outside, and I wore nothing on my feet but socks and an old pair of loafers that had a small hole in them. I had no hat or gloves, just an old, threadbare sport coat, clutched together at the lapels as I ran. My toes were numb already by the time I'd stumbled halfway up the river. My ears, my fingers, the flesh on my cheeks, were all gone, too, as if they'd somehow hardened and become separate from the rest of me.

The secret, of course, is to strive for oblivion. There can be some real comfort in that.

It's only if you choose to make it back to the warmth that you pay for the unfeeling.

It took me only minutes, gasping and wheezing for breath, to reach the spot in the river immediately underneath the small clearing in the woods where much of Sandy's family is buried. From the middle of the frozen river, I could see, in the distance as I ran past, the top of an ornate monument that marked some of the graves.

Her great-great-grandparents were there, under an epitaph that had already faded. Near them, under more modest stones, were great-uncles and far-removed aunts, Sandy's grandparents, and, already, some distant cousins, too.

Last in line, unseen from the river though I knew it was there, sat the small, dark, polished gravestone of Sandy's father. He was only fifty-nine years old when he went, and Elizabeth, who is Sandy's mother and a practical and committed sort, put her name on that stone as well. Sandy's own plot, empty and covered still in snow, was ten feet away, just off to one side.

Sandy and I were different. I grew up in a little bungalow with two brothers I no longer know, and parents whose graves I cannot bear to see. She, on the other hand, made her own private procession beside that same river and to her father's stone almost each and every day. An only child who grew up alone and in affluence, she kept him with her, drew him in; just as he drew her to him as well.

I knew of Sandy when I was young, as almost any Catholic boy who lived in Droughton and went to her church would. She was a child of privilege dressed in Sunday finery who seemed part of the bygone ritual of another age. I think now, especially now, that I loved her long before I met her and there was a time, I know, when she felt of me just the same.

Do you find that romantic? I once considered it that way myself, evidence of some ethereal bond or fate. I think I thought it even as I ran to her that night. Today, I will confess with all that has happened, I wonder if we imagined in each other beautiful things that, in a real world, could never be conceived.

We did not date when we were young, when the differences of a few blocks and more than a few dollars were the differences of entire worlds. It was only later, after I went out with Haley, the woman who would become her law partner, that we met formally at all.

For me, the attraction was instantaneous, almost to the point of cliché, the kind of thing that quickly obliterates one's past. In Sandy I saw all the things I'd never known: unbridled confidence, intelligence, compassion, a sophisticated sort of beauty—things that penury, I thought, had robbed from the less fortunate. That it was all interspersed with periods of deep depression and self-recrimination only made it all the more mysterious.

Sandy, like generations of Crosses before her, grew up along that river in a house that was magnificent. It was a white, three-story Victorian surrounded by hundred-foot pines her great-great-grandfather had planted. The trees provided anchor and shade, Sandy often said. Stability. Succor. While all else changed and turned from one season to the next, the trees stayed still, never wavering, always green, standing sentry over the oldest and most prominent house in town.

It was a grand house to live in during the warmer months, when the French doors opened up onto a spacious terrace that overlooked the green river valley below. In the spring and summer the sounds of lumbering barges wafted up with the smells of lilac bushes and freshly mowed grass.

Like all serious homes in this part of the world, however, the Cross House was built for winter. It was then, when the solid workmanship and stately efficiency was left bare, unmitigated by the burgeoning shrubbery and manicured lawns, that she was at her best. Built long before the invention of fuel-efficient furnaces and double-paned thermal windows, she was dominated by fireplaces. Not small, ornamental fireplaces like the ones in the newer jerry-built houses on the south side, but fireplaces with character and purpose. The one in the living room was large enough for a full-grown man to walk into without bowing his head. Others—in the study, the bedrooms, even the kitchen—were smaller, but intricate in detail.

We were married not long after Sandy graduated from law school and, because her father died within a week of the ceremony, immediately returned home from our honeymoon. Until then, I had gotten by on a bartending job at a local microbrewery, serving pale ales and martinis to some of the same kids I had grown up with and telling myself it would be foolish to take a real job in a place where I had never been certain I wanted to settle down.

After the funeral all that changed. Sandy helped her mother with the estate and took a position in the local public defender's office. I, uncertain what else to do, took a low-paying job as a reporter at the local paper. My plans to rent a large and airy apartment for us above a downtown shop seemed almost excessive to me until Elizabeth learned of what she called "Will's game." Within days, she announced she was moving permanently to Arizona, where she spent her winters anyway, and wanted to sell us the Cross family home. I hesitated, but Sandy, having grown up with just that expectation, was enthralled. She told me it would be silly not to succumb.

"Let's at least pay her what it's worth," I said.

Sandy chuckled.

"Yeah, Will, we could buy the garage. Course, it doesn't have any plumbing but, hey, we can just pee in the flower beds."

In the end, we bought it, but at a greatly reduced price that made it seem more like charity than a business transaction. The deal was such that, even on relatively modest incomes, we could easily make the mortgage payments every month.

Having children was not as easy. Before we were married, Sandy went on the pill briefly but it made her bleed and left her, she felt, bloated. The thought of sex, she said, was repulsive.

For some time, we used various other types of birth control, but it was inconvenient and after we married we used nothing at all. It was not really a choice or a decision. It was just convenience, and we expected sooner or later that Sandy would get pregnant. When she didn't, we eventually became concerned and went to a doctor who said Sandy had a mild case of endometriosis, not something that should cause infertility.

"The best advice I can give you is not to worry about it," said the doctor, a young specialist who wore tennis shoes and a short-sleeved shirt. "Some people just take longer to conceive, and no one really knows why. There are plenty of couples—basically healthy couples—taking years to have a child. Even more. I don't see any reason it should take you that long. Okay?"

After another couple years of trying unsuccessfully, Sandy decided the doctor had been wrong and went to get another opinion. She found a specialist in Minneapolis and made her trips there on Mondays, driving over the river in the afternoon and heading northwest for tests I came only vaguely to understand. It wasn't an inordinately long drive and she always arrived back home early in the afternoon. If she was going to be late, she called.

It was one of those Mondays in March, over a year ago now, when I pulled into the driveway and found her car was not there. I presumed that she had gone to work out, but found quickly when I walked through the back door that that was not the case. Her green nylon workout bag remained on a wooden peg in the entryway where it had been for several weeks.

As I stepped out of the cold, a wave of warm air hit me and I smelled the familiar fragrance of the Cross House—the residue of burnt cedar and oak, of smoldering ash and poplar. There was a reassurance to it, an intimacy. It was the smell of a home—and a family—with a history. It was a house that lived with you and became a part of you, sucked you in and changed you just by the fact that you slept in its beds and knew where the wine was in the cellar.

Like most old houses, it required constant attention and, although neither Sandy nor I was mechanically inclined, we had learned the necessity of tinkering. All sorts of Phillips screwdrivers, regular screwdrivers, pliers, and other tools, nothing more complicated, we kept handy in a drawer in the kitchen. Right above that drawer, resting on the counter, was an answering machine and I could see from where I stood that Sandy had not called.

"Sandy," I yelled out into the darkness, not expecting a response. "You here?"

It was the irrational call of a concerned, if not exactly frightened, husband. There was no reason to believe she was home, no footprints along the snow-dusted walk, no lights on in any of the silent rooms. Still, I yelled again.

"It's me!"

Cricket, our old, mottled terrier, gingerly padded through the kitchen and peered into the entryway.

"Good girl," I said. "Where's your buddy?"

Sandy was an independent person and lived a life quite apart from me during the day. But at night, even when her job demanded twelve-hour days, she would almost invariably come home—and certainly call if she couldn't. She would spend an hour eating and chatting in front of the fireplace in the living room and then, if she had to, head back to work. If she didn't, we would sit and read or talk until nine or nine-thirty, then work our way into the bedroom.

When she didn't answer, I checked the mail. There were some magazines and bills and a letter from Elizabeth. By the time I'd taken a shower and made a fire, it was almost seven-thirty, and there was still no sign of her. After calling her office and getting no answer, I walked out to the garage to make sure her car was not inside. Someone had evidently pulled into the driveway after me because there were fresh tire tracks in the snow, but no car. I don't know if it was that oddity that worried me, or the simple fact she was not home, but I conceded to myself my heightening concern. I went back inside, sat down at the kitchen counter, and dialed the police. I knew I was manifesting my paranoia, but there was no harm. I was only calling Deiter.

Deiter—no one used his first name and there were people who had worked with him for twenty years who didn't even know it—had a deep, resonant voice that matched his height and bulk and he liked to joke that he used the King's English so no one could tell on the phone what color he was. That had led to some uncomfortable moments for a few of Droughton's old-timers who would call up the police station to complain about the influx of young blacks moving in from Milwaukee and Minneapolis.

"Nooo," he'd say, leading them on.

"Yes!" they'd assure him, launching into tirades of racist profanity destined to remain unheard. Deiter would have by then silently placed the phone on his desk and, as they yammered on, walked away to get a cup of coffee. If they called back, he would route the calls to a disconnected number until, indignant with frustration, they would finally give up.

Deiter, of course, had more proactive ways of dealing with such things as well. More than one Droughtonite, for reasons unfathomable to them, found themselves pulled over for speeding, or for a defective taillight, or not wearing a seat belt, time and time and time again. And more than one questionable remark or action or vote by a local politician or public official had mysteriously made its way into the paper. Deiter, whom I had met years earlier when I'd first gotten a job at the *Courier*, was, unbeknownst to anyone else in town, my very best source.

I got his voice mail. "You in?" I said nonsensically.

Calls to Deiter's personal number, I had double-checked long before, were not recorded by the same devices that taped most other department calls. We could communicate this way in confidence.

Deiter was my friend, but he was also a cop and, suddenly, I felt funny about bothering the police simply because my wife was late coming home. I almost hung up. He was a workaholic and had better things to do than chat with me.

"I'm a little worried about Sandy," I finally stammered. "It's probably nothing. She's a couple of hours late and I haven't heard from her but I'm sure it's nothing. Gimme a call when you get a minute if you're still in. . . . I'm gonna see if you're around . . ."

I pressed zero and got a dispatcher, who said Deiter was working and promised to page him. Then I hung up and looked for what must have been the fourth or fifth time on the refrigerator and the kitchen counter for a note. I looked also in the bathroom to make sure that her toothbrush was still there, that she hadn't gone away for the night at the last minute to take a deposition. Or, it crossed my mind, simply packed up and left.

Her toothbrush was there, along with shelves and shelves of soaps and creams, lipsticks and rouge. There were powders and pastes, all manner of shampoos and conditioners and moisturizers, tubes and bottles with names I didn't recognize that did things I couldn't fathom. I teased her that she could have opened a retail store with all of those supplies.

Sandy had not been a beautiful child. She was chubby and carried her baby fat all the way through the first years of high school. Thick glasses and twenty-eight months of braces—she had counted—had not helped. Blessed with a wealthy family and a quick, sharp-edged mind, she had been deprived, she thought, of the more basic gifts.

She thought wrong.

There was, it became evident as time passed by, nothing plain about Sandy. She had dark hair with a bit of a curl and she could never decide whether to keep it long or short. She would commit herself to growing it down her back, then, when it reached her shoulder blades, drive past the hairdresser one day and, for no other reason than she felt compelled, stop and have it all lopped off. Her brown eyes dominated her face and, from the side, were like big luminous marbles suspended in pure white cream. They opened so wide it sometimes surprised me she could keep them in that position.

Sandy's lips were thin, but malleable, and when she smiled one side stretched upward so that it seemed to pull the other over as well. Her nose was straight, almost aquiline, slightly freckled, and modest in size. Her chin was dimpled and strong, but not protuberant. It was a face capable of a million different moods or expressions, and I think I had seen them all.

As high school progressed, her weight began to dissipate and she got a pair of contacts to complement her straight, white teeth. It was then that she began to paint her nails and perm her rich, dark-chocolate hair, began to experiment with makeup, never wearing too much, but always enough to make sure no one ever forgot about her again. With a child's complexion she carried up through her thirtieth birthday the previous spring, Sandy Cross was a woman of uncommon gifts.

She was already two hours late, and a vague unease metamorphosed into the first twinge of panic. I knew Sandy, knew everything, I was sure, about her, and I knew, with a disquieting certitude, that she was not coming home. I put on my sport coat and shoes—boots would take too long—to look briefly around the outside of the house, made one last irrational search of the inside for a note, a clue, maybe a missing suitcase, and began to head for the door.

Then the phone rang.

"Will?" said Deiter, almost whispering. His voice was solicitous and soft. Full of pity.

"Will?"

They'd found Sandy's car, he said, beneath the cliffs just north of the house. It had traveled in the air almost all the way out to the banks of the river.

2.

The Cross property abutted the public land where Sandy had gone over the bluff and I could see, as I hissed and wheezed and blew billows of warm breath into the cold air above the river, searchlights shining down into the trees. A helicopter was lifting off.

I ran another quarter mile, my chest heaving, until I came almost to the point where the old Percy Avenue Bridge cantilevered out over the water. There amid a stand of pine and oak stood a small cadre of police and rescue personnel.

"Where is she?" I sputtered. "Is she okay?"

I knew this area. There were twenty or thirty yards between the road and the cliff up above. And off to one side, behind a thicket of trees, was a place that was used as a lovers' lane. Officially, in local history books and maps, it was called Promontory Park, but local wags had shortened it; and "going to the prom" had long meant more in Droughton than it did everywhere else.

People were not moving here the way I expected. They were standing around, talking, as though it were some sort of subdued cocktail party. It seemed to me there should have been sirens and lots of people, more of a crowd. I looked for dark splotches of blood in the trampled snow. But there was none. This, I realized, was the sad aftermath.

As I got closer, someone in a snowmobile suit grabbed me and I saw a flash of charred, silver metal flickering in the lights. Sandy's Mazda was almost directly ahead of me and it was nothing, really, but a burned shell. We'd bought it at a little dealership outside Minneapolis, and for several years buffed and shined it, took care of the dents, didn't allow anyone to smoke inside. Sandy had traded an old Corolla to get it. Had spent a good hour asking the salesman questions about everything from how the compact disc player worked to what we could expect for highway mileage.

"I'm her husband!" I cried, but still the arms held me tightly and a voice told me to wait. I asked again if she was all right.

"She was thrown from the car. There's some pretty bad internal injuries and, apparently, some to the head, too," said the voice. He was a cop.

"Where is she?" I said, trying to catch my breath.

"At the hospital already. . . . How did you get down here?"

I could see that the car had probably landed on its front bumper. It was upright now, sitting half embedded in snow and brush. The hood had been pushed up into the front seat. All the side windows were smashed out and the seats were oddly askew. The dashboard was still in place. Good, I thought. There would have been room for her legs.

The arms eased up on me and, almost in hyperventilation, I took a few slow steps to one side for a better angle. The windshield had been knocked out either by the impact or, I found myself imagining, from Sandy being thrown right through. One of the doors was open and everything was covered with a thin veneer of ice.

Water, shot in a stream from the cliff above apparently, had been used to put out the flames, and in spots—near the rearview mirror, underneath the wheel wells—small icicles had formed. As one patrolman or another flashed his light on the wreck and the trees and brush around it, countless miniature stalactites glimmered and flickered in the night, and I remember resisting the thought that it was really quite beautiful.

After another moment, one of the arms pulled me back slowly by the sleeve.

"What happened?" I asked, trying to suppress the panic. "Do you know what happened?"

"We got a call at about six-thirty saying there was a fire down here. Apparently the car exploded when it hit."

"Was she burned?"

"No. She was thrown away from it."

There was a time when I knew most of the police officers in Droughton. But in the decades since Sandy and I were kids, things had changed. As the economy boomed and the high-tech companies prospered, the Twin Cities exploded to the south and east. Much of what we had known was now unrecognizable. Droughton was no longer a small city. The yuppies and corporate climbers were using old river homes and cabins as year-round residences. Small subdivisions began to sprout up out of the farm fields, then bigger ones. Droughton had gone from a small place of less than 60,000 to over three times that. Outlying areas prospered and a small high-tech corridor with computer and telecommunications firms added significant sums to the tax base. The city, at the same time, developed a much poorer, urban core. Poverty, in some neighborhoods, became entrenched; serious crime was suddenly quite common. Police were hired by the dozens, and often without adequate background checks.

There was a time when police officers in town had to go through rigorous physical and psychological exams. Now, partly out of fear of lawsuits charging discrimination from those who might not pass and partly because low pay meant few applicants anyway, there were frequent complaints about lowered standards.

"We had to go a hundred yards over just to find a path down here," he said. "And the face was too steep to get her up. Had to have the helicopter come down and land on the river."

"She missed the turn?"

He hesitated. "I don't know," he said. "Give me a minute here and then we'll talk."

He let go of me and started to turn away. But I grabbed his shoulder.

"About what?"

He had a full head of blond hair pushed back from his forehead under a hood, and as he talked he constantly raised his fingers up to his brow, which sat atop gray eyes. Above his mustache was a prominent Roman nose. Below it, teeth that were so straight I suspected they were false. He had an athleticism even in the features of his face. One suspected that his body, inside the winter coat, had the musculature of a weight lifter.

"Nothing," he said, dismissingly. "Let's get to the hospital. We'll worry about it later."

"Worry about what?" I could hear my voice getting louder and I could see I was trying his patience as I enveloped us in the clouds of my frozen breath. He had a look on his face that told me he was about to say something he didn't really want to.

"What?" I repeated.

"The car's quite a ways from the base of the cliff," he said finally. "And there don't appear to be any skid marks up above. . . . Course, those could be hard to see."

"What's that mean?"

"Look," he said, shifting the weight from one foot to another. "Let's not talk about this now."

He started to turn again.

"I want to talk about this now!"

He stared at me and nodded, almost imperceptibly, and I grabbed his arm, which perturbed him.

"Okay," he said, evincing a great effort to keep calm. "Was your wife having any problems?"

"Problems? . . . She didn't have any problems," I said slowly, nursing the implication, feeling it fester.

"Financial problems?"

"No."

Sandy had more money than someone on a cop's salary could possibly imagine.

"Marital?"

A plume of steam, warm breath frozen by the night air, flowed from my mouth.

"What's your name again?" I had not asked previously.

"Czubak."

"Look, Officer Czubak—"

"Detective—"

"Do you really think . . . ?" Here I stopped.

"Where's your boss?" I said, turning away.

He pointed to a man about fifteen yards away and, suddenly, I realized it was Deiter. He was on a cell phone, talking to someone, holding an accident report form in his gloved hand. I moved toward him.

"Deiter . . . ," I was saying.

He met me halfway, and clasped my arm, tightly. Then held it. Steam, his own, was rising up from the mouthpiece, dissolving into darkness. After a moment, he let go of me, held a finger up and motioned for me to wait.

"Just a second," he said, eyes open wide as he listened to whatever the person on the other end of the phone was saying to him. Czubak was behind me, like a schoolboy rival waiting for the attention of the teacher and, irritated, I turned to the side to wait as Deiter backed away a little and continued his conversation.

I could see from where I was that the blackened glove compartment was open, and its contents, those that had not burned—some old pens, a windshield scraper, the remains of a flashlight—had spilled out. In the dim light, I could see Sandy's keys still dangling from the ignition.

"Deiter!" I urged him in a low voice, feeling the waves of panic starting to rise up inside me again. "Deiter!"

But he held me off.

What I felt then was unlike anything I've felt before or since.

It was amorphous and expansive and it rose up in my throat like yellow bile. I don't know if it was fear or sorrow or maybe just the ineffable sickness and horror of sudden realization.

"Yeah," I heard Deiter say into his radio as he turned away from me, trying to shield me from the words. "It looks like a suicide attempt."

3.

That night it snowed. Not much of it seemed to hit the ground at first. The winds were strong and forceful and pushed it almost horizontally across the streets and fields so that one imagined it would never actually touch down, just keep circling the globe until spring came and melted it.

By the time it stopped—what seemed like days later—Sandy had been moved to the critical care unit and placed in a bed by a window. She could not know it, but in the afternoon the dull, yellow light would shine in through the frame and create a little rectangular box full of dust motes that moved slowly across her stone-still body. First it would illuminate her feet, one of which was enclosed in a cast, the other covered with a pink booty that Haley had placed there. Next, it would warm her abdomen, then move up across her chest to her face. Almost every inch of her was either entombed in plaster or wrapped in gauze. Wires and tubes shot in and out like so many roots to a tree. When the sun shone directly on her head, I was struck—as if I had not seen her in ages—by how gray her hair had become. I knew that she'd lost a lot of color, but I suddenly realized that her roots were almost pure white.

Sandy had started pulling long gray strands out of her scalp when she was still in high school, first one or two along the sides, then dozens. Then, one day when she was home from college out east, she succumbed. Too embarrassed to buy coloring down at Hasberger's Drug Store, she sent away to a small boutique in New York City. Forever after, once every month or so, it would arrive in a small pink box with a bow, a package of chocolate-brown dye and a glass bottle of clear, scented shampoo that the package said was supposed to smell like pear nectar. It was called Inamorata.

When I returned after going home for supper one of those first nights, I believe it was Tuesday, I brought the bottle of dye from Sandy's bathroom back with me. I asked one of the nurses if, when Sandy got a little better, she would give me a hand with it but the nurse just put a hand on my shoulder and, emitting a small breath, did not answer. Later in the night I asked another, and when I got the same sort of nonresponse, I decided to ask one of the doctors who came into her room.

"Will," he said softly. "Sandy does not need colored hair."

He was an older Asian man by the name of Kerry Tsau, and he had a very dignified, quiet demeanor that made it hard not to listen. He had known Sandy's father and perhaps that gave him the license, or the obligation, to be even more forthright and personal than usual. As he talked he gently lifted me up out of a chair by the elbow and pulled me close, as though what he had to say would be too difficult for anyone else—even Sandy—to hear.

"She has little," he said, "if any, brain function."

He had in his speech an exaggerated and utterly clear enunciation, an overcompensation for a slight accent that still attached itself subtly to certain sounds and words. It gave one the impression he had thought deeply about each utterance, parsed each sentence before he spoke it, and said nothing he did not mean and know.

"There is really no likelihood," he said, "that she will ever be able to eat or drink or even go to the bathroom on her own. You ask me to be honest, and I am sorry, but that is all I can be. . . . I am sorry. You should not worry about colored hair."

Sandy had been on a ventilator from the time she entered the hospital Monday night, and it was the ventilator along with the feeding tube, he said, that kept her alive.

"So, you're telling me she is brain-dead?" I said.

"That is a very imprecise term. But she has severe, extensive damage to parts of what people often refer to as the higher brain, the part that controls speech, thought, memory, consciousness—irreversible damage."

"What's left then?"

"It is hard to say. The damage is extensive, as I have said. She was without oxygen for a prolonged period of time. There is activity in the brain stem, although it is difficult to say how much. Without the ventilator, it is unlikely she would continue to respire."

"To breathe?"

"To breathe. She would, in all likelihood, stop breathing."

His grip on my elbow tightened till it almost hurt.

"And with the respirator?"

"She could live indefinitely."

"And could she regain some function?"

"As I said, there is extensive damage caused by the trauma of the accident. In my opinion, she has lost all cognitive functions."

"She'll never think."

The doctor nodded. "I'm sorry," he said. "There is no good way to put it. Once the neurons of the brain are destroyed, they can never be regenerated to any significant extent. She will remain in what we call a persistent vegetative state without any self-awareness or response, at least any purposeful one, to external stimuli."

"You're saying she's just a body," I murmured.

He started to speak, but hesitated. "Mr. Dunby—"

"Will."

"Will—"

"What?"

"What constitutes a person," he said, seeming to contemplate his own words, "is something I cannot answer."

He directed me down into the chair and placed a firm hand on my shoulder as I sat down.

"You should consider, when you think you can, disconnecting the respirator," he said, never averting his gaze from me for even a moment. His eyes were brown, with large, dark bags underneath and he looked exhausted. For some reason I wondered if he ever had time to see his family.

"We will talk again later," he said.

I don't remember much else about that night other than that as I was about to leave a nurse walked up to me and handed me a large plastic bag with the jewelry Sandy had been wearing. Plus a set of keys. I murmured an acknowledgment, accepted them without really looking, the artifacts of a life. When I got home I placed the jewelry in Sandy's jewelry box in the bathroom and realized, as I pulled the keys out of the bag as well, that they were not Sandy's. Sandy's keys, I remembered, had been left in the ignition of the car. Those that I held in my hand were on two little key chains linked together. One of them, I now noticed, had keys marked "House" and "Barn." The other set was for a car.

I had not slept or even eaten much for days, and a stultifying numbness seemed to infuse my arms and legs and extend upward toward my neck and head. It was then that I heard a barely audible gasp and I wondered for a moment if it had really come from me. I reached out with my right hand and, suddenly collapsing, hit my head on the side of the vanity.

I realized, as I lay on the floor a moment later, that I had passed out. And when I pulled my left hand out in front, away from my head, I found it covered with a surprising amount of blood. I had cut myself quite severely. There were no towels nearby so I reached up for a white, terry cloth bathrobe that Sandy had given me as a Christmas gift. I tried to pull it down off a hook, but a searing pain shot through my forehead and forced me back down. When I opened my eyes the second time it took me a few moments to focus, and when I did all I remember seeing was my right hand lying out in front of me, fingers tightly curled around those keys.

Sandy's mom flew in from Phoenix that evening and I picked her up at the airport. I have only a vague recollection of that, of looking for her as she came through one of the small portable tunnels where, at the end, young wives with their children waited eagerly and embraced their husbands with great fervor, kissed them on the lips when they finally appeared, and caressed the back of their trousers when they thought no one was looking.

Elizabeth Cross was a woman of considerable stoicism who kept her emotions well in check. Even before Sandy's father died, it was Elizabeth who kept the family and the medical practice, and even her husband himself, together. And perhaps because it was so uncharacteristic of her—perhaps because it so shocked and transformed me, made me realize the enormity of our tragedy—I remember mostly her uncontrollable sobbing. It came in the form of great, tumultuous, almost violent heaves. I held her hand and in the frozen parking lot of the Droughton County Airport tried to explain what I myself did not want to believe.

"I'm just telling you what they're saying," I said. "I don't know what to think."

"I know," she said, sobbing. "I can't believe it. I know."

The next morning, still only a few days after the accident, I signed several sets of papers, then walked to the chapel on the hospital's third floor. Elizabeth was a lapsed Catholic, but she knelt in a pew in the front row of the small, darkened room and clenched her hands in tight, anguished fists. I knelt down next to her, wondered about the presumptions one must make to pray after so long an absence, and got no further before I heard her whisper softly in my ear.

"I think," she said, "it's time."

Together, we walked to the elevator and rode it three flights to Sandy's room on the sixth floor. Kerry Tsau was there with a hospital chaplin, who performed the last rites and said several prayers for the repose of Sandy's soul. Then he stepped aside.

I felt, that afternoon, I suppose, all the reflections and feelings of a lifetime. Grief. Anger. Fear. Compassion. Relief. Love. All of the things one imagines—yes, imagines—when one tries to conceive of such scenarios. I will tell you, I will admit to you, that I had imagined what would happen, had tried to imagine it long before Sandy had her accident even. I imagined it, I suppose, the way anyone does, the way a superstitious man would imagine, create, caress his talisman, his charm, his way of averting the worst of what he fears and abhors. I feared that day and hoped that it would not come. And when it did, I did not cry or wail. I only felt then that it could not be true, and that I had never imagined it at all.

We each kissed Sandy, Elizabeth on her forehead, me on her cheek and then her lips. It surprised me how cold and hard they were. Then we waited for one last sign. A blink of the eyes, a gasp from the silent mouth, even just a quiver in the fine, pale skin where some bandages had been removed. There was nothing.

When he did it, it seemed to be without warning. For all the prelude and preparation, there seemed to be no moment of pause, no momentary cessation, no hesitation on his part before Kerry Tsau stopped the ventilator. I had expected some final salvo, some symbol, some tangible mark, but there was none of that. It was like a burial. One keeps waiting for them to lower the casket, to toss the dirt and cover the dead, for some finality. Instead, there are prayers and words, more prayers and words, and then the funeral director says: "This service is ended. You may return to your cars at your own leisure."

There is nothing, really, so very different from the moment before. The people stand still in a semicircle in the late afternoon sun. They do not turn to go, at least not yet. The casket rests atop the earth. Everything looks the same.

I am one of the lingerers. I stay and watch and wait. I see the people approach the casket, shiny and smooth, and touch it with their quivering fingers. I see them dab their eyes. I linger and I watch. And even that is not good enough for me. I need to see the casket lowered.

Elizabeth turned away, sobbing. She had seen what she needed to see. I reached out and touched her arm as she left the room, but she did not respond. Sandy was her only child.

I lingered, hoping to her God that Sandy would not go yet, asking too that she would. Pleading that she would not linger in some amorphous state of limbo, neither here nor there, not really present at all, but still here next to us like an old hairy-faced lady dreaming dreams of years and times when no one lived, no one at least that lives still.

I stayed. I stayed and watched and waited for Sandy's final breaths. I waited there forever, still as polished granite, silent as a gravestone. But the casket never fell. The faint and gentle undulation of Sandy's chest never ceased.

Sandy breathed that evening, and she breathed that night. She breathed gently and steadily into that night until I could no longer watch, until I fell into a fitful sleep on the chair by her side and dreamed myself.

And when I finally awoke, she breathed still. I lingered for hours, and so did she. But Sandy's coffin did not fall. She lay inside. I knew that. But it did not fall. Sandy breathed. And I think—no, I know—that, but for me, Sandy would breathe still.

That is what I want to tell you. That, here, now, with what follows, is what I need you to know.

4.

In the beginning when she first got her law license, Sandy worked out of a small, cramped office in the basement of the Droughton County Courthouse with about half a dozen other underpaid, overworked public defenders. Most, like her, took the job right out of law school when money meant a lot less than ideals. And most, unlike her, lasted two or three years. She lasted five.

Her first year she spent representing small-time thieves, prostitutes, and drug addicts, people who as often as not, she liked to say, were victims—usually of their own inadequacies and mistakes, but victims nonetheless. Later, as she gained seniority, her clients were of a different ilk. A tireless and passionate advocate, she was tabbed to represent murderers and rapists, perverts and impenitents of the worst kind. Quite often, they resisted her counsel. Some swore at her; others threatened. Despite the ingrates, however, Sandy only rarely became disillusioned or despondent. She sympathized and empathized, loved to get on the other side of a self-righteous prosecutor and poke holes in his shining white, prelapsarian world.

Born with all the advantages of wealth, Sandy had none of the usual preconceptions. Instead of siding with the establishment, assuming that success and accomplishment were always earned, she came to assume the opposite: that they were not. Conversely, those who failed, or faltered, were almost always to be forgiven.

"People make mistakes," she would say, "sometimes serious mistakes, and it isn't always because they're evil or bad."

"Well," I'd argue, "sometimes I don't care why. I just care if it happened. Some things are right and some are wrong."

"Yeah, and sometimes it's not so easy to tell the difference."

This was more than an argument about the law. This was, in time, an argument Sandy used to preserve our marriage.

"I'm human," she would say, time and again, repeating it over and over through long, cold winter nights when I would sleep in one of the guest rooms, and she would come to try and draw me back. It was her mantra, but also her siren call, and it worked. People falter, she told me. She believed that men—and women—carry a lot of sin around with them, that it kind of flows in the blood along with the little corpuscles. I, if I wanted to stay at all, at least had to hold out some possibility of acknowledging the same.

That I did not somehow find out about the affair sooner surprised even Sandy, I think, who once accused me of being "overly attuned to the minutiae of life."

"The guy who has spreadsheets on the relative costs of romaine, Boston, and iceberg lettuce," she once called me.

"I know," I replied, "I should have just given the maid a calculator when I was a kid."

"We didn't have a maid," she said.

"Bullshit."

"Well, not one that lived here."

I was, it was true, far more in tune with our finances, how much we had—aside from Sandy's trust fund—and what we spent. And money, whatever other limitations it might have, is a very fine divining rod. It points and bends to show the trail. It pulls you along into the recesses of another's existence—though not, apparently, always.

Sandy was careless with money. Having always had it, she took it for granted, spent it freely and gave it often—except, it seems, when it came to hiding her affair. When it came to the affair, Sandy was careful about where she went and what she spent, and that was evidence of a premeditation that made it hurt all the more.

When I did find out it was not by accident. There were no late night phone calls. I did not find a scrawled love note in her purse, or discover suspicious charges on the credit card bill. It was nothing like that at all. I suspected it only through an odd sense of disconnectedness that, one night after we had made love, metamorphosed into a wash of tears.

Sandy seemed several times on the verge of telling me something, and then backed off. It took several more days before she would even hint at what had happened, but by then I knew in my heart and had only purposefully failed to articulate it.

"I do not want to lose you," she would say, lying there unclothed, bare to me at least in the corporeal sense. And, before the confession, I would respond, "Why do you think that you would?"

After a few days of postponing what became inevitable she approached me one night and sat down next to me as I read the paper in the living room.

"We need to talk," Sandy said, and as my heart pounded I knew, before she had again opened her mouth, what we were going to talk about. He was a doctor of some sort by the name of Moylan, though not an M.D.

"A doctor," I murmured.

"Please don't make this a bigger deal than it is."

I complied, at first, acknowledging stoically that I had been hurt but pretending that, from Sandy, I expected no less. Of indifference or placidity, however, I found myself incapable. I had a hidden temper, one that had occasionally surfaced during my youth but that I had successfully suppressed ever since. Suddenly it reappeared in shouts and accusations, strings of expletives. I would have felt embarrassed to say such things on a golf course, but for some reason not in the confines of our own bedroom.

Sandy, for her part, evinced dutiful sorrow, but also, somehow, reminded me of my own seeming indifference. There had been, it is true, periods in our marriage of what Sandy called my "emotional disengagement," and they'd lasted for months.

"I'm sorry, I am," she said months later. "But we should either get past this, all of this, or not." She was standing in the bedroom, having just walked out of the bathroom.

"What's that mean?" I wanted to know.

I had been getting ready for bed.

"Shit, Will. Whatever you want it to mean! At least talk to me instead of giving me this everlasting silent inquisition!"

"Silent inquisition? What the hell does that mean? I'm not the one with the secrets."

"Oh, no?"

"Don't try and turn it around on me, Sandy! I'm not the one who was out fucking her doctor!"

"He wasn't my doctor."

"Okay, I wasn't the one out fucking *a* doctor. Whatever. I'll try to get the articles and pronouns straight."

She turned away disgusted.

"Yeah, there you go. Walk away."

"I was never the one who walked, Will!" she screamed, turning toward me in a paroxysm of rage. "Never was!"

Sandy always said that I lived my life through some blind faith in fate, letting the rivers wash over me and move me where they decided, hoping where they left me and what I did there would be right and good enough. And a good deal of what she said was true. Able to see others with sometimes surprising clarity, able to deduce quickly all their dreams and failings, I found my own self less readily fathomable. Unable to convey to Sandy any of it, I eventually moved out, then, of course, drifted back, asked her to promise, swear, that she would stop seeing him.

"It's over, Will."

"So you're not going to see him anymore?"

"It's over. I won't even talk to him."

"Not at all?"

"It's over, Will. I don't want anything to do with him—anything."

Still, I could not seem to set it aside.

It did not help that some time shortly thereafter I was anonymously sent a picture of them in the mail, a black-and-white photo of them standing outside somewhere, just standing there smiling, she delicately touching the sleeve of his coat. It hurt me far more, for some reason, than any erotica possibly could.

"Who the hell would do such a thing?" I asked Sandy.

"Will," she said, "this scares the hell out of me. I have no idea."

It helped somehow, at that time, that Sandy was changing jobs; it magnified the illusion, or perhaps the reality, that she was ready for change. She had decided to leave the public defender's office and join Haley in private practice.

"I guess," she said, "it's time to grow up."

It wouldn't be one of those fancy, downtown partnerships whose goal was to do nothing but make money, Haley said. Money would be made, of course, and they still defended their share of drug dealers and perverts, but there would be pro bono work, too. There would be a choice of clients. Finally, Haley told me, they would be able to choose the people they wanted to represent, help the people they believed really needed help, leave all the other "hassles and assholes" behind.

"And still," added Haley, "make a living."

Sandy and Haley established their offices in downtown Droughton on the fourth floor of an old building with an orderly, impressive, neoclassical look to it. One of the reasons that they chose the area was that it was in close proximity to the courthouse and the municipal building that held the police department and most of the city offices. The *Courier* was just across the quadrangle as well. They could get to the courts in a matter of minutes when they needed to. We could have lunch, although we rarely did. Grab a beer after work, Haley and Sandy and me. Share a ride.

Early in the morning of that first Thursday—still just three days after the accident—I made my way to Sandy's office. The temperature was rising up into the low forties and the sun was beginning to melt the snow.

The lobby was cramped and closed. It had undergone far too many modifications, and as I walked in I was immediately greeted by a set of elevators and a door that led to a set of stairs. I chose the former, and pressed the button that was marked CROSS & ARNOLD.

It was a large building and Sandy and Haley had taken over just a portion of one of the upper floors. Little had changed since I had helped her move in. There were double doors made of glass about fifteen feet in front of me. Inside, an oriental rug sat atop polished hardwood, and on it an antique cherry-wood settee, two smaller cushioned chairs, and toward the back of the reception area a large, polished desk. There, staring dutifully at a computer beside a big ficus, sat Sandy's secretary, Margo.

I greeted her and asked if Haley was in as I opened the door.

"Will!" she said, looking flustered. "No. Not right now. Sorry! Will! How are you? Do you want to leave a message?"

This is the way I was often greeted in the days after Sandy's accident. People tripped over themselves to express shock or commiseration or empathy, but many were unsure how to go about it. It came off as nervousness.

"Would it be okay if I waited?" I asked. "Is she going to be back?"

"Oh! Haley?" she effused. "Sure! I'm sure that would be okay. Sure. She shouldn't be gone long. Do you know where it is?"

A young girl with a pockmarked complexion and oversized

pinkish glasses, Margo got up and motioned toward Haley's office, which was next to Sandy's on the other side of an open area that served as their law library–cum–conference room. "It's right down there, but you know that," she said.

"Thanks."

I started to walk down the hall, but paused.

"Can I ask you something?" I said.

Her head bolted in my direction.

"Sure!"

"Did you talk to her Monday, the day of the accident?"

She looked perplexed.

"Sandy," I said. "Did you talk to her at all before it happened?"

"She called me from Minneapolis," said Margo, nodding, her voice suddenly gone soft, "just like she always did, to get messages."

"Did she have any?"

"Just one."

"From whom?"

"A client."

"Who?"

Margo paused. She was trained never to talk about clients to anyone under any circumstances and for a moment I thought she would resist. But I had put her on the spot. Ask like you expect an answer, I was told when I first started reporting, and more often than not you will get it.

"Uh, a woman," she said. "A woman who had been arrested and wanted to know if Sandy could come and see her at the jail."

"Did Sandy return the call?"

"As far as I know. From what I understand, she went there."

"To the jail?"

She nodded.

"What was the woman's name?"

She paused, but only momentarily, and I did not blink.

"Billi Stroud."

"Who is that?"

Finally, Margo balked. She scrunched her head down into her shoulders and was, I suspect, about to protest when I spoke.

"That's okay," I said, indicating that she should not answer and heading down the hall toward Sandy's office. I knew I would get no more. "Thanks."

Sandy's office much resembled our house: small parts were well ordered and clean, but there were other, disorganized areas as well. Closets and corners were full of tangled masses of old notebooks, boxes, books, and bags. Somehow she kept it all straight, knew what was important and pressing, knew what could be deferred or delayed. Never did I hear anyone complain about her missing an appointment or forgetting something of any real consequence.

It was typical of her. Sandy worked in rushes of intensity, immersing herself in briefs or trials for days, even weeks at a time and letting all else pile up around her. Then, when whatever she was working on was finished, she would sleep for days and lie about the house, gradually, eventually, work her way back to the office and begin to sift through the refuse that had gathered.

Except for the day she moved in, when we had simply stacked boxes and bags and furniture in this room pell-mell, I had never been in this office, not since it had been furnished and worked in. Some of the boxes were still there, piled one atop another near an overflowing file cabinet in one disheveled corner of the room near her desk. The rest of the office, though, was like something out of a glossy magazine. I was struck by its formality and beauty. Tasteful oriental rugs covered the hardwood floor and expensive-looking tapestries hung on the walls. The ceiling was an intricate pattern of pressed tin, highlighted by a flood of natural light cascading in through arched windows along one wall of exposed brick. The other walls had been put up during a period of refurbishment, and were papered in off-white with a decorous pattern of small scales and gavels. At one end of the room was a small coffee table and two mauve, Queen Anne–style chairs.

This was an office that exuded confidence, intelligence, and aspiration, if a bit of disarray. This was how others saw Sandy. While I went to work every day and sat at a small metal desk covered with Formica and surrounded by five other small metal desks—each of which had an occupant—Sandy came here. It was another world and one I was suddenly quite sure I had not understood. Sandy had lived a real life, grown up, and flourished. I had sensed it. Known it, perhaps, in the silent, intuitive way that one spouse knows the other. But I had never articulated it, not even to myself.

Sandy's desk was a formidable, solid antique that looked heavy enough to put a dent in the floor if left sitting in one place long enough. It was stacked high with folders and papers amid the customary accoutrements: the phone, a coffee cup, a calendar turned to Monday, the day of the accident. There was the appointment in Minneapolis at two in the afternoon, and nothing thereafter. The rest was a blank. The appointment with Billi Stroud, I reasoned, would not have been planned in advance.

I sat down and pulled out her desk drawers one by one. They were a mess. The largest, the one that ran across the length of the desk above where Sandy's knees would have rested, held assorted office supplies, pencils and pens, paper clips, keys, and change. Old pictures and dozens of notes on little yellow pieces of paper that Sandy had written to herself were all thrown together.

The drawers on the left and right held files with names handwritten on them—Anderson, Bates, Bissinger, et cetera. However, most of the files, I quickly found, were in a generic stand-alone cabinet, dull gray, with two drawers, that sat off to the desk's right side. I reached down and from the back pulled out one titled "Stroud." Like all of Sandy's files there was an address typed under the name and I recognized it as the location of a shelter for battered women. Inside was a copy of a letter addressed jointly to Sandy and Billi Stroud by the chief of the Drougton police.

It was dated several months earlier.

"Dear Officer Stroud," it read,

This is to inform you that your resignation effective today is hereby accepted. Per conversations with your attorney, Sandra Cross, charges related to Section 34.1(a) shall be excised from the record. Please submit your shield and service revolver, Glock 10mm #EE516US.

Thank you for your service.

Stroud had been a cop, but had resigned, it appeared, for some unarticulated reason. There was nothing more in the file and I removed the letter, placed it in my jacket, put the file back, then fingered through the rest of the drawer without taking anything else out.

"Will?"

"Jesus Christ!" I said, lurching.

For a second I had actually thought it was Sandy, or some doppelganger. They could seem eerily alike, Haley and Sandy, not in appearance really, but in the tone of their voices and their mannerisms.

"You scared me!" I said, jumping up in embarrassment and sliding the drawer shut with my leg.

She was standing in the door.

"Sorry to barge in like this," I said. I could tell she was a bit miffed.

"Don't be an ass, Will," she said flatly. "And I mean that."

Haley was of medium height, and had blond hair and piercing blue eyes. In the summer, when she was in the sun, freckles still popped up on the bridge of her nose, and in the winter her skin faded away into a pallid and smooth translucence. She was wearing faded jeans and a red cardigan sweater. I was not surprised. Sandy, too, had often gone to work in casual clothes when she did not have to appear in court or meet clients. And she and Haley were more alike than either of them had ever cared to admit. The two had been friends since high school, had bonded in the unpredictable and mysterious way that two girls—despite coming from vastly different families—sometimes do. Haley's parents, from what I knew of them, were hardworking and supportive, but lived in a wholly different economic strata than Sandy's. They were like mine. We, in fact, Haley and I, were from much the same background, lower middle-class. When Haley and I dated, that may have been what initially attracted us. It may have been, I think now, what eventually separated us as well.

At times, of the three of us, it still seemed it was Haley and I who had the most in common. We teased Sandy relentlessly about her affluence and she mocked us for a lack of culture. Often, Sandy insisted that she didn't really like either one of us but did find "slumming" with us sort of "titillating."

The two of them went to different colleges. Haley, as did I, went off to the state university with about 50,000 other kids. Sandy got into one of the small and exclusive "Little Ivys" out east. We didn't think she would ever return, and when she did come back for a time after college, before law school, we threw a party. For a while, Haley and Sandy even ended up living together. It was only when Sandy and I became serious that they put some distance between themselves, although, to my way of thinking, not quite enough.

Sandy told Haley everything, sometimes before she even told me. If Sandy was mad at me, I could tell just by exchanging greetings with Haley on the phone.

"Now what did I do?" I'd ask Haley.

"Ask her yourself."

They picked up each other's habits, borrowed money from each other and even wore each other's clothes. Much to my amusement, I discovered at one point that the bra I had taken off of Sandy had Haley's name on it. They were, Sandy said, laughing, the exact same size.

"But," she said, "you probably already know that."

Not everything was so funny. When Sandy and I first started going out and I would sleep over, we would try to be as quiet as possible, but I was acutely aware that, as we made love, Haley was only separated from us by a wall, sometimes no more than five or ten feet away. We were like the boys in boarding schools who, sleeping in bunk beds, learn how to masturbate without so much as an audible sigh. Still, there was no way to keep the bed from squeaking, no way to negate the plain truth of what we did there.

In the morning Haley would let it be known that we had not been alone.

"Thanks," Haley would say, hunched over her bowl of fruit and not looking up, "for saving me from setting my alarm."

Or, "When are you guys going to buy some oil for that bed?"

Sandy found it amusing that Haley would speak so freely of such things. I, on the other hand, found it uncomfortable, perhaps because Haley and I had gone out, and done the same things, not so very long before.

Haley walked in front of Sandy's desk and sat in a black leather chair. She had done every low-paying job imaginable before becoming a lawyer. She'd been a waitress in a seedy bar. She'd been a janitor. There was a rumor I liked to think was true—even though she denied it—that she'd been a stripper. She could be vulgar and base and still remembered what it was like to be scraping by. She seemed to like to get down in the dirt and fight. Still, there was something reassuring and casual and, when she wanted, utterly feminine about her. The first thing she did, after she graduated from law school and started making some money, was get her teeth capped.

"What's going on with her?" Haley said, once she was seated. Her hair was tousled as if she had just taken a hat off, and her cheeks were pink with cold.

"She's the same," I said.

Haley had been at the hospital numerous times, the first night falling asleep sitting on the floor.

"Find anything out?" she asked.

"Maid in a house owned by an old lady name of Terrlich or something like that, up above the accident site, called it in," I said.

She opened her mouth in a small circle. Then she raised her eyebrows, and the little circle metamorphosed into a ponderous frown.

"Shit, Will, you know, I keep saying it, but she seemed fine, as far as I could tell. A little tired, maybe. She'd been working pretty hard. But fine."

It had been only three days since the accident and already we'd had the same conversation a dozen times. Disbelief was reiterated over and over again.

"You been home at all?" she said.

"What do you mean?"

"Just have you been home? You look like crap."

"Thanks."

"Yeah, well I mean it. You were wearing that same shirt last time I saw you, and that wasn't today. You getting any sleep?"

I had always been a sound sleeper. Sandy once told me that the average person takes seven minutes to fall asleep. She said I was usually out in less than two. Now I couldn't get to sleep at all. Memories of Sandy, things she had said and places we had been, came back to me during the day, almost like a dream.

"I don't know," I told Haley. "I feel like I'm half asleep all day, and then when I lie down I'm wide awake. Just can't seem to get to sleep. That's never happened to me before. I haven't really slept since it happened."

I was up most of the night, pacing the hallways of the hospital until they told me to go home, then walking in and out of the rooms of the Cross House. It was an odd sensation for me, and

I was not tired as much as somehow altered. Things looked different; I wondered time and time again if I was using the right words. I suffered from aphasia.

"Maybe you should try some pills or something?" said Haley.

"Oh, I don't want to get into that. . . . It's just worry, stress."

"Could be, I suppose," she said. "Or guilt."

"Guilt?"

Her face was deadpan, and she waited a long moment before responding.

"Course, I guess you reporters are used to rummaging around in other people's legal files."

I sat up straighter.

"It won't happen again," I said.

"No, it won't. Puts all of us in a bad position, Will. You, me, and Sandy alike. Client confidentiality and all that, don't you know."

"I'm sorry," I said. "I'm just trying to figure out what the hell is going on. Okay?"

Haley looked at me, expressionless. "Aren't we all."

5.

The Droughton County Correctional Facility, DCCF, was three blocks north of Droughton on Highway 3. From the road, at first sight, it resembled a huge mansion set in a bucolic field of towering elm and maple trees. But the first sight was deceiving.

Built in the early 1880s as an asylum for the criminally insane, the building was converted into a jail sometime in the 1920s and had remained one ever since. Since it was a larger facility than the county needed, the state also sometimes used it as a state prison. Most of the state inmates sent there were minimum-security risks, not those who were a danger to themselves or the people who were guarding them. But over the years there had been two separate riots and two murders had occurred within the walls. One inmate was stabbed with a crude knife, another bludgeoned to death with bare fists.

To get to the prison, one had to turn off Highway 3 and drive up a long, tortuous entranceway. As the prison grew closer, so did its flaws and imperfections. What appeared to be a partially snow-covered lawn from the highway was actually an expanse of dirt mottled with enough grass to make it appear somewhat green underneath melting patches of gray snow. Many of the age-old trees that towered above seemed to be dying of Dutch elm disease. A few had already fallen and appeared to be rotting into the dank earth near an old swamp. In the winter, they formed an almost surreal entry into the prison as they seemed to melt down sideways into the snow.

Long before, all of the windows at DCCF had been taken out and replaced with cinder block. The original stonework on an arch over the front door and around the eaves and cornices was still intact, as were a dozen or so gargoyles peering down from their perches beside dormer windows on the third-story roof. The general effect was that of a large, muted tomb. Much of the lawn, what there was of it anyway, had been paved over near the front entrance and turned into a parking lot. Prisons were designed—or renovated in this case—by the ultimate pragmatists.

Shortly before noon that Thursday, I got out of the car, made my way through the slush—it was getting warmer—up a series of steps and entered a two-story foyer about the size of a living room. On one end of the large foyer, near where I entered, was a row of molded plastic chairs similar to the ones in a bus station. On the other end was a female guard holding a clipboard and sitting on a waist-high stool next to the rectangular, eight-foot-tall frame of a metal detector. On the other side of the metal detector was a massive steel gate with bars four or five inches apart.

"Over here," she said to me. She wore a slightly rumpled brown uniform with epaulets on the shoulders. Her hair was pulled back in a bun, and she looked Hispanic.

"Who you here to see?"

"Billi Stroud."

"Family?" asked the guard.

"No."

"She know you're coming?"

"No."

"Says here," she said, flipping through papers attached to the clipboard, "that she ain't taking visitors. 'Less you're an attorney. You her attorney?"

"My wife's her attorney. I have some things for her."

She looked at me, unimpressed.

"What's your name?"

"Dunby. Will Dunby."

She looked back down at her clipboard.

"You're not on the list," she said.

"I know I'm not on the list. But my wife is her attorney."

"You're not on the list, you're not getting in."

She looked directly at me as she said it, as if it were a challenge and I returned the glare.

"Do you have a phone I could use?" I asked.

"Right there," she said, pointing to a phone on the other side of the small foyer. "It's a pay phone. Help yourself, champ."

I walked over to the phone, dialed the operator at DCCF and asked for Perry Ludin, an assistant warden. Within minutes, he was in the foyer talking to the guard, telling her he would take care of me.

"Well," she finally said, pissed that she'd been overruled, "he's still gotta sign."

Perry took the clipboard out of her hands, and thrust it at me.

"Sign," he said.

I did, then handed the clipboard back to the guard in a somewhat exaggerated fashion. She was not amused.

On the other side of the metal detector was a cavernous, cupolaed room with glossy, pale marble floors that reminded me of a dance hall. All around the periphery were stout pillars that stretched up two stories and supported a balcony running the oval perimeter. This was, at one point, the old building's cafeteria. Now, it was simply an unused rotunda that led to the rest of the jail.

Perry inquired about Sandy and I gave him the standard "wait and see" reply. "It's hard to tell anything, the doctors tell me, after only three days."

"So what brings the assassin to us?" he said. Given the circumstances, it was somehow comforting that he felt it appropriate to joke—as much as it was a joke.

Perry, short and muscular, with thinning red hair, was the prison's media contact. His little nickname for me was supposed to be short for "character assassin." He always smiled when he said it, but meant it only half in jest. He had started in with it shortly after I wrote an exposé some years earlier on the amount of contraband ending up in the prison with the acquiescence of guards. Perry, as the spokesman for the warden, denied any improprieties and claimed in a letter to the editor the articles were an "ambush, one-sided as the Anschluss, and about as fair."

I knew he didn't believe it. The letter was strongly worded but it was also predictable and he later admitted that the warden had made him write it. There were serious problems in the prison at the time and, although none of the guards was ever prosecuted, two of them were eventually forced into early retirement.

"Always good to see you, Perry," I said.

"Why do I suspect I can't say the same?"

"This is personal," I said. "You know about a Billi Stroud?"

"Sure. One of our new ones. Segregated. Former cop."

"Any idea why that gig ended?"

"Don't know," said Perry. "She was just a trainee, I think. Still, wouldn't be good to put her in with the other animals. Why?"

"One of Sandy's clients. I guess Sandy was here the afternoon of the accident."

"I didn't know that," he said. "Here I am the public information officer and I'm the last one to get public information."

"Well, it's not exactly public—yet. Can you ask Stroud if she'll see me?"

"I can ask."

He led me through a long, narrow corridor that housed the administrative offices of the prison. When we got toward the end, he unlocked a door on the right side and held it open. I walked in and was in a small anteroom to his office. His secretary, a plump, thirtyish woman with long, dark hair who looked like she would have been pretty in high school, was on the phone, and apparently not on business because she immediately hung up.

"Why don't you wait here," he said to me, pointing to an undersized, vinyl-covered chair. "I'll have Dorry bring you the file. Then we'll see if Ms. Stroud cares to talk."

The secretary followed him into his office and I heard her giggle. A few moments later she walked out smiling, with the file in her hand and Perry following close behind.

"She was a cop for less than a year," he said. "Resigned just a few months ago from DPD. Sandy was here the afternoon of the accident. You're right about that. Talked to her for a little while it looks like, collected some of her stuff, and took off."

"What stuff?"

"Just the usual. She was booked so we had her clothes, money, whatever. . . ." She looked down at the file. "Keys, stuff like that. Attorney asks for that stuff, we hand it over. Here, you want the file?"

Billi Stroud had been pulled over on a little road outside town for a defective taillight, the file said, and for speeding. She was only four miles per hour over the limit. For some reason the cop asked to search the blue van in which she was riding and he found a joint in the ashtray. After that, he asked to search further and Billi, ostensibly surprised at the joint, agreed. She was shocked, she told the officer, when he later found a larger amount of marijuana hidden behind a door panel.

There was a considerable amount of other stuff in the van as well, according to the report, including common household and personal goods, suitcases full of clothes, and toiletries. Some old lamps and kitchen utensils, a tennis racket, some tools, including a hammer and a set of screwdrivers, a plant. She had apparently been in the process of moving. I took a few minutes to look the list over before I glanced up at Dorry.

"Perry put her three doors down on the right," she said. "She's waiting."

I handed the file back to her and walked out into the hall. The lighting was poor and I stopped for a minute to gather my bearings, then poked my head in.

Wearing blaze orange, Billi Stroud sat in a chair in the middle of the overly lit room. Her hair, pulled straight back off her face into a greasy ponytail, was the first thing one noticed. The ends, a good four or five inches, were bleach-blond and frizzled; the roots were a dark shade of brown with a few interspersed strands of white. Billi Stroud could not have been much over twenty, was my first thought, and yet she, too, like Sandy, was turning gray.

That was about the only physical similarity between the two. Stroud's skin was imperfect, scarred by lingering adolescent acne, her face slightly gaunt and sallow and, somehow, overaccentuated. She looked like someone who had lived a hard life.

She stood up, expectant almost.

"You're Sandy's husband?"

I nodded.

"How is she?"

"Not good," I said. "It's still early, they say. Just three days. But not good."

Other than an expressionless guard and two chairs, including the one she had just gotten out of, the room was empty.

"What do you mean 'not good'?"

She had her arms crossed, as if she were cold, or protecting herself. She was nervous, and trying not to be.

"Just that. It was a pretty serious accident."

"But she'll be okay?"

"We don't know that."

Her mouth dropped slightly, and she seemed genuinely concerned.

"She's unconscious, Billi. I thought you'd know that."

"No."

Her voice, in that one syllable, moved higher, like a child trying to suppress a cry.

"I don't know shit in here," she wheezed, turning away, her arms folded. "You saying she's in a coma or somethin'?"

Her voice was barely audible now.

"I guess you'd call it that."

"But she's unconscious?"

"She is."

"She gonna die?"

"I hope not."

She threw her head back incredulously.

"Think I could see her?" she said.

"I don't know. . . . You'd have to go to the hospital. You can certainly ask. . . . But you know you're entitled to another attorney."

She turned toward me.

"I don't care about another attorney," she said, shaking her head. "Sandy was . . ."

She paused.

"What?"

She turned away from me.

"My friend," she said.

Then she turned back. Her eyes were watery and she rubbed them.

"Why are you here?" she asked.

"Just trying to find out what happened. On Monday."

"I don't know what happened," she said.

"But you called her, right? I mean I presume you called her?"

"Yeah," she said, looking off into one of the corners. "I called her. I needed an attorney for help with my arrest."

"What kind of arrest?"

"I don't know. What's it matter . . . ?"

"It matters."

"How?" she said. "I don't really know anything. I got pulled over, and the cop for some reason searched the van I was in. Found a bag. It wasn't mine so I called Sandy."

"Why'd they pull you over, you think?"

"I don't know. All I know is it wasn't my pot and it wasn't my van."

"Whose van was it?"

"A guy's."

"You tell Sandy that?"

"Sandy knew that."

"How?"

"The van belonged to a guy I'd been staying with."

"I thought you lived at Stone Soup."

"How'd you know that?"

"I asked around."

She looked at me for a moment, and paused. Nobody ever knew who stayed at Stone Soup. That was part of the appeal. But she let it go.

"So, you'd moved in with your boyfriend?" I asked.

Stroud dismissed the possibility with a grunt.

"Yeah, he'd've probably liked that. . . . He wasn't my boyfriend."

"Who was he?"

She turned toward me now.

"You don't know?" she said.

"No."

She looked slightly bewildered.

"Look," I said. "I'm just trying to figure out what happened. . . ."

"With me or your wife?"

I sat down in one of the chairs.

"My wife," I said.

I had brought a pack of cigarettes and pulled one out now and offered it to Billi. I rarely smoked. Sandy, Haley, and I had all made a pact to quit years before and, for the most part, stuck to it. But I thought Stroud might want one.

"Are we allowed to smoke in here?"

"Smoke 'em if you got 'em," said Stroud. She raised her voice to a high pitch on the final few words, mimicking somebody, somewhere.

I extended the pack and Stroud reached out for it but fumbled it. It fell to her feet.

"Damn," she said.

She crouched over and retrieved the pack, and tapped one out as I lit a match for her. She took a long hard drag on her cigarette, like a teenager sucking on a joint, then leaned back and blew a stream of gray smoke toward the yellowing ceiling.

"Think we could have an ashtray?" she said, looking at the guard leaning against the wall. But he just grimaced to himself, ignoring the question and her, looking off into the nothingness. Billi shook her head slightly, then glanced at me, and took another drag.

"Fuck," she muttered, trying to decide where to put her ashes.

"You drop those ashes and you're the one who's fucked," said the guard.

Billi murmured incredulously to herself as I pulled a page out of my notebook, folded it into a small ashtray and handed it to her. She placed it on the ground next to the chair she was now sitting in and flicked some ashes into it, then she got up again and crossed her arms across her chest. She held the cigarette no more than a few inches from her mouth at any one time, and started pacing, two or three steps toward a wall, then back again.

"I'm just trying to piece it all together," I said.

"Piece what together?"

"Why she did it."

"You saying she did it on purpose or something?"

Billi Stroud had hazel eyes, a fact that, even in the bright light, was not easy to discern. Most of the time she squinted in a way that left them almost closed.

"Appears that way."

"That's impossible."

She took another drag on the cigarette, as if she weren't even listening.

Stroud was thin, and the prison jumpsuit appeared at least a size or two too large. It was zipped to the top, but the neck was so oversized that it hung down like a low-cut dress. She had rolled the sleeves up to her elbow. On her feet she wore white socks and cheap plastic sandals, blue ones.

"Did she say anything to you?" I asked. "What'd you talk about? Was she depressed, or seem distracted. Anything?"

"Was there some reason to be?"

"I don't know. You must have talked about something."

She looked at me.

"We talked about what you'd think we'd talk about in here," she said. "She wanted to know why I was here, and I told her, far as I knew, which wasn't much. I asked her to help get me out and she said she would. Said she was going out to talk to the guy who owned the van, guy I'd been staying with. She said she'd be back."

She paused and shook her head. "I just sat here and waited. . . ."

"Did you tell her where to find him?"

She looked at me for a long moment, shaking her head slightly from side to side.

"Couldn't have been hard to find," she said slowly.

"What do you mean?"

Billi Stroud leaned back and blew smoke up at the ceiling, then sat there for a moment and stared at it until it dissolved into the old, yellow tile above us.

"She's the one who set it up so I could stay there in the first place."

Stroud was utterly still now, for the first time. She was gazing into my eyes.

"So she knew him?"

"Yeah."

"What's his name?"

She took a final drag on the cigarette, then bent over and put it out as the smoke worked its way up into the pipes and dust and dirt of the ceiling, turning everything a sickly shade of gray and yellow and white as she looked back in my direction and told me what I had, by then I think, come to expect.

"Tommy Moylan," she said, the residue of the smoke still seeping out of her mouth. "Name's Tommy Moylan."

6.

Billi Stroud was right. Tommy Moylan was not hard to find.

He had inherited a beat-up farmhouse on a parcel of land near a waterfall on the creek just west of town. The house had once belonged to his father, and he and his younger brother, Bobby, had grown up there. After the family moved to town, it was left vacant and eventually stripped of most of its value. Vandals had torn out everything from the copper plumbing to the solid oak mantel that sat over the fireplace. As a final indignity, someone had started a fire in the middle of the living room and destroyed most of the innards.

Moylan, who fancied himself a cerebral sort but was also good with his hands, rebuilt the house almost from scratch, moved in, and tried to firm up an old dilapidated barn that sat about fifty yards from the homestead down next to the two-lane highway. It was there that he kept his tools and his van.

When I arrived late that Thursday—still just three days after Sandy's accident—a squad car was parked at an odd angle along the highway and to the side of the barn just off it. I presumed the police had come to search for more marijuana. It would make sense after finding drugs in the van to come out and extend the search to the rest of the place.

Only one cop was visible, and he was standing there talking to two young boys, one of whom, the smaller one, was holding a hockey stick. The cop was asking them questions, and he had his notebook out.

"Can I help you?" he said as I approached. It was a warning, not an offer. He recognized me as a reporter, and did not wait for a response before he added, "You'll have to stand back there."

He pointed to a cordon of yellow plastic tape, then turned back to the boys. He must have been finished because a moment later he turned and walked into the barn, where he began sifting through some boxes. A few minutes later, his walkie-talkie crackled and, after exchanging a few words with someone, he disappeared out the other side.

"What did he want?" I said to the boys.

"Don't know," said the older one, the one without the hockey stick.

He was wearing a jean jacket and had his hands in his pockets. The sun was still relatively high in the sky and the snow continued to melt but it was still chilly enough not to want to leave one's fingers exposed for too long.

"Let's get out of here," the older one said, turning to the younger one. "Just go get the sled."

The younger one looked reluctant.

"Go ahead, numbnuts," urged the bigger one.

The younger boy resisted.

"I already looked. It's not there. Maybe somebody stole it."

"Who gives a shit enough about your stupid baby sled to steal it?"

The barn was almost fully enclosed, but Moylan had incorporated a conventional garage door and there was another, smaller door as well. It was on the other side of the cordon, and the older boy walked over and slipped inside. Part of the inside had been transformed into a workshop and there were several wooden workhorses. There were lights all along one wall and a workbench—probably twenty feet long—stretching out underneath. There were only a few tools visible, an electric sander, a drill, and a circular saw. On the very top shelf sat a variety of cleansers and other supplies. I noticed a row of SOS pads lined up one in front of the other. Tommy Moylan was apparently a very well-ordered man.

By moving over a little, I could see a pile of skates and hockey sticks leaning up against the wall. On one side was a maroon-colored Saturn, and near it the boxes of what looked like clothes. I guessed that Billi, halfway through her move when she left that prior Monday, had intended to come back for them.

The sled must not have been there after all because, a moment later, the older boy came out and, muttering something, walked around the side of the barn.

"You guys live around here?" I asked the younger one, who was holding the stick, but not playing with it. He looked preoccupied.

"Not far."

I assumed they lived in one of the subdivisions starting to sprout up a mile or so down the road. The barn and homestead still stood alone in the middle of a large tract of farmland, but that would soon change. Gradually, For Sale signs were sprouting up in the adjacent fields along the two-lane highway and, if nothing else, the barn would someday be lost because it sat so close to the shoulder of a road that would need to be widened.

"Where do you sled?" I asked the younger one.

"Out back on the hill," he mumbled. "After school."

"Not much snow out here now," I said.

He was looking off toward the end of the barn where the older boy had walked off. Wisps of thin hair fell into his blue eyes, and he still had the look—and the sound—of innocence. When he spoke, he tried to deepen his voice, but all that came out was affectation.

"What'd Tommy do in there?" I asked, motioning toward the inside of the barn.

"Dunno," said the young boy quietly. He had a baby face, round still in the cheeks, smooth-skinned, and freckled. "Anything he wanted, I guess. Who are you?"

"I'm a reporter," I said.

"Like from television?" This sparked his interest.

"Newspaper."

"Oh," he said, deflated.

He looked again to the end of the barn and was about to go look for the older boy when I grabbed his hockey stick.

"Hey!" he said.

I shot a tiny little clump of frozen gravel toward him, intentionally missing but close enough that he had to jump to the side.

"He shoots," I said as the imaginary puck flew by him, "he scores!"

He smiled.

"Do you play?" I asked.

"Naw. I suck."

"Bullshit."

He almost laughed.

I took advantage and, tossing the stick back at him, pulled a picture of Sandy out of my wallet. It was one of my favorite pictures, taken when her hair was long and unfettered. Her smile was more like a laugh, exuberant and joyful.

"You ever see her here?"

He glanced at it.

"No. She's pretty."

"That's my wife."

"Why would she be here?"

"She was a friend of Tommy's. Do you know where he is?"

He shook his head, but almost too quickly. There was a small hint of concern.

"When's the last time you saw him?"

He didn't say anything.

"Do you know?"

"He's okay," murmured the boy, getting sullen again.

"Any reason he wouldn't be?"

"No reason."

He turned away from me slightly.

"What's your name?"

"Adam."

"Adam what?"

"Dougherty."

"I'm Will Dunby," I said, extending my hand.

He shook it.

"When did you last see him, Adam?"

"Monday."

"Monday when?"

"After school. I came to go sledding. But he was working on Billi's car."

He was pointing at the Saturn inside the garage.

"You tell the police that?"

He nodded.

"What was he doing to it?"

"Don't know. Just saw him through the window."

"You didn't ask?"

"The door was locked and I couldn't get in. But he was working on it. I could see his feet."

"Did you knock?"

"Yeah, but he must have been wearing his headphones cuz he didn't move. He likes music."

I nodded.

"Kyle and I came back later, after dinner, but he was gone."

"That your friend?" I said, gesturing toward the other side of the barn, "Kyle?"

"Cousin."

"You talk to Tommy then?"

"No. He wasn't there."

Just then, we heard something that sounded like the whimpering of a puppy. Then I realized it was the older boy, standing at the end of the barn. He had come back. And his demeanor was totally different.

"Adam," he murmured softly. "C'mere."

"What?" said the younger boy.

The older boy was convulsing almost as he spoke, motioning for the younger boy to come with him.

When we followed him around the side of the barn, there was a thirty- or forty-foot plateau above a fairly steep hill that sloped quickly into the creek near the falls. It would have been a good hill for sledding, although the water ran by quite close to the bottom and would be dangerous, especially during a thaw.

At the bottom were two police officers, the one I had seen earlier and his partner, and as the older boy moved toward them the younger one followed.

"Hey, guys," I said to the boys, trying to get them to reverse course, but they were not listening.

When we got closer to the creek, I could see that, as the air had warmed, the open waters that normally gurgled beneath the falls had expanded outward. For some twenty or thirty feet from the base, water was starting to push up frantically from below.

"Hey, thought I told you to stay up there!" yelled one of the cops at Kyle.

But it was too late.

Protruding from the melting ice on the edge of the open water about ten yards from the shore was the rounded edge of a plastic, red sled with a white stripe on it. "Slider!" it read, in cursive letters above the stripe. Most of the rest of the sled was still beneath the ice, though not far from the edge of the open water. If one had thrown it in the falls, I imagined, it would have been shoved far enough under the surface to be obscured. A thaw would quickly resurrect it.

"Hey, Kyle!" said Adam, catching up and, hurriedly, moving a little closer. "It's my sled. How'd that get down there?"

Kyle was shaking his head as small puffs of breath steamed from his mouth. He was pointing and, by then, I saw it. Near the sled, as I moved closer to the edge of the creek, I could see the dark tip of a shoe that looked brand-new jutting up out of the melting ice near the red plastic. It was not old or worn. It looked like it was just off the shelf, and had plenty of tread. I could see the frozen shoelaces, and one of them formed almost a perfect circle. Both of the cops had moved out there, and Kyle, too, now walked out over the ice and onto a protruding rock. The cops were screaming at him to get back, and I joined in.

"Hey!" I said. "Let's go back up to the barn!"

Kyle was clearly not going to listen, so I turned to the younger one, Adam, who looked scared and was hanging back. His lip was quivering.

"Let's go," I said. But he wouldn't answer. It looked like he was trying to catch his breath. Both cops were now using batons to flail away feverishly at the ice and around the shoe. There were jeans that could be made out, scrunched down toward the red and white rubber bottom of the Nike.

"Hey, buddy!" I yelled to the older boy. "Kyle!" I screamed.

But there was no response.

The ice was thin and, in another moment, it had been broken almost completely away and we all knew, by then, what we were about to see. When the hair appeared, it was like a doll's, brown and mussed. The flesh around the eyes, as the corpse floated toward the top of the water, appeared a little swollen and yellow. I could see, even from my distance as this body turned up toward the clouds, that it—a man in his late thirties with sharp features and high cheekbones—was cleanly shaved. The ice and cold water had preserved him almost perfectly.

There were no scratches or bruises upon the face, and but for the small round hole in the middle of his forehead, he could have been sleeping.

I do not remember when the screams and yelling stopped, only that, when they did, the young boy stood by my side as pale and silent as the moon and looked at the body of a man lying frozen in stunning inanimateness next to his sled. And as we stood there I recall thinking then that it must have been a particularly incongruous and surreal exercise, giving that body one last ride down the icy back hill where these little boys, on other nights, yelled and screamed and barely dared to curse as they flew out over the ice they hoped would save them from going too far into the black ink of the water.

Adam's mouth was agape. And when he spoke, he spoke the only words I heard him say the rest of that day.

"Tommy," he said, gasping. "It's Tommy."

7.

I watched Droughton County Circuit judge Eddie Nevers lean back contemplatively in his black, high-backed, leather chair, slowly place his interlocked hands behind his head, and, arms akimbo, digest what he had just read. It was the first bullet in the forehead that killed Tommy Moylan, sent his body reeling amid the oil spots and dirt and bits of sawdust on the floor of his barn. It was the second bullet that made the murder so macabre and gruesome and media-worthy.

For, after he fell to the floor and the horror of the act was plainly evident, or should have been, the shooter knelt down on the concrete beside him and unzipped his jeans. Placed the gun on the floor probably for a moment while pulling Tommy Moylan's pants and underwear down over his hips, then pressed the tip of the cold, steel barrel firmly up against the soft, pliant flesh of his testicles—and squeezed the trigger. The second bullet traveled straight up through his interior organs and, like a pinball, veered off a bone toward his back and nestled up next to his spine.

Looking out at the courtroom filled with lawyers, cameras, reporters, cops, relatives of Moylan's, and assorted other spectators, the judge sighed.

He was a handsome white-haired man of average height and fine features who, despite having reached his fiftieth birthday a few years earlier, still had the frame of the star miler he had been at Wisconsin State College thirty years before. An only child whose mother had died early on, he put himself through school and, defying the odds of the neighborhood he grew up in, became a cop. Deciding after a few years that he wanted something different, he went back to school and became a lawyer.

The truth, and one that was easily overshadowed by the praise and accolades of his later years, was that he had not been a very good one. He had an acute sense of the law and what it meant, but lacked both the judgmental indignation of the prosecutor and the moral turpitude of most defense attorneys. More interested in the law than money or politics, he secured a seat on the bench after a few years in private practice and had been there ever since.

"What is this?" he asked, looking toward Carney Thorpe and holding up the information in front of him.

"Background material, Your Honor," said Thorpe, a rotund, graying man whose complexion seemed to redden a shade with each minor exertion.

"On what?" said Nevers, staring at him.

Thorpe, a deputy district attorney in his midfifties, shifted slightly from one side to the other while all eyes in the courtroom focused on him.

"The defendant," he said, almost in a whisper, gazing down at his shoes as he said it. Thorpe was a florid, large man easy to imagine sitting at a big round table in a smokey basement, drinking beers and smoking an oversize cigar—one of his favorite pastimes, in fact. But he was not a buffoon. He knew already that Nevers was not going to buy what he was offering, not that it hadn't been worth a shot, and presented himself as appropriately cowed.

"My docket," replied Nevers, looking down at some papers on his desk, "says this is an arraignment on charges of possession of marijuana and possession with the intent to deliver. Also a possession-of-stolen-property charge. I don't see anything else. 'Less I'm missing something? Am I missing something?"

"No," said Thorpe. "I don't think you're missing anything. . . .

It's just background. . . . And whether it is relevant is, of course, up to judicial discretion."

Nevers continued staring at him, waiting for more, but Thorpe didn't offer it. He just looked from the papers on the table in front of him to the judge, then back again. Nevers peered at him for a long moment before, in a deliberate and exaggerated motion, placing the report he had been reading on Tommy Moylan to the side.

Then he looked at his watch.

"Let's do this the right way," he said finally, in a low, steady, somewhat irritated voice. "This appears to have happened Monday. Why are we not here for an initial appearance until Friday afternoon? Four days later."

"She waived the time requirement, Your Honor," said Thorpe. "Her initial attorney was Sandy Cross, as you know. When the defendant finally realized she was going to have to find substitute counsel, there arose a matter of whether she could afford to retain another private attorney. Turns out Ms. Cross was probably going to do it pro bono. The short of it is that it has taken this long to get her to accept a public defender."

"This true, Mr. . . . ?"

Nevers paused, focusing now on a piece of paper in front of him as Thorpe stared over at his counterpart, looking for all the world like he was going to belch.

"Phinney, sir," said Stroud's attorney, a tall, lanky, and bespectacled public defender about three years out of law school. "Dennis Phinney."

Phinney looked young and haggard. He worked sixty hours a week at a job that paid less than $39,000 a year. Largely bald by the age of thirty, he compensated by growing his reddish-brown hair long in the back. He didn't have a beard, but sprouted a full mustache and wore perfectly round glasses that made him appear more like a graduate student than a grown man who'd had responsibility for a person's fate in his hands.

"Yes, sir," he said. "All true. I—"

"Okay," said Nevers, cutting him off. He looked back at Thorpe and then, again, at his watch. "What were the circumstances of the possession arrest?"

"I'll make this quick, Your Honor," said Thorpe. "Quick as I can."

Thorpe was the great-grandson of a former governor to whom he bore an uncanny physical resemblance. He conceded it was not a wholly comforting inheritance, for the governor had died at his desk of a massive heart attack while still in his fifties, right around Thorpe's own age. He'd gone face-first, legend had it, into a bowl of mulligatawny.

Carney Thorpe had secured his own "humble position," as he referred to it, after successfully engineering the election of a friend as district attorney some twenty years earlier, and he had been there ever since. He spent much of his time tending to the red tape and administrative duties of the office, but was by no means a dull-minded man. He was an adept prosecutor, the one the office turned to when it had a particularly sensitive case that needed to be handled by someone aware of, as Thorpe would say, the "nuances of the situation."

The nuances were that the police, confident they had in custody a killer who was until quite recently one of their own—Billi Stroud—were going to push hard for a quick trial and, for the time being, simply needed to keep her in custody. Thorpe's job was to use all his bluster or obsequiousness or anger or whatever else the occasion called for, as well as whatever legal strategy was necessary, to make that happen until they could bring the murder charge. Unfortunately for him, the case had been randomly assigned to Nevers, who, though occasionally bemused by the prosecutor's wiles, was rarely swayed by anything but a legitimate legal argument.

"The police received an anonymous call that Ms. Stroud here would be traveling along Route 3 and that the car she was in contained a quantity of marijuana," said Thorpe.

As he said it, he gestured toward Stroud, who was sitting in her prison garb at the defense table next to her attorney.

"An anonymous call?" Nevers interrupted.

The judge looked off into the distance now as he spoke. His tone was polite enough in a dry, businesslike sort of way.

"Yes—"

Nevers, again, cut him off.

"Any idea who it was?"

"No."

Nevers was moving already into the legal no-man's-land between the judge and the attorney, taking control of proceedings before they had scarcely begun. Thorpe had no choice but to be the picture of civility.

"Judge," Thorpe said, "it was apparently no secret that Ms. Stroud had a predilection for marijuana. In fact, that was the reason she was leaving the residence in which she had been staying."

Thorpe straightened his arms now and, with some resignation, stepped back a bit from the lectern and looked down at his feet. This time, it was more a gesture of casual disinterest meant to convey an air of experience or control, however, than obsequiousness.

"And the residence. That was Dr. Moylan's?" asked Nevers.

"Yes," said Thorpe, looking back up. Perhaps submission of the report had not been a mistake after all. "He was a psychotherapist and he had an office there, too, sort of practicing part-time. He'd been upset about her drug use and asked her to leave. We have three or four witnesses who could testify to the fact, if necessary—folks who were told as much by either Ms. Stroud here or the doctor."

"Mr. Phinney?" said Nevers, turning toward the public defender. "You concede this?"

"Yes, sir."

Nevers raised his eyebrows a little—defendants typically admitted to nothing at this stage of a proceeding. Billi Stroud grasped Phinney's arm and anxiously whispered something in his ear. She wore the same sort of oversized jumpsuit I had seen her in at the jail, and appeared, if it were possible, even more nervous than before. She was having a hard time sitting still.

"Except that I want to make it clear here," Phinney added quickly, listening to her and trying to quiet her at the same time, "that it is our position that the marijuana found in the van was not hers. In fact, the van was not even hers. She had been given permission to use it by Dr. Moylan to move her things."

Phinney had long fluttering fingers and an earnest, high-energy disposition that, as he tried to talk to both Stroud and Nevers, made his head swing manically from one side to the other and threatened to catapult his glasses off into a distant corner of the room.

"He let her use his van even though he kicked her out of the house?"

"They did not part on bad terms," said Phinney, straightening up. "In fact, they parted on quite decent terms. He was, it is true, perturbed about her marijuana use, but he simply explained to her that he could not condone that kind of behavior and he did ask her to move, but he also said she could use one of his vehicles to do so. There was no bad blood. Quite the opposite, Judge. The doctor had more than one vehicle so it was not an inconvenience in that way. It's true he did want her out of there. He said he felt like an accomplice to her activities if he let her stay and he didn't want that for various reasons. So he asked her to leave but also let her use the van for a day. She was making a trip and was going to head back and make another."

"There's no doubt he knew that she used marijuana?" asked the judge.

"Yes, he knew."

"Mr. Thorpe," said Nevers. "What time did this anonymous call about the marijuana in the van—Dr. Moylan's van, I now gather—come into the police department?"

Thorpe looked at some notes in a folder, then back at several police officers standing in the rear of the room. One of them, I now noticed, was Deiter.

"If I'm not wrong," said the prosecutor, "that call came in at around . . . one-thirty. Early afternoon."

Deiter and the others, some in white shirts and ties, the others in short sleeves even though it was still under forty degrees outside, were nodding in the affirmative.

"About an hour before she was picked up?" said the judge.

"Yes."

"So, the officer was sort of lying in wait?"

"Well, the police had a tip that she would be transporting marijuana," said Thorpe, still standing at the lectern. "They responded as they would in any instance."

"And do you have an estimated time of death for Dr. Moylan, according to the coroner's calculation?"

"The coroner's calculation? No."

Thorpe again turned and peered toward the back of the courtroom and, when he didn't see whomever he was looking for, walked back to the prosecutor's table.

"No," he was saying as he riffled through some papers. "Given where the body was found, there was little decomposition at all to gauge the time of death," he said. "The water was cold. We are, however, interviewing—"

"Okay," said Nevers. "So, it's at least possible that Dr. Moylan—whom we know had knowledge of her marijuana use and had asked her to leave the house—could have been the one who called the police."

"Well, the call came from a pay phone and I guess, theoretically at least, he could have made it," said the prosecutor, moving back now toward the lectern.

Nevers mulled this over.

"What about this stolen-property charge? What's the basis of that, Mr. Thorpe?"

"There is evidence some of the possessions that Ms. Stroud had belonged to Dr. Moylan."

"She stole them?"

"We believe so. We are trying to sort that out—a difficult task, obviously, without the defendant."

"I'd imagine," said Nevers. "What sort of possessions?"

"Tools. Namely, a tool box with a hammer and ratchet set, some screwdrivers, that sort of thing. All with his name on them and all discovered in her boxes intermingled with her stuff during a search of the van."

Billi Stroud again whispered something in Phinney's ear.

"Mr. Phinney, your client have something to say?" asked the judge.

Phinney held up a forefinger, as if to ask for a moment's pause. When Stroud finished, he looked to the front.

"Judge, Ms. Stroud is just reiterating to me that Dr. Moylan gave her the tools and a few other things before they had their problems, that he had won new ones in a raffle of some sort and mentioned it to her, and when she expressed interest in buying the old ones he simply gave them to her—as a gift of sorts."

"Of sorts?"

"They were a gift," said Phinney, correcting himself. "He never asked for them back and my client never gave them back. They were hers so she took them with her when she left. She didn't steal them."

Nevers turned toward Thorpe. "Where's your proof she stole them?"

"They were his—they had his name on them. And she had them with her possessions."

"That it?"

"For now."

Nevers was shaking his head from side to side, smiling.

"That's not gonna do it," he said.

"But," started the prosecutor, "we expect to be able to do

considerable investigation into this whole situation prior to the time this gets to trial—"

Nevers interrupted.

"If it ever gets to trial. You have anything else on the stolen-property charge?"

Thorpe was rocking slightly again.

"No. Not right now."

"Well," said Nevers. "As I said, that ain't gonna cut it."

"But, if I may . . . ," began Thorpe.

"What else do you have here? Intent to deliver? On what is that based?"

Thorpe shook his head, digesting the loss he had just suffered even as Nevers forced him to move on.

"The amount, Your Honor," he said quietly, throwing one hand briefly up into the air. "In our estimation that clearly signals an intent to sell."

"Mr. Phinney?" said Nevers.

Phinney was standing behind the defense table now, slowly shaking his head.

"Well, yes. Just that, while we in no way concede that the marijuana in the car was my client's, it was not—"

"You concede that she used marijuana, but this particular batch was not hers?" interrupted Nevers.

"The marijuana in the van, Judge, was not hers and, moreover, I would submit that whether it was hers or not, it was not enough to justify an intent-to-deliver charge. One person smoking marijuana on a regular basis could herself use that quantity alone over a relatively short period of time—"

"How much are we talking about?" the judge said to the prosecutor.

"About twenty-five grams," said Thorpe.

"So, less than an ounce?"

"Slightly less."

"That's not much," said Nevers.

"That's somewhere between fifty and seventy-five joints," said Thorpe. "Enough to raise questions about what her intentions were."

"Well," said Nevers, leaning back again in his chair, looking off into the middle distance with a slight smile. "No one's saying she couldn't have sold some, at least theoretically. . . . Just that she could also easily have used that amount by herself over time. Granted, it would have taken her a while—but I, for one, have never seen this type of charge based on this sort of amount. Not in this jurisdiction anyway, and I have to be guided by precedent. This is just marijuana we're talking about, right?"

"Yes," said Thorpe. "Just."

That last word was a mistake, and Nevers stared at him a moment longer than normal.

"Your Honor, may I have a sidebar?" asked Thorpe.

"If you have something to say, say it out loud," said Nevers.

"I'd rather a sidebar."

Thorpe was no longer smiling. He pulled out his handkerchief and wiped his brow.

"For what purpose?" said the judge.

"Judge—"

"I don't know that there's much to discuss," said Nevers. "You have something else on the intent-to-deliver charge, other than quantity, that is, that indicates she planned to sell it?"

Nevers said it with slow deliberation and Thorpe looked down at a legal pad in front of him as if the answer lay there.

"Not right now," said the prosecutor.

"Okay," said Nevers. "I'm throwing out the possession-with-intent-to-deliver charge, and the stolen-property charge as well. This is clearly a plain old possession case—and not a huge amount at that."

Thorpe, losing ground swiftly, shifted his weight from one foot to the other, then back again. And he appeared to redden a shade.

"Your Honor—" he said, clearly surprised.

"Tell me about the drugs that were found," said Nevers, cutting him off. "They were concealed in a door panel of the van and there was a marijuana cigarette in the ashtray, is that correct?"

"Yes," said Thorpe, in a low voice, standing now absolutely ramrod straight and looking concerned. "It's in the report."

"I know," said Nevers. "That's the report I did read, Mr. Thorpe."

Thorpe pursed his lips.

"Anything more from you?" said the judge.

Thorpe contorted his mouth slightly and stared at his feet as he shook his head, as if he were trying to compose himself.

"No, sir," he muttered.

"Mr. Phinney?" said Nevers, switching his gaze to the defense attorney.

"Nothing other than the fact it was not hers," said Phinney. "The marijuana was not hers."

"But you don't contest the fact it was found in her possession?"

"Well, it was in the van she happened to be driving."

"Okay, this one's obviously gonna stick. You can argue it at some later point. Now, what about the bond?"

"I would suggest a personal-recognizance bond," said Phinney. "She has an unblemished background, was a police officer until recently leaving the force, and is no risk of flight. Judge, she doesn't have many assets. As you know, I'm representing her and I'm paid by the state. She can't even afford an attorney."

"Mr. Thorpe?"

Thorpe was shifting back and forth, faster now.

"Sir, this is a very serious issue," he said, his voice wavering slightly. "She doesn't even have a local address. She lived in a homeless shelter for some time, or a women's shelter, and then at the Moylan house till she got kicked out of there for, by her own admission or the admission of her attorney, using illegal drugs.

She quite obviously can't go back there." Thorpe was talking a million miles a minute, trying to get as much in as possible before Nevers interrupted again. "Apparently she was on her way to an apartment that, since her arrest, is no longer available to her. You know what the booking papers say for a home address? They list the county jail." The prosecutor was shaking his head, almost in disdain. "We suggest, on this charge, a fifty-thousand-dollar bond."

Nevers actually chuckled out loud.

"On a possession charge? For this amount?" There was derision in his voice.

"Look, Mr. Thorpe," he said, picking up the report on Moylan's death and waving it in the air, shaking his head slowly. "Look, I know you have a bigger fish to fry here. We all know that all too well based on what has transpired here today, but you're going to have to fry that one in a different pan, okay? I mean, you know that. Now, forgive the extended metaphor, but that one ain't even on the stove that I can see, is it?"

When Thorpe did not immediately respond, Nevers got a little bit louder.

"Is it?" said the judge.

"Not this stove, apparently," said Thorpe, staring back at him.

That got a few smiles out of the gallery, but Carney Thorpe was in no mood for laughter, and the district attorney and the police wouldn't be either if Billi Stroud was released. Thorpe had scant legal basis and knew it, only a fleeting hope that Nevers would, out of deference to the prosecutor's office, or maybe just out of recognition that he was a judge who had to stand for election at some point a few years down the road, stiffen the bond, give them some time to solidify a murder charge against Billi Stroud. But, clearly, it was not going to happen.

"Very well," said Nevers. "I will set the bond at two thousand dollars, with the usual conditions." Now he turned toward Stroud. "If you have the money, you can pay in the clerk of court's office down the hall here, and they'll advise you as to what happens next. Any questions?"

He lifted his gavel.

"Can I pay it today?" said Billi Stroud.

It was the only thing Stroud had said aloud during the entire hearing.

Nevers held the gavel in the air for a moment about a foot off the top of the desk.

"You can pay it whenever you can come up with the money, as long as they're open in the clerk of court's office. Talk to your attorney about that, okay?"

Almost everyone in the courtroom now glanced at their watches. It was five minutes past four. The clerk of court's office had closed five minutes earlier—a fact, most of the courtroom suddenly realized, the judge had no doubt been aware of all along.

"That means I have to spend the weekend in jail?" said Stroud, just realizing what had transpired.

The gavel, still suspended in the air, wavered now, like a bobber on a wave.

"Like I said," said Nevers, "whenever the clerk of court's office is open, you can pay. If it's not open, you can't. That's the way it works. Your attorney knows all about it and, I'm sure, can fill you in on all of it. Till then, you remain in custody. That's it. That's all. Court adjourned."

He didn't wait for a response. The gavel smashed into a small block of wood on top on his desk, then Nevers rose and moved out through the door behind his bench that led to his office, leaving behind the simple fact that Billi Stroud was headed back to a cell. And the lingering realization that if murder charges weren't brought by the district attorney's office by Monday morning, she would be free to go.

8.

Sandy did not need a ventilator and could breathe on her own, but her breaths were labored and shallow and the slow undulation of her chest was one of the only movements her body was capable of making.

The nurses periodically would empty her urine bag or give her an enema. Once a day, they would change the sheets and rotate her body so she did not develop bedsores. Some of them remembered her as a little girl, visiting the hospital with her father, and they had taken to using her formal name, Sandra, the same way he had.

“Here, Sandra,” they’d say, adjusting a pillow or the contour of the bed. “This will be much better.”

Through all of this, the expression Sandy wore was one of complete and utter neutrality, never once altered. Still, on occasion, I had noticed, she sometimes seemed to be chewing the way a newborn does, instinctively. A few times, she had seemed to yawn, and I imagined that she could remember the past even though Kerry Tsau assured me it was not possible. To him, although he would never put it that way, she was a body, and nothing more.

“She’s still going,” I had told Elizabeth the night, some days earlier, when the doctor had removed the ventilator.

“What do you mean, still going?” she said, kneeling in the hospital chapel, dabbing at her eyes with a tissue.

Somewhere in her midfifties, Elizabeth was a diminutive woman with white hair. Cut short and layered, it framed a face of small, sharp features, perpetually dark, tanned skin, and well-ordered, pearly white teeth.

"She's breathing," I said. "On her own."

"What?"

"They say it's unusual, unpredictable. But she's breathing."

Elizabeth was originally from the east coast, and still carried an eastern accent, although it had been largely muted by time and geography. Now in moments of emotion, it returned with a vengeance.

"For how long?" she said, her voice breaking, a tear sliding down her face. She dabbed it with a forefinger and searched a pocket for another Kleenex.

"I don't know. They're surprised that she's breathing at all."

"Could it go on indefinitely?"

"I don't know."

She thought for a long moment.

"Could she recover other functions as well?"

I touched Elizabeth's hand, which was now resting on the pew. "I don't think so. Not from what they tell me."

She buried her head in her hands.

"I don't think they know what they know," she muttered.

The wife of a physician, aware of all their faults and limitations, Elizabeth was already less inclined than most to accept their pronouncements as sacred. And from that point on, she began to rely more heavily on her own counsel. She started talking about moving Sandy home, putting her on a hospital bed in the living room of the Cross House. Then she said she would move back to Droughton and care for her only daughter.

I said little and attempted, like a diver trying to ignore his yearning for the surface, to stay focused on the present; for there was no way to rise quickly toward the air and the light and the open space. I had been designated as the trustee of Sandy's funds in the event of her incapacity and, somewhat sheepishly, felt I should assure Elizabeth we would spend whatever money was necessary on nurses.

"Do you really think we'll need them?" she said. "It's not like you're working."

What she really meant, I felt, was, "I suppose that now that you are rich you will no longer bother."

Elizabeth and I were polite enough with each other, and sometimes even shared a laugh. But there was, barely disguised under the surface, a deep distrust. It was, perhaps, nothing more than the normal hesitations and doubts of a mother toward a son-in-law. Banal as it sounds, I was simply not good enough.

"If you would like," I said, "I would be glad to transfer the funds to you, all of them."

This seemed to surprise her.

"There's no need to talk about that," she said.

If there was any solace, it came from the fact that it was not just I who would occasionally feel such awkwardness. Sandy, although she knew her mother loved her, had often said she felt it as well. Both of us suspected that Elizabeth thought we had wasted something of ourselves, that neither of us had really challenged ourself in the ways that counted. We sought refuge from the suspicion by noting that Elizabeth was largely unfathomable—something Sandy occasionally said about me.

Sandy's father was different.

He was a successful doctor, an internist. But he had his struggles. It was when he was still a young man, when he would work sixty- and seventy-hour weeks at the hospital or at his office, then spend ten hours over the weekend in his gardens, that he had what the family sometimes later euphemistically called "his spells." They were nothing overly dramatic, not from the outside at least. He just slipped into a depression, one that he was, at least in the beginning, able to mask. For days, he ate little and slept not at all, wandering the Cross House at all hours in an increasing state of incoherence and abstraction, crying inconsolably in the large, cavernous rooms of the first floor.

"Please!" he would plead to no one at all. "Pleeease!"

Finally, when he could no longer care for himself, he was admitted into what they then called a sanatorium. He spent weeks there, unburdening all his fears and disappointments, which were not, I gathered in later years, all that out of the ordinary, until it was found that a drug known as Depokote was the real answer. After that, the ghosts no longer roamed the hallways at night, shrieking and babbling, but neither did he whisper and giggle quite so cherubically in the midday.

"There are compromises," he would say.

And Sandy herself would come to know them.

Night creatures and ghosts are the stuff of a little girl's nightmares. To have them manifest in one's own father is to see the world inside out, to have roles and attitudes, responsibilities, thrust upon you that are not yours, or shouldn't be yet. Sandy had witnessed early on the fragility of life and it gave her a maturity that others her age did not have. She began to think of herself as her mother's daughter; saw Elizabeth, all her steadfastness and strength, in herself, and used it to get where she wanted. As time went on it became evident, however, that there was, too, a part of her father in her, the part that had been so long muted, the unchecked emotion in which she would throw herself into projects and trials for days and weeks at a time, never sleeping, moving about on rushes of adrenaline, bolts of energy that infused and moved her, gave her so much compassion and empathy—then the inevitable sharp despair.

The world, Sandy knew, was very much with her, crowded and sometimes teeming with expectation and intimacy and vibrant beauty. Instead of fleeing it, receding into herself as her father sometimes had, she embraced it and held it tight, allowed it to embrace her, exposed herself to it fully, sometimes allowed it to carry her with it, like the last surge of wave upon the beach before the tide starts to pull back again. Her favorite flower was the tulip, the brightest burning and shortest lived.

Over the weekend after Billi Stroud's initial hearing, it warmed considerably. The last, most resolute clumps of frozen ice melted and, although the ground was still hard as concrete it was not too early, I decided, to try to rake the leaves out of the flower beds. Many of them were still stuck to the ground and it would be a largely futile effort, but it was, at least, a diversion.

"You want some help?" asked Elizabeth.

"If you'd like. Sure," I said. "Most of the stuff's in the garage."

I dutifully asked Elizabeth several times in those days after the accident to come stay in the Cross House. With Sandy gone, it—like the money—seemed much more hers than mine. But she repeatedly declined. She said she was doing a favor for an old friend who had gone south for the winter and wanted someone to stay behind in her house. But both of us knew the truth. The two of us living together in the same house—the Cross House that I now owned—would be unbearable.

That did not mean that Elizabeth would stay away. That would be unbearable for her in its own way. She needed something to occupy her, something to do. She needed a distraction and, despite her affluence, wanted to work. Elizabeth was not lazy; quite the opposite. When she met Sandy's father she had been a nurse. They met during his residency at a hospital in Minneapolis. She had, since then, so easily assumed the yoke of wealth that it had sometimes been hard for me to imagine her in her younger days changing bedpans and giving sponge baths. But Elizabeth was nothing if not efficient, and I could see now that she would approach those tasks the way she approached everything: with determination, pragmatism, and little overt emotion. She'd married into this family, I sometimes remembered, the same way I had, and had a lot more experience learning to deal with it.

Sandy and I didn't often park our cars inside the garage and it was obvious. When I lifted the door, there were several garden chairs, a lawn mower, a full cord of wood, and a workbench full of tools—those that had not ended up in the kitchen drawer—pliers and wrenches, an electric sander, levels and saws. Cans of paint sat on shelves. Old buckets and bags of drywall plaster, driveway sealer and sand sat on the floor. The only things not in view were Sandy's tools.

"All her stuff's upstairs," I said.

Sandy had added the second story to the garage, and a set of steps just inside the garage door led up to the second level. They were exceedingly steep, and Elizabeth went up first. I followed behind. About halfway up, we moved into the musty smell of dirt and garden chemicals Sandy had once used, then abandoned when she went organic. I instinctively ducked down so as not to hit my head on the roof that slanted down almost to the floor.

"Sandy's haven," I said.

"Kinda dark," said Elizabeth.

The place was full of bags of wood chips and seed and fertilizer, all sorts of gardening tools and implements, hoses and peony rings and covers for the rose bushes when it got cold. Each year, Sandy would plant row upon row of multicolored dahlias and impatiens, begonias and gladioli. They were truly fragrant and, at times, astonishingly beautiful, and Sandy cared for them with an almost maternal and heartrending devotion.

There were rows and rows of flowering spirea and rose bushes, pale orange lilies, bee balm, and brilliant orange Chinese poppies the texture of crepe paper. Sandy was particular about her flowers, and planted them in a very specific order. In the back of most of the beds she laid cosmos and zinnias that would grow up over the windowsills. Then there were calendula and salvia in shades of blue and gold. In the front, she placed white alyssum and creeping phlox of all varieties and colors. The answer to why, I think I know.

Spring was always a hard time for Sandy, and I suspected this was her way of recognizing, or reaffirming, the hope of rebirth. It was no coincidence that when she planted she often talked of babies. Mused about whether she would like to have a boy or a girl and what we might choose for names.

"I don't want a Will or a Sandy," she said.

"Why not?"

"Every kid deserves his own name. There are too many of us around already."

"I kind of like my name."

"Yeah, but isn't it vanity to think there has to be another one?"

She read books on baby development, knew when and how she was most likely to conceive. She was fascinated by the fact that through the first month or two of pregnancy, all babies—even ones with Y chromosomes—develop like girls. Only then, it seems, do the hormones mandate whether to change course and make the child a boy. Sandy reasoned that this was why there were always slightly more girls born than boys. Nature is more inclined to stay the course, to finish what had begun.

"The better models get the accessories," I told her.

"Yeah, but they never work quite right."

She was a quick wit.

"There's a light right above your head," I told Elizabeth, when we got up the stairs to the second level of the garage.

"Where?"

"Pull the string."

"Oh," she said, reaching into the darkness and pulling downward.

Nothing happened.

"Must be out," she said.

There was a small window at one end of the garage attic that provided some light, along with what seeped up from down below, and gradually our eyes adjusted.

"S'pose we need the metal rakes first," said Elizabeth, reaching for a rake that hung from the front wall and pulling it down. "Got any bags?"

"Just the compost pile. We'll use these baskets to get the leaves over there. I'll get them."

There was a pile of baskets in a far corner and I moved toward them.

"Sounds like a plan," she said, moving down the stairs again, rake in hand, ducking her head.

In the summer, when Sandy was doing a lot of gardening, this place was a mess. Boxes and bags were used and discarded. Tools strewn about. But in the fall, after the frost, she would come up and spend a Saturday cleaning up and rearranging. Making right with it all. Putting her implements in perfect order for the winter so she could leave them, and be away. The small bags of seed and fertilizer were lined up against one wall. Then she had arranged the stakes for her plants, the hoes, spades, shovels, trowels, bags, boxes, and at the far end, baskets, the wooden kind with small wire handles. These were what she used to haul leaves to the compost pile and they were stacked upside down, one upon another. There were three or four and I pulled at the top one, expecting it to come free.

I found them wedged so tightly together, however, that all four unexpectedly moved up off the floor in my hands.

I was standing alone just then, at that time, with all my carefully constructed tangents and diversions, thoughts of calendula and barefoot baby's feet and surface air, whole worlds of it that, in a moment, evaporated like a wisp of moisture. In a moment, that moment, it all went, and quicker.

I don't think there was an exclamation from me, perhaps because at first I did not make the connection. Then it came, and I went to my knees. Breathless.

"Elizabeth?" I sputtered, too softly for her to hear. "Are you there?"

She was already down the steps.

It was, when I saw it, a dull gray, the color of the sky on a dark and overcast winter day that you hope will break, but never quite does. Spring is there almost and yet it is never further off. I picked it up, checking to make sure it was empty as I turned it over and over and over again in the palm of my hand, looking at it, staring at the serial number, afraid to let it drop. Worried even as I held it. Making my mark.

There is a detachment, I tell you, that comes with sudden revelation, and it lifts one like a specter out of the real and tangible. I felt it that day, an aura of lightheadedness so dizzying that I thought it would lift me right up into the rafters. Perhaps I, too, I felt, would dissipate with my dreams and fabricated notions.

I moved across the floor toward the steps—I don't know after how long, but Elizabeth was not to be seen—and with my left hand held tight to that wooden railing. I anchored myself to those stairs and the garage and the very earth that spun beneath it, while with my right hand I clutched in disbelief the heavy, metal grip of Billi Stroud's service revolver.

9.

On the news that evening there was a live picture of Phinney and a couple other men, investigators I presumed, at the bottom of the cliff where Sandy's car had landed. They were walking in concentric circles that started where the car had hit and slowly got bigger and bigger. Phinney wouldn't comment so it was just pictures mostly, shot from the top of the cliff.

I was surprised when, before the news was even over twenty minutes later, Phinney was knocking on the door.

"Hey, Clouseau," I greeted him. "Saw you on the news."

He smiled, but only slightly.

"May I come in?"

"Of course."

Phinney was wearing old brown corduroys and a baseball cap.

"How's Sandy?" he said.

"I think she's comfortable. Hard to believe it still hasn't even been a week. I guess we can take some hope from that."

"It's early," he said.

"It is. Something I can get you?"

"Sure."

"I'll be right back. Take a look around."

People were fascinated by the house. I had grown up in Droughton and, like anyone else, had walked or ridden past it a thousand times as a kid, each time wondering what it was like to live inside. It could rightly be described as a mansion, so large that in the summers it always seemed there were at least half a dozen painters scraping or sanding or reapplying a fresh coat of whitewash. It had the natural beauty, the intricate carvings atop the windows and doors, to be a painted lady. But that would have been considered garish. Instead, it remained a dull and dignified off-white, with the trim always painted a slightly different shade of the same colorless color. Three stories tall, it was capped off with a mansard roof that had four chimneys coming out of it. Most of them, passersby were unaware, led to more than one fireplace.

But the house was not why Phinney was there. Never once in the years I had known him had Phinney ever been there, not that I could remember, not until he surprised me and knocked on the door that night. He was a family man. Married young, in his late teens, he had at least four children by the time he was thirty, and when he had a free night usually spent it at home. His wife was no older, but looked like she was almost fifty. She was overweight and perpetually harried with dark circles under her eyes, the result, Sandy had said, of caring for all those kids while her husband spent his days working some sort of retail sales job and his nights going to law school. Now that school was over, he wasn't making much more money than he would have managing one of the little clothes stores in the mall. Sandy, when they'd worked together, called him Papa, but said it as if he were her younger brother.

I walked into the kitchen, opened the refrigerator and found three or four different varieties of beer.

"You want a domestic or the good stuff?" I yelled.

There was no response so I picked out a couple of each, and walked out into the living room, which was empty.

"In here," he said.

He was in the study, standing in the middle, looking around, and turned toward me.

"Beautiful place," he said.

"Would you like the full tour?"

"No, that's okay. I'm really sorry to bother you, Will. As you might suspect I'm sort of here on business, unfortunately. Need to ask you a few things if that's not a problem."

"No problem at all," I said, letting him choose one of the beers. He chose an import, took a sip, a tiny one, then placed it down on top of a filing cabinet. I wondered if the beer had touched his lips at all.

"You mind if I take a look-see at Sandy's files, see if there's any records that might be helpful to me, might be able to sort of clue me in on the background of all this stuff?"

"I don't think she'd gotten too far looking into the drug charge, if that's what you mean."

"Actually, I'm trying to be a little more proactive."

I took that to mean he was looking for a way to dissuade Thorpe from bringing murder charges against Billi. Sandy had always said that the best way to fight a charge is to never have it issued.

"Maybe there's a file here on Billi Stroud or something," said Phinney.

"Here?"

"It's just a shot in the dark."

"I don't know anything about that. I'd never even heard of Stroud until after the accident."

"Never over here or anything as far as you know?"

"At the house?" I said. "Stroud? Not as far as I know."

"You have any idea how long they'd known each other in whatever capacity?"

"What do you mean?"

"Were they friends?"

He sat down behind the desk now, as I remained standing in front of it, beer in hand.

"They knew each other," I said. "I know that. Why don't you ask your client?"

"Well, sometimes there are better sources than one's client, unfortunately."

"She not talking to you?"

"She's talking. Sort of. I know she resigned from the police department," he said, "and that Sandy was involved." Phinney, I noticed for the first time, had a bit of a nasal tonality to his voice.

"Why did she resign, if you don't mind my asking?" I said. "Was there some disciplinary action or something?"

He picked up his beer, but brought it back down swiftly.

"Not sure exactly. You ever hear Sandy talk of a kid named Chucky Ware?"

"No. Who's that?"

"Friend of Billi's, I guess. Someone she got involved with somehow before she was kicked off the force. Thought actually there might be something on him here as well." He was leaning down toward the filing drawers of the desk. "Mind if I look?"

"Sandy didn't keep anything at home," I said.

"In the desk, maybe."

He was reaching down.

"Actually," I said, moving toward him, "don't take this the wrong way, Dennis, but, yeah, I do. I do mind. I don't know what's in there, but I don't think Sandy would want somebody rummaging around in her files."

Hunched over, halfway toward the file, he stopped.

"Well, I wouldn't be rummaging," he said, looking up from underneath the bill of his cap. "I'm just trying to pick up where Sandy left off. Her client deserves continued representation. I think that's the way Sandy'd see it."

He sat up straight now.

"I don't know how Sandy would see it. No offense, but I don't think it's a good idea."

"Really? How come?"

I was surprised at his persistence and how quickly the tone of the conversation had turned.

"I just think if you want to know something, there are legal avenues, Dennis. You know that. And at a very minimum, I'd need to talk to Haley. Sandy's files, really, are hers now. Why don't you talk to her?"

He contemplated this, then said, "I did."

"You did?"

He nodded.

"And?"

"And she said she hadn't had a chance to even start going through Sandy's files," said Phinney.

"And then she sent you here?"

He paused again.

"No."

"So, you came here because you didn't have any luck there?"

"I came here because I'm trying to help my client."

"Well," I said, "I would think there are better ways to do it than being duplicitous."

He digested this and leaned back in the chair, as if it were his.

"Am I the first to ask?"

"For what?"

"For whatever. Stuff relating to Stroud or Moylan."

"Moylan?"

"Well, Stroud."

"What do you mean?" I said.

"Just if anybody else has asked about this stuff."

"Who else would?"

"I don't know; prosecutors, maybe."

"Why? Even if they wanted to, it's all covered by attorney-client privilege, isn't it? I mean, they couldn't use that stuff even if they wanted to. Even if there was anything."

"Depends," he said.

"On what?"

"It's covered, I would think, in most instances," he said.

"When would it not be?"

Phinney picked up a pencil and pretended to examine the tip, then leaned forward. His shirt was wrinkled and had a small, barely perceptible ink stain at the bottom of the pocket.

"Well," he said, "I suppose, hypothetically, if Sandy were acting in some capacity other than as Billi's lawyer."

"I don't get it. What kind of other capacity?"

"Well, that's sort of what—what I'm here asking about."

He had stammered slightly.

"I thought you wanted the legal files?"

"I do. I want whatever is relevant."

"I don't know why Sandy would keep anything on Billi Stroud that was not a legal file. I mean, I don't think she'd keep notes on their friendship, even if they had one, any more than she'd have kept notes about her friendship with you—course, maybe there just aren't any in that case."

He didn't laugh.

"What are you talking about here?" I said bluntly, still standing in front of the desk. "You're not suggesting that Sandy was acting somehow illegally?"

"I'm not suggesting that . . ."

"But you're wondering."

"Will, I'm just trying to do my job, okay?"

"Is Sandy being implicated?"

"You mean by something other than the circumstances?"

Now there was silence, and he averted his eyes. Then he took his cap off and ran his right hand through his thinning hair. He was uncomfortable.

"I think," I said, "it's time for you to go."

He nodded, and started to rise.

"Look, Will," he said, "I'm just trying to do what lawyers do."

"Do it somewhere else."

10.

The newsroom of the *Courier* was on the fourth floor of an impressive, yellow-brick building that looked more like a bank than a newspaper. It had been founded exactly a hundred years earlier by a printer named Harold Thomes who used it mainly to preach fundamentalism to a town of German and Irish Catholics. Thomes lasted almost two decades, far longer than anyone would have expected, writing fire-and-brimstone editorials that resembled church sermons and were ignored by just about everybody in town. When he died, an editor by the name of Frappeau purchased it from Thomes's widow, paying her one thousand dollars cash, and it had been passed down through the generations after that. The family still owned it and the publisher was a great-great-great-grandson. But everyone knew who ran it.

"What the hell are you doin' here?" said Terence Hemper.

I had hurried to the *Courier* immediately after Phinney left. "Just visiting," I said.

Hemper, a Droughton native, had worked his way up from copyboy—when there still was such a thing—to managing editor. He was a workaholic and came in every night, even on the weekends, to oversee the final makeup of the next morning's paper. He was a relatively young man in his midforties with an unkempt, graying beard, large, oversize glasses and a gruff demeanor that some considered intimidating. Aside from running the paper, he wrote many of its editorials, and many of those who read them took what he said as gospel. He didn't bother with superfluities.

Hemper had called the house earlier in the week and told me to take as much time as I needed. The paychecks, he said, would keep coming. Sandy, of course, didn't have the security of working for someone else but there was enough money in joint accounts that I could get by for a time, even without tapping into the trust.

"Don't even think about this place," Hemper said. "Stay outta here until Sandy gets better."

That was as sentimental as Terence Hemper would ever get. He patted me on the shoulder, walked in step with me for about ten feet, and then veered off someplace else as others converged. One after another, at least a dozen people, everyone who was working that night, rose up out of desks or walked out of offices, expressed condolences, and shook my hand. They asked about Sandy and I told them we, Sandy and I, were "okay" or "adjusting" or "hopeful." It was not, at that point, a total lie.

"Hey, mister," said a voice from behind me.

Mozzy was in her early forties, and had already been at the paper for over twenty years. She had been the gossip columnist for most of that time and had an iconoclasm about her that endeared her to some, like me, and nettled others, like the paper's publisher, Steven Frappeau. When she wrote about his first divorce, he stopped talking to her; when she wrote about his second, he waited three months for her to make a mistake—no one remembered what it was—and then demoted her to the police run. Then he got pulled over for driving under the influence, and she wrote about that, too. He could have prevented publication in all instances, but it would just have worked its way into one of the bigger regional papers or magazines and he knew it.

I walked her over to her desk, which was in a corner of the newsroom away from the traffic. Piles of old, yellowed papers reached up three or four feet off the floor throughout the newsroom.

Many of the desks, buried in notebooks and documents and

assorted books and magazines, were barely visible. Even the walls, covered with pictures and plaques and bulletin boards, seemed crowded. But Mozzy's desk was an oasis of organization and clarity. She kept on it exactly one picture of her husband, Liam, a coffee mug full of pens and pencils, a phone, a notebook, and a folder with whatever she was working on at the time.

"Thanks for all the cards and stuff," I said. "The casserole, the sandwiches, the dessert. Little excessive, don't you think?"

"Liam says he thinks we're having an affair."

"Guess he figures I'm available," I said.

Mozzy had brown hair, cut in a bob, thin features, and glinting, green eyes. Her face scrunched up into a frown. "*Ohhh.* Don't say that."

"What's goin' on around here?" I said, looking around the room.

"Same old same old. We think Frappeau's diddling Wendy."

Wendy was one of the secretaries, and not particularly comely.

"Whoa," I said. "I hope she got a raise out of it."

"Or a rise."

I laughed.

"Gonorrhea more likely," said Mozzy. "What are you doing anyway? You shouldn't be here. You're not coming back yet, are you?"

"I don't know."

She shook her head slowly. "Stay out of here for a while," she said. "We'll survive without you."

"Yeah, I come back in a month or two and you'll be sitting in my desk."

Although we were both reporters, I had the better job, a loosely defined general-assignment beat that gave me considerable latitute to do both features and hard news.

"You're good at this shit," she once told me, "because you can be so totally fucking dispassionate."

We had been in a bar at the time, after work, with many of the other reporters.

"Did you," I asked, "just call me a prick?"

She laughed. "Yeah, but in a good way."

"Hey, I just tell it like it is—the truth and nothing but the truth," I said, trying to mock myself, but somehow falling short of parody.

She pounced.

"Make that a sanctimonious prick."

"Ouch."

"No, really, you have absolutely zero emotion or compunction about this shit."

She was drunk.

"What shit, Potty Mouth?" I said.

"Destroying people."

"I don't destroy people. I just don't let it all be personal. It's not."

"Ever?"

"I hope not."

"Yeah, well, wait until you're on the other side of pen."

"The other side of the pen?"

"Fuck you. You know what I mean."

"Hey, if I get shit-faced drunk here and slam into some kid on the way home, I hope they'll assign you to write it."

"Why?"

"Cuz, you'll make me look like a prince—probably blame the kid. I can see the headline: KID GETS IN WAY OF DRUNK." I laughed.

"Either that," she said, "or: SANCTIMONIOUS, GODLESS, DRUNK PRICK WITH NO FRIENDS FUCKS UP. Nothing personal. No offense."

I drank the rest of my drink, and smiled at her.

"None taken."

Back in the newsroom, Mozzy was standing up, patting her desktop with mock affection.

"I don't want your desk," she said. "I've got my own."

'Well, use it if you like. I'm not really here to work. I need a favor."

"Oh," she said, lifting her chin and giving me a smug little smile. "Something personal?"

I pulled the letter from the police department to Sandy regarding Stroud's resignation out of my pocket, handed it to her and watched her read it.

"I found that a couple of days ago."

"Found it where?"

I ignored the question, and ignored, too, the vague awareness that I could be putting her in a bad position.

"There some sort of police rules book or something, sort of a code of conduct?" I asked.

"You mean for the officers themselves?"

She wasn't smiling anymore.

"Yeah," I said.

She turned around and started sifting through a bookcase against one of the walls, then pulled a blue paperback off a shelf.

"Been wondering what happened with her," said Mozzy, referring to Billi Stroud. "What's that number in there again?"

I looked at the letter I had pulled out of Sandy's file.

"Says thirty-four, sub-one, sub-a. Is there something like that?"

"I don't know. Let's see, let's see," she said. "Thirty-four, sub-one . . . looks like conduct unbecoming an officer. Sub-a . . . Sub-a has to do with consorting with something or other. Here's the verbatim. Says an officer shall not, separate and apart from customary law enforcement practices, associate with any person known to be or suspected of having been engaged in any enterprises in violation of state or federal criminal codes. Basically, looks like it's the department's don't-consort-with-criminals rule—you know, the kind of thing that got that chief of police over in Minneapolis fired some time back."

"Rodriguez, or something," I said.

"Yeah, some Hispanic name. I think most departments have them now."

I looked at her, incredulous.

She chuckled slightly, and said, "I mean codes of conduct."

Mozzy loved to be politically incorrect.

"So, what are you thinking?" she said.

"I don't know. Could you see if the name Chucky Ware gets any kind of response over there? Be a little discreet about it. Stroud had some kind of involvement with a kid by that name, and Phinney's sort of interested in it for some reason. I guess Stroud may have been accused of something, or involved with something with the kid that might have gotten her fired. I just thought it might be worth looking at, maybe even getting in the paper."

"Oh, yeah," she said, "the paper."

"Maybe see if Stroud's got some kind of history of problems. Might be better, you know, if you're the one doing the checking."

"Sure thing," she said, sitting down. "I'll get right on it."

I had noticed Hemper eyeballing me and now he walked over and stood in front of Mozzy's desk as she dialed the number. He was wearing a stained, light-yellow shirt, either that or a very, very old white one.

"What's she doin'?" he said, gesturing toward Mozzy.

Mozzy had jotted down in black marker the name "Chucky" followed by a question mark on the letter I had just handed her, which, as Hemper approached, she had turned over so he could not read it. He noticed, picked it up and scanned it quickly. Then he kept it.

"She's just makin' a call," I said to Hemper.

He didn't smile.

"Yeah," he said, "I see."

Mozzy was trying to keep her voice down, but we were standing right in front of her desk and both of us could hear her say Stroud's name to somebody.

"I'll let you know if we find something," I said, turning away, starting to walk.

"Hold on, smart-ass," said Hemper.

He was looking up from the document now and leaned back, taking his glasses off, and rubbing his eyes. I had started toward my desk.

"Over there," he said, motioning for me to follow him into his office.

I did.

"Sit down," he said. He sat down on the edge of his desk.

"I'll stand."

"Sit."

I did.

"Look," he said, folding his arms. "I can only imagine how hard it is, what you've gone through in these last few days, and I'm gonna be the last guy in the world to tell you not to seek out answers to every single question you can. I think you should if you already haven't and, frankly, it's something we oughta be doing around here, too—as journalists. But we both know you shouldn't be the one doing it here. These have to be separate things, okay?"

"I'm just a source," I said. "I'm just passing something on. Like any source would. We give each other tips around here all the time. Mozzy can do what she wants with it. I'm not trying to influence her. Since when do we not share what we know?"

"So, you don't have any problem with us putting whatever we find in the paper?"

"None at all."

He looked at the letter to Sandy regarding Billi Stroud.

"Where'd you get it?" he said, reading it.

"It's authentic," I said. "There's no doubt about that."

"That's not the question."

"Just happened upon it."

"Don't give me that bullshit. What else do you have?"

"Nothing."

I saw Mozzy lingering near my desk. Hemper saw her, too, opened the door, and yelled.

"Get in here," he shouted at her. "What do you have?"

"Nothing," she replied, walking into the office and sitting down in one of the chairs. She leaned back so that only the tips of her shoes touched the ground and her head rested on the wall behind her.

"That the cops you were talking to?"

She nodded, and her chair rocked back and forth as she did.

"What'd they say?" said Hemper.

"Nothing."

"What do you mean nothing? Goddamnit, quit that rocking!"

"Nothing!" said Mozzy, straightening up. "Geez! They didn't say anything. Said they don't know what we're talking about, even off the record. Said we have our facts wrong. Said Stroud quit and they don't know why. Wasn't related to any discipline or any kid named Chucky Ware."

"Who's Chucky Ware?" said Hemper.

"That's what they said," said Mozzy.

He was re-reading the letter.

"Some kid Stroud was investigating, I guess—got her fired somehow."

"Did you tell them about the letter we have?" said Hemper.

"No. I don't think Will wanted me to. I got as specific as I could. Asked if she was disciplined at some point for consorting with someone she wasn't supposed to consort with, and that's the response I got: supposed bewilderment. Said you got your facts wrong. Said, 'I'd be real careful if I were you about what I planned to put in the paper.' You know, one of those."

"Write it up," said Hemper, handing her the letter. "And include both the fact we have the letter and who we got it from. Put Will's name in there. Write it up, just like we would anything. Include the denial and get it in tomorrow morning."

"What?" I said.

"If you're gonna be a part of this—and you are—we're at least gonna be up-front about it."

"What?"

"You heard me."

"It has to be today?" said Mozzy. "Maybe we could get more information tomorrow."

"Today," said Hemper.

"You sure I should be the one doing this?" said Mozzy.

"Will seemed to think so," replied Hemper. "Anyway, to the extent there might be a conflict, everybody here is going to have it. I think we should be okay, as long as we treat this like every other story, everything aboveboard."

He turned to me.

"I trust there's nothing," he said, "you haven't told us?"

"I'm telling you what I know," I said. "That's why I'm here."

"Good," said Hemper, turning back to Mozzy. "By the way, who's the prince who issued the denial?"

"Who do you think?" said Mozzy. "The only guy dumb enough to be working the weekend. Deiter."

11.

Cyprus Avenue was a street like most of the others in that part of town, once neat and well kept, now largely boarded up and deserted, windows covered with plywood, plywood covered with indecipherable graffiti. At one time, this had been a flourishing blue-collar neighborhood sustained by several large tractor and heavy-equipment plants. But they had long ago closed down, metamorphosed into rusted, hulking shells infested with rats and littered with used condoms and drug paraphernalia. Ubiquitous red and black caps of crack vials festooned the streets. Having worked hard for thirty years to pay off the mortgage on their tidy, brick bungalows, the old, unemployed factory workers realized now that it was all for naught. Even if they wanted to sell, no one in his right mind would buy. Property values had plummeted. An average house in decent shape would go for less than $30,000.

Deiter had grown up in this neighborhood, and still lived there, knew more about what went on than probably anyone else in the whole city. But he was not why I made the trip.

Cyprus was a block about two streets over from Deiter's own. Number 768 was right in the middle, one of the few houses late on Sunday afternoon with any of its lights on. I knocked.

The sidewalk was cracked and the concrete that led up three or four steps to the generic aluminum door was slowly being chipped away, but the house itself looked like it had been taken care of. I had waited until I was certain the occupants would be back from church. I could tell someone was home, and I was about to walk down the steps and peer into one of the windows when the knob turned and the door opened a crack.

"Yes?" inquired a pale, white woman who was crisply dressed in a skirt and blouse, but who looked tired.

I identified myself, conscious that I was still breathing heavily from the hurry, as she opened the door. She had large, vulnerable, blue eyes, graying hair, and a small round face. She looked out into the street, then focused again on me.

"I'm from the *Courier.*"

"We don't want the paper," said the woman, starting already to close the door.

"No, I'm a reporter. Are you Chucky Ware's mother?"

"Sister," she said, flatly.

"Oh."

"What do you want?"

"Nothing, really. I just wanted to talk to him for a minute if he's around. . . ."

"He's not. What'd he do?"

"Nothing, I don't think. It's not really about him so much. Do you know where he is?"

She paused for a long moment, then looked over my shoulder, from right to left. Inside, I could see from the stoop that the living room was dark with the exception of a couple of small lamps that gave the entire place the tint of an old sepia-colored photograph.

"It'll just take a minute," I said.

She glanced at the press card I had pulled out, then nodded almost imperceptibly. I moved inside, pausing to take my boots off, and she emitted a breath that bordered on a chuckle.

"Keep goin'," she said, before I had unlaced even the first one. I wasn't sure if she meant keep going and take the boots off or keep going into the living room.

"You comin' or not?" she said, as I pulled off the boots.

It was quiet inside, dark and silent, and it took me a moment to notice why: In a recliner was a man with his head bent forward, asleep. In the dim light, I could see at least two crucifixes in the room, one hanging on the wall near the door and the other above the TV set. She dragged a rocking chair out of a corner, and placed it directly in front of the couch, motioning for me to sit in it. The man with the bent head grunted. He was unshaven and overweight, a white man probably around fifty who looked like he was asleep. They were probably one of the last white families left in that part of town.

"You can sit there," she said, pointing at the rocking chair, not bothering to introduce or wake him.

There was a framed picture sitting on a nearby table of a handsome, young kid with close-cropped, black hair. He was standing in front of the house I was in, holding a small dog in his arms, and smiling at the camera. He was a stocky boy, wearing a blue-and-gold football jersey with the number 22 on it, and a big, almost cocky, smile.

His trouble had started young, I would later learn. First it was minor stuff: shoplifting, small items mostly—candy and gum, a pack of shoelaces. Another time, he was inexplicably caught taking a ball of string and three nuts out of a hardware store. Then, things got more serious. There were fights, a breaking-and-entering, and two assaults, both of them against girlfriends, one of them with sexual overtones. The district attorney's office sought an adult charge on that one, but a judge decided against it and sent him to a youth home for about eight months. Deiter, I saw in the file, had been involved in several of the cases.

"That Chucky?" I said, pointing to the picture.

"That's him."

"And he's not around?"

"No."

"This is your parents' house, isn't it?"

I'd checked the property records. In the modern world, with the Internet, you can do a lot on a Sunday.

She pursed her lips, ever so slightly.

"My parents have passed, my mother just a year ago," she said. "It's just me, most the time, sometimes him." She gestured to the man on the recliner without identifying him. "And Chucky . . ."

Her voice trailed off.

"Can I ask where Chucky went?"

"That's actually a hell of a good question."

She picked up a pack of cigarettes on a table in front of her and turned it over and tapped the bottom of it, then put it down again without taking one out. She had a face of experience and sorrow, but I thought it had a certain softness to it as well. I pulled out a picture of Billi Stroud that we had been running in the paper. It was one taken when she was arrested and showed her much the same way she looked the day I visited her in jail.

"You recognize her?"

She took a hard look, then reached for some glasses on the table, put them on and looked again in the dim light.

"Don't know," she said. "Hard to tell."

The cigarettes gave her voice a gravelly sound that, I presumed, would only get worse as she aged.

"She a friend of Chucky's? Maybe a girlfriend?" I asked.

She looked again, a little closer, then put it down.

"I don't think so," she said, picking up the cigarette pack and nervously tapping on the bottom of it until one slid halfway out, then putting it down again. She was younger up close than she at first appeared, probably not much more than midthirties.

"Who is she?" she asked.

"That's Billi Stroud."

She turned her head slightly, as if it sounded familiar but didn't quite register.

"The cop," I said. "One who's been on television."

She picked up the picture and looked at it again, puzzled. The local television station had been running a much different picture, one of Stroud in her police uniform with her blue cap on, smiling slightly for the camera. That one made her look much younger, less worn, more innocent.

"That's her?" said the woman, for the first time exhibiting some interest in the conversation, some animation. She held the picture with both hands, squinting as she examined it.

I nodded.

"Damn," she said. "Why are you showin' me?"

"She knew Chucky."

"How?"

"Thought maybe you'd know."

She was shaking her head back and forth. "Was she doin' something she wasn't supposed to?"

"Like what?"

She didn't answer.

"Where is Chucky? Can I talk to him?"

She handed the picture of Stroud back to me and paused for a moment.

"Truth is," she said, "I wish I knew. Haven't seen him in a while. He left his pickup at the bus station. We asked if the bus company knew where he went but they said they'd had no idea. Just told us to move it. It's in the garage."

"Any idea where he went?"

"That's just it," she said. "There's no place I can think of that he coulda gone." She fingered the pack of cigarettes again, and her voice grew noticeably softer. "Acted like a hotshot around here, what with the drugs and the boys all following him like a bunch of puppies. But he was lost once he stepped out of this little neighborhood. He didn't know anything else, never even really went anywhere else. Don't really know why he would."

"He was dealing drugs?"

She bowed her head now, just slightly.

"Look," she said. "What's your name?"

"Will Dunby."

"Mr. Dunby, look. Chucky had his troubles, and I don't excuse him for it. He had a hard time, Lord knows, and when our mother died, well . . . But at some point you have to grow up, you know. That's what I told him, but he just didn't seem to take to that. Maybe just wouldn't. He was fooling around with stuff I didn't approve of. Had people comin' by all day and night. They'd sit in there . . ." She pointed down the hall. "Here, too, right at this table here. Do God knows what. I tried to stop it but most of the time I'm at work. And she . . ."—she pointed to the picture of Billi Stroud—"I don't know anything about her."

"Are you worried about him?"

"Truth is, it wasn't unusual for me not to see him for a day or two, maybe three or four if I was busy working and our paths didn't cross. But he never stayed away like this. Being honest, it worries me to death. Been sick about it. For months."

"You haven't seen him for months?" I asked.

She looked me straight in the eye.

"At least," she said.

"Why didn't you report it to the police?"

"Who says I didn't?"

12.

Deiter's house was a brick two-story place with a large metal gate surrounding it and an immaculate front yard. Either he was meticulously neat or the kids in the neighborhood knew better than to mess with him because there was not a scrap of paper or refuse within ten feet of his property. He was just getting out of his car as I pulled up.

"Hey," I said. "Got a minute?"

Deiter was close to fifty, if he wasn't there already. He was a large man, with not a hint of fat on him, and despite the fact he lived in one of the rougher sections of town, he claimed never to have been so much as sworn at. To look at him was to believe it.

Never in all the years I had known him had I come to his house and the greeting quite literally stopped him in his tracks. He was not smiling.

"Will," he said. "What the hell are you doing here?"

I walked quickly up his driveway from my car, and repeated my query. "You got a minute?"

He looked around furtively. "Yeah."

He was clearly perplexed. Most of the people he worked with still had no idea we really even knew each other and we were used to meeting, if we had to at all, in dark and out-of-the-way bars. He had been to our house, but only occasionally.

"Sorry," I said. "I need to talk."

He ushered me in through the back door and into the kitchen. Like the outside, it was neat and well ordered, in no way ostentatious. The dishrag in the sink, I noticed, was folded into a perfect square. A moment later an attractive middle-aged woman in a dress came in. She looked like she had just returned from church.

"Jennie," said Deiter, "this is Will Dunby."

"Oh!" she said, smiling warmly and extending a hand. I shook it, but she must have gathered something from Deiter's demeanor because she quickly excused herself.

"Need to see if I can figure out Del's algebra for him," she said. "Nice to meet you."

Del was their son, a high school senior who would have been about Chucky Ware's age. Del, as anyone who lived in Droughton knew, was a star athlete, not in basketball or football or one of the sports that white folks expect black kids to excel in. He was a star hockey player, good enough, despite being out much of his senior season with a case of mononucleosis, to be given a full scholarship to Boston College. Moreover, he was smart, a National Merit Scholar semifinalist. He was only eighteen, and already his name was in the paper more frequently than his father's.

"How is Del?" I asked.

"What do you mean?" said Deiter, curtly.

"Nothing. I mean how is he?"

"He's fine. What do you want?"

Deiter was still holding a bag of groceries in his arms and, only now, put them on the table. Then he turned toward me without asking me to sit. Instead of saying anything, he just lifted his hands slightly toward me as if to say "What?" He was not pleased that I was there.

"I need to ask you about Chucky Ware," I said.

"I sort of thought you already did."

"Why'd you deny knowing anything about it when Mozzy called?"

"The way I recall it, it was more of a 'no comment.' You know I'm still entitled to that."

"But you do know him?"

"You know, Will," he said, "we've known each other a long time and I've noticed you've got a funny habit of asking a lot of questions—but answering very few."

"Hey," I said, not backing down. "Sandy's my wife."

"Yeah, I'm actually quite aware of that small fact. I got a wife and kid myself." He paused for a moment, not taking his eyes off me, then said, "Of course, I know him."

"Do you know where he is? It's off-the-record."

Deiter turned away from me now.

"Look, buddy," he said, and I really could not tell if he used it as a term of derision or friendship. "There is no more off-the-record. Not with this."

"What do you mean?"

"Just what I said. I'm glad you're here, actually, because we need to talk."

He turned back toward me.

"About what?"

"About what do you think about what? We need to close out this investigation of Sandy's accident, first. That's number one. I need to ask you a few things and I need you to be straight with me."

"I'm always straight with you. And for the record—"

"You weren't listening. It's all for the record."

"Fine," I murmured.

"What was goin' on with Sandy?" he asked.

"I told you before. Sandy was fine," I said. "I haven't slept, thinking about it, but I can't come up with anything. She was fine—"

"Thinking about what?"

"All of it. Anything. Whatever. She had her problems you know, but they were like anyone's."

"What problems?"

"Just like her dad, you know, occasional, mild depression. She was on Depokote. But that had been the case for years. It was okay, never that severe. It was manageable."

"Had she stopped taking it?"

"Not as far as I know."

"I'll need the pills. No questions, doubts, anything like that about anything that was going on with her? Suspicions even? Hunches? Intuition?"

"Not really."

"Something with Moylan?"

"No."

He looked at me long and hard, and I wondered what he knew.

"I mean, sure," I said. "Yes, I have questions. But not really."

He nodded slowly. He knew I was not trusting him with the truth. I had never said anything about Moylan out loud to anyone other than Sandy, and at that point silence was just not a habit I could bring myself to break.

"You know," he said, "these are the things that tend to come back at you, Will. You know that?"

"What things?"

He just stared at me again, and didn't answer.

"And where," he asked, "do you come up with this stuff about Chucky?"

"I got some of it from one of Sandy's files," I said, trying to redeem myself with some small measure of honesty.

"From the letter about Stroud?"

"Yes."

"That's what I figured."

"What was all that about?" I asked.

"No comment."

"Could Chucky have killed Moylan?"

"What?" he said. "Why would you possibly think that?"

I didn't answer. I didn't know. I was grasping at straws.

"He's a stupid kid," said Deiter. "He's a criminal. And a drug dealer. But that doesn't mean . . ."

He stopped in midsentence, as if it were not worth his time explaining. He blew out of long stream of air.

"Look, Will," he said, "this is going to be hard on all of us—no matter which way it turns. I don't know where that kid fits in, frankly, and he might not fit in at all. It's just one part of what I'm trying to figure out. But don't muck things up now by sticking your nose into it. You're way too close to it to know what you're looking for and when I tell you to back off you need to trust me."

But it was too late. We'd both just found out that I didn't.

13.

The cameramen and the reporters sat on wooden benches and drank lattes and complained mildly about having to work so early on Monday morning while, gradually, the crowd around them grew. Courthouse gadflys, youngsters hoping to get on television, hangers-on attracted by the lights and the familiar faces of TV reporters, passersby wondering what all the hubbub was about—all gradually stopped and lingered.

At a few minutes before nine, Phinney showed up and waved off the reporters who approached him for a comment.

"She's ready to get out," was all he said, sitting down on one of the benches with a coffee. "She didn't do anything and she wants to get out."

Several reporters spent a few more minutes peppering him with questions until, finally, it became clear he was serious about the no-comment.

The clerk's office where Phinney would have to post bond was supposed to open at nine o'clock sharp, but they were late opening the doors. Finally, about ten minutes past the hour, Phinney got a little agitated and got up and looked into the offices and gently tapped on the glass door. A couple of women were standing behind a counter, talking in what looked like serious tones and glancing occasionally at the crowd but did not make a move. Finally, just as Phinney was pulling out a cell phone to try to call inside, Thorpe walked down the hall.

"C'mon, Carney," said Phinney, when he saw him, the cell phone open in his hand. "Why aren't the doors open?"

"Change of plans," responded the prosecutor, not bothering to look at his adversary, turning toward the bevy of reporters.

It was as if a switch had been thrown. Almost instantaneously, the lights and the cameras snapped on. The courthouse hallway lit up like a crèche on a dark winter's night, obscuring everything that was outside the perimeter, bathing Thorpe in bright white like some sort of self-anointed savior. Phinney stood up, downed what little remained of his coffee, and threw the cup in a garbage can.

"What are you telling me?" he said.

"She's not going to be posting," said Thorpe, still not bothering to look at him.

Thorpe was at the center of the fishbowl now. The cameramen formed the initial row, four or five of them with huge lenses eyeballing the prosecutor like a herd of open-eyed cyclops. In between, jutting through the openings, were countless small microphones and tape recorders at the ends of the outstretched arms of radio and print reporters.

"Everybody ready?" said the prosecutor.

The cameramen stopped fiddling, and held still.

"We got the ballistics tests back," he said into bright lights, "and the bullets pulled from the victim's body came from the gun issued to Ms. Stroud." He paused for effect. "It was her weapon that killed Dr. Moylan," Thorpe said. "We're charging her with first-degree homicide."

"How do you know it was hers?" said one of the reporters.

"She was issued a ten-millimeter Glock, serial number EE516US. It's a gun that, before she owned it, was carried by another officer. That officer, it turns out, fired the gun at one time a few years ago outside a tavern. No one was seriously hurt but ballistics tests were done. The bullets found in Tommy

Moylan's body came from that gun. Same caliber and markings."

"Where is it?" someone asked.

I stood there immobile, seeing an image of Billi Stroud pacing her cell, waiting for someone to show up with a key.

"Where is the gun?" reiterated another.

"We don't know," was all Thorpe said. "We still don't know."

part TWO

14.

Sandy, when she got home from the health club, used to wear one of her old cotton shirts after she got out of the shower and before she came to bed, one that reached down well below her belly button but did not conceal her fully.

"Hey!" she'd say, laughing, crouching so that she could pull the shirt down toward her thighs. "Quit glowering!"

"Glowering?"

Now, when she was not wearing a diaper, it was surprising almost to see the dark patch of hair above her genitalia. It was as if I had expected her somehow to have regressed to a state of prepubescent dependence and innocence, for that is how, most times now, I thought of her.

Within a few months, Sandy had been stable enough to bring home. We set her up in the living room with a view of the gardens that were, by then, in full bloom. Surprisingly quickly, despite a diligent routine of therapy, she was losing all muscle tone. She also developed sometimes acute respiratory problems. Much of the time she was wheezing and gurgling, struggling to suck enough air into her shrinking body to keep it functioning. Some days, I marvelled at her resilience. Other days, especially if I had been away from her for a period of time, I would return to be utterly struck by the sadness and apparent painfulness of her condition. She was clearly deteriorating.

I could not know how it registered with her, the pain, for her mind and her nervous system were utterly unfathomable to me.

But I was certain it was no less a part of her than her hands and feet and the blood that flowed through her veins.

Sandy was still breathing on her own, but her breaths were labored and shallow. Drinking a glass of water or lifting a Popsicle to her mouth would have been a miracle. It was never even discussed, and I had stopped dreaming about it. We would occasionally dab a wet sponge on her lips but they were chapped so badly that in places they cracked and even bled. They had been coated with Vaseline, but it had not seemed to help. Her graying hair was pulled back in rather severe fashion off her forehead and tied with a ribbon that Haley had bought. Haley was well intentioned, but the ribbon looked so incongruous it was absurd, like placing a television in front of a gravestone. The visiting nurses still administered enemas, but she also need the diaper. Once a day, they would change the sheets. She couldn't even move her lips, at least not intentionally.

"Does she remember?" I asked Kerry Tsau, leaning forward with my elbows resting on my knees and my hands propping up my chin.

He came to the house occasionally, a vestige of small-town courtesy, wearing hospital scrubs and a pair of old sandals with black socks.

"Why shouldn't she remember?" I wanted to know.

"Will," said Kerry, pensively, sitting up on the edge of the chair. "Will, I never really expected that she could even breathe spontaneously. That she can means only that her brain stem is essentially intact—and that her body is capable of some other spontaneous functions. Sleep, maybe in a sense, is one of them. Blinking sometimes, maybe. Memory is not something I can gauge."

"She's on autopilot." I said this derisively because it was a term he had used before.

"Yes," he said, ignoring my tone. "There is a part of her brain that still maintains body temperature and blood pressure and all the other functions it takes for a body to physically live. At least most of them. But, yes, you might say she is on autopilot."

"Sometimes I think she's listening."

"It is a normal reaction. She is still living, Will. And maybe in some way she does hear." He turned fully toward me. "But she does not listen. She does not register things the way we do. She can't."

Kerry did this often, I thought. Momentarily raised my hopes. Said she had something akin to a capability. Then redefined it. Drew a line. Said, "Yes, she can hear, perhaps, but she cannot listen," when most people would think of them as one and the same.

"You don't really know," I said, irritated. "Do you?"

"Know what?"

"Whether anything really remains in there, whether there is any vestige?"

He sighed.

"Will," he said. "Will, you can see it as well as I can."

"Some physical vestige, sure. But I mean of something essential."

"What's essential?" he said bluntly.

"I don't know," I said. "Something, at least, of what she was."

"You're asking me to look inside her mind and I can't do that," said Kerry. "It's not up to me to define who she was, or is. It's a fact that Sandy cannot think the way that we do. But even the best neurologists can't be certain whether the cessation of higher brain function entails a total and complete loss of all forms of consciousness and awareness, a loss of self, whatever it is. There is no evidence that those things can still exist, but it's difficult to prove a negative. Impossible to prove a negative. I can't prove to you that it doesn't exist."

"So she may still be there in some essential way?"

"I don't know what you mean."

I turned away, convinced that he really did.

Elizabeth rarely took part in these conversations. She stood at a distance with her arms crossed and her head tilted and listened intently until he was done, then silently left the room.

As time went on, she began to comment to me, casually and offhand at first, that there was no way Sandy could suffer like this indefinitely. At first, it was said in a way, or perhaps this is simply how I chose to hear it, that implied that surely the fates would not allow this type of suffering and unresolvedness to continue forever. But Elizabeth was not one resigned to the caprices of fate. She was proactive, a word Sandy once told me I didn't know the meaning of.

"Hey," I told her, "I'll learn it when I have to."

Elizabeth became more explicit one day in midsummer not long before the trial of Billi Stroud was to begin. Whether it was because she had settled in her own mind upon the exact genesis of what happened the day of Sandy's accident, or because whatever happened outside the walls of the Cross House was, to her, simply extraneous, I was not sure. But she had no interest in the legal proceedings that were about to begin in earnest. Elizabeth was focused elsewhere.

She was standing beside me, changing a diaper. It was, of course, an unpleasant task, and Elizabeth knew that I tried to avoid it, but not for the reasons I think she assumed, not because of the smell, or the distastefulness. My hesitation had a different origin, more to do with the past than the present, or perhaps the vivid juxtaposition of the two. I was trying to preserve memories, not let them be wholly overrun, while Elizabeth was focused on the moment at hand, and what the future held. She evinced no hesitation at the task, just a workerlike fastidiousness.

She took the soiled diaper and walked into the bathroom, where we had a little container that was supposed to hide the smell, but didn't. She placed the diaper inside and washed her hands, then paused, looking toward the cabinet to one side. The closet was open and even from where I sat I could see the shelves of medicine, the aspirin and antibiotics, shelves and shelves of soaps and perfumes, gauze and bandages, small sponges and needles for stitch-making. There were old bottles of lotion, metal containers of Band-Aids. These were Sandy's things, bought by the case, compulsively, and often never used, strewn about with what had been left behind by her father and mother in no predictable way. Most of the bottles held harmless cough syrups, iodine, or penicillin. But there were stronger medications as well. Codeine, barbiturates. Lithium. Sandy's Depokote. Even curare, or at least the purified form—tubocurarine chloride—used by doctors as an anesthetic. The real stuff, Sandy's father would say in one of his little impromptu lectures, was extracted from two plants that grew deep in the Amazon and Orinoco River Basins of South America. The tribal doctors would mix it up in a brew with everything from vines and leaves to red ants, scorpions, blood, and human hair.

"Many of the ingredients were superfluous, of course," I could hear him say, sitting in an overstuffed leather chair in the den. The Indians down there used it for hunting. They'd dip their blow darts into the dark, brown, tarry resin that came out of the pot, wait patiently for their prey, and then blow the tiny stick thirty or forty yards into a bird no bigger than a small hen. The time needed for death depended on the size of the animal. Even a relatively large curassow could drop out of the sky and die in just a few minutes. A peccary, the little white-lipped swine—or a human, perhaps—would take somewhat longer. Paralysis was immediate, but not painful. The drug would disconnect the nerves from the muscles, first numbing the toes, then the ears and eyes. If administered in large enough doses, it would go to the neck and limbs as well. Those who got a big enough dose just stopped breathing as the drug surrounded the respiratory muscles. Disconnected them. Cut them off.

Elizabeth picked up the curare, then realized that I was looking at her through the open door. Emboldened, she carried it with her out into the living room and sat down at the side of Sandy's bed. Then she sat there and did not move for what seemed like an eternity of separate and distinct moments.

"What would you want for yourself?" she asked, finally, looking at me for the first time.

Elizabeth still spent most of her nights at her friend's house, but each day she arrived early and stayed well past supper, sometimes caring for her daughter, sometimes simply sitting beside her, sometimes taking long walks through the fields and woods. In the months that Elizabeth had been there, the subject had lingered like yellow fog in the distance, held there immobile by the other questions and suppositions, moving in slowly, showing no sign of dissipation. And yet I was not prepared for it.

"What do you mean?" I said.

She looked at me briefly, sternly. We both knew I was being disingenuous. I knew what she meant, and she turned back to Sandy, grasping one of her hands and stroking the hair away from her forehead.

"I'm asking," she said, slowly and clearly, enunciating her words, "if you were in her position—"

"I know . . . I know what you're asking. . . . and the truth is that neither of us has any idea what it would be like, what it is like," I said. "I don't know . . . and I don't know that it matters."

She nodded, absorbing it all, preparing a response, a strategy.

"You're right," she said. "We really don't know what it's like . . . not exactly. But we do know what it's probably not like." She pulled Sandy's gown down over the diaper, and stood up straight, looking at me now.

"What's that mean?" I said.

"It's unlike anything we know," said Elizabeth, with the air of someone who has thought her words through. "Unlike anything she knew. Where she is, or what she is now, Will, it's just completely removed from us, from the whole world."

"Elizabeth, I can't help but feel, I think, that somehow she still has a connection to us. Knows we're here. That we still care. She's still there, Elizabeth. She hasn't gone away. She's right there."

Elizabeth nodded, not in agreement, but as though she were taking this in, too, taking measure of me, and she continued to nod as she caressed Sandy's forehead and held her hand, as if my response was wholly expected and had somehow harmed Sandy. Elizabeth was her savior and protector.

"I just think sometimes," she said slowly, enunciating even more carefully, "more than sometimes now, that if I were in this position I would want some resolution. And I think that Sandy would want the same, wants the same, if she's even capable of wanting. She might just be better off, not—"

"Not what?" I interrupted. "Being?"

I had said it loudly and quickly, with no hesitation or regret and Elizabeth seemed struck by the force of the words. She stepped back, and after a short moment, a brief repose, she moved around to the same side of the bed that I was on, leaned back into a corner and, facing me from about a foot away, crossed her arms.

"Tell me this," she said. "What are we trying to prove?"

"I don't know about you," I said. "I'm not trying to prove anything."

I was still sitting, looking up at her.

"Oh, no? Will, we've known each other a long time and maybe it's different for you, I don't know. Maybe it is. For me, I will admit there are things I wish I'd done differently, things between me and Sandy, and I think maybe she would feel the same. Lots of things, believe me. I wish she knew how proud I was of her, how much I admired what she accomplished and what she was, how good and decent a person she was. How caring. I wish I'd treated her differently in ways I can't really express to you even now, to anyone, to myself. It's too painful, and that's not an easy thing for me to admit to you. But doing—doing this!" Her arms came apart now and her hands burst outward. "Doing this just doesn't have anything to do with that, with the rest of it, with whatever else is going on, or went on. You understand what I'm saying?"

"There's nothing going on," I said.

She glared at me.

"I mean who are we doing this for?" she shouted.

I don't know that I had ever heard her shout.

"I'm doing it for her, for Sandy," I said.

I was still speaking in a calm and level voice, and of that I was proud.

"Are you? Are you really?" said Elizabeth, moving even closer. "I mean, if you are, fine, okay. But, Will, she doesn't see . . . or smell . . . or taste." Elizabeth now was leaning toward me, talking in a low voice, as if she were tired already of explaining. "She has no idea who we are, or what we do—and that's if she's lucky! She can't even make a sound. She's in pain, for God's sake! It's demeaning!"

"To whom?" I said.

I regretted that immediately. Elizabeth, I knew, had no compunction about changing Sandy's diapers and wiping her nose. She was more than willing to do it, and I believe would have done it for the rest of her life. She would have.

"To all of us," she said, ignoring the barb. "Pretending that she's living because her intestine still works. Or because she can breathe. Or bleed! She can bleed!" Elizabeth said it as if it were a revelation. "Like the plain truth isn't right there in front of us!

That's not what made her human! It's not what made her, Will! My God, do you remember how much more than that she was? Her intellect? Her personality? Everything! It's gone! All of it! And it's not coming back!"

I had never till then, nor have I ever since then, seen quite the same look in Elizabeth's eye as I witnessed at that moment. But there was something in me, too.

"She also had determination," I said, whispering. "Do you remember that?"

"Do I remember?" she said, her voice quavering. "Will, I remember things you never knew. Could never know." Her eyes were welling up now. "I remember the day she was born. It was twenty degrees below zero. We wrapped her in four blankets when we took her home. I still have one of them. I remember the first time she took a step. She was wearing green pajamas, standing on the porch of our old house on Hasser Street." She wiped a tear away. "I remember I was sitting in a wicker rocker and she was standing there in front of me holding on to a table. Just walked into my arms. . . ."

The tears flowed down her cheeks, unabashedly.

"I remember her first date," said Elizabeth, reminding me, I was sure it was intentional, that I was far from Sandy's first boyfriend. "She was my girl, Will. I remember all of it. Everything. And I don't care what you say." She was sobbing now. "This has nothing to do with me except that she's my daughter, and I raised her the best way I knew how. I love her. And I would take care of her for the rest of my life if I thought she would want me to. . . . If I thought it for a second."

She turned away and plucked a Kleenex out of a box on a table where we kept Sandy's medications. Scattered tears were still flowing freely down her face as she looked at the curare there on the table at the end of the bed; she just left it sitting there like a challenge as she walked, without another word, out into the kitchen.

A few feet away, Sandy lay unmoved, gasping and wheezing and, maybe if she could have, wishing she had never been so lucky as to have been thrown away from the burning wreckage of that car as she drove out over the treetops toward the clear, gray, everlasting, unfathomable sky.

15.

Phinney, as part of the discovery process, attempted to have Sandy's legal records, and anything else germane to Stroud's case that might be present on the Cross property, subpoenaed—but Haley immediately challenged it in court. She called the subpoena everything from "vague" to "oppressive" to "ambiguous" to "a fishing expedition" to "overly burdensome," and then raised the attorney-client privilege issue to boot. Nevers sided with us, and quashed it.

"How do I pay you?" I asked her.

"Just buy me a martini," said Haley.

Haley, Sandy had often teased her, liked her martinis. And lots of other stuff with alcohol as well.

Sandy and I first formally met the night that Haley and I graduated from college. Haley threw a party in an apartment in Droughton she had started renting the week before and put a keg on the back porch. She started drinking early in the afternoon and by the time most of the guests arrived was already drunk enough to twice accidentally lock herself out. When we laughingly refused to let her back in, she shrugged, sat down on the porch and directly inserted the end of the tap into her mouth.

"Resilient, isn't she," said Sandy.

Haley and I were dating at the time but as the party grew we lost track of each other. The music was loud, and by the time it was dark the smell of marijuana drifted out of the bedrooms as bleary-eyed twenty-two-year-olds tried to shout incoherent conversations over the din of music. A few people had lined up jobs, and a couple others—like Sandy and Haley—were going on to law school. It was something Sandy had always wanted to do and something Haley concluded she would be good at as well. I had vague plans to go to graduate school but was going to tend bar for a while to make some money first. Further schooling was a way of deferring the inevitable—a real life, a real job, responsibilities.

I knew who Sandy was, of course, but it was not until Haley introduced us that evening that we talked. She was wearing jeans with holes in the knees and a casual T-shirt but appeared older than most of the rest of us. She was drinking Coke and munching on pretzels and was completely clear-eyed.

"I think Haley might be in love with you," she told me.

"Actually," I said, "she spends most of her time talking about you."

"I suspect it's a slightly different sort of affection."

"I hope so."

She chuckled. I had once thought I was in love with Haley, it is true, perhaps even still felt it at that time. If it had not been for Sandy, I sometimes suspected in the years after, Haley and I could easily have ended up together, perhaps indefinitely. There were many ways in which we were cut from the same proverbial cloth. We came from similar backgrounds, we had fun together, basic as it might sound, and were, in Haley's words, "quite sexually compatible."

And yet I couldn't escape the feeling that it was circumstance that brought us together more than who we were exactly or what we did for each other.

"You're dumping me because it's too easy to be with me," she said, incredulous, when I told her I wanted to date other people.

"I'm not dumping you," I said.

"Sure feels like it," she countered.

"I'm just not sure it feels right in my heart," I told her finally.

"Maybe you don't know your heart."

I thought I did.

"Maybe," I said, "you don't exactly know yours."

The beginning of the end, I think, probably started the night of that party. I did not have a car that night, and Haley was too inebriated, by the time it was midnight, to give me a ride home. So when Sandy, who was not drinking, offered me a lift to my parents' house, where I was temporarily staying, I accepted. What we talked about I have no idea—until Sandy pulled her car into the driveway.

"He's a night owl, eh?" she said.

I didn't, at first, know to what she was alluding. Then, I saw my father slouched over in a chair on the front porch. I immediately knew what had happened and tried to hurry out of the car.

"Is he all right?" said Sandy.

"I'm sure he will be in the morning."

I quickly thanked her for the ride, but she did not leave. She stayed in the car with the headlights on as I rushed up on the porch and tried to rouse him. He stirred, but I could not get him to sit up.

"You're sure he's okay?" she said, standing now beside her car with the door still open. "You're sure?"

"It's okay," I said. "Thanks for the ride."

He'd gotten drunk enough to throw up on himself and when I came back out from inside the house with a warm rag I found Sandy on the porch, already using some tissue to try to clean him up. I'd dated Haley for months, and she knew nothing about my father's problems, which I resisted defining as alcoholism. I'd only just met Sandy and there she was cleaning vomit off his T-shirt and his pants.

"Should we get him a fresh shirt?" she said.

"Let's just sit him up in the living room," I said. "Keep his head up."

"Not in the bedroom?"

"I don't think my mother lets him sleep in there anymore."

"Oh."

Sandy placed herself underneath one of his arms and I got underneath the other. After we put him in the living room and got him into a clean T-shirt, Sandy and I sat on the porch and sipped glasses of Coke.

"I'm sorry," I said, "that you had to witness that."

"Must be hard," she said.

"More so for my mother."

My father spent his life, I told Sandy that night, working seventy or eighty hours a week at a wholesale fruit distribution business, hauling baskets of apples and peaches and oranges off the produce trucks and lugging them into coolers, then out again when the grocers arrived. It was physical work of a sort not very different from what transpired in those same buildings almost a century earlier. My father would have fit just as well, perhaps much better, in a far earlier age. That the buildings were still there at all, still used as they had been for a century to sell fruit to the city's merchants, was testimony to one thing: money. The handful of ragtag wholesalers who walked around the open-air market in white, dirt-encrusted bibs, made so much of it that they alone had been able to resist the generous offers of the developers and investors who had tried for years to convince them to move their fruit businesses elsewhere. So, while the rest of the city changed and grew, transmogrified from a manufacturing and factory town into a city of lawyers and accountants and computer programmers, the grocers stayed still. They bought their oranges from the big growers in Florida, their grapes from the vineyards in California, their corn from the farmers in Iowa and Wisconsin and Minnesota. And then they sold it. Always for a tidy profit.

None of which was ever seen by my father.

He worked the docks, unloading trucks and keeping track of invoices. Did it for years. Saving a nickel here or there, going to church on Sunday morning, and waiting, he told himself, for a chance to buy one of the four or five operations. For decades he worked. And he waited. And for years he never made more, I bet, than ten dollars an hour. He lugged crates of cantaloupe from one truck to another until, the previous fall, he'd collapsed in a cooler and been forced to stop working altogether. He collected a small amount of disability pay and tapped into his pension early and came to realize rather quickly that, for him, that would be it.

"Life," Sandy said, "sometimes weighs you down."

She was sitting right next to me on the top step, so close that when she turned her head in my direction to speak her hair swept across my shoulder and brushed my cheek. And although she was, to me, stunningly attractive, I felt nothing so much as overwhelming comfort.

"Why am I surprised," I said, "to hear someone like you say something like that?"

"Don't let the nice car fool you."

I laughed. She was driving a Subaru that night.

"It's not yours?"

"Sure it is. But that's not what I meant."

"You just strike me as someone who floats above it all."

"Nobody floats above it all."

"No? You're beautiful. Rich. Intelligent. You're going to law school."

She smiled. "I'm not going to sleep with you."

I laughed again. "I don't expect you would."

"I'm lucky," she said. "I admit it."

"You've got something figured out."

"You think? Like what?"

"How not to get drunk at your third party this week, for one."

"Hey," she said, "it's the season."

"Yeah."

"Anyway, I don't abstain out of maturity."

"What other reason is there?"

"Nothing so mundane."

"So you're just a lightweight?"

She chuckled in a self-deprecating way.

"Not the kind of lightweight you think."

We sat there for a moment, in a stillness that seemed almost preternatural. In the distance you could hear the sound of cars on the highway, but not one drove down my parents' street that whole time we sat there. It was as if no one could find us.

"I don't drink much," she said, "because I'm not supposed to. It doesn't mix well with my medication."

She said it all matter-of-factly, had nothing to hide.

"What's it for?"

"My dad's been on it—or something like it—for years. Helps us cope, I guess."

"With what?"

"Stuff. Your dad drinks. I take a little pill."

"Sounds illegal."

"Hardly."

"Are you okay?"

She paused for a moment, then burst out laughing. She laughed so loudly that it seemed to bounce off the houses across the street and echo back at us and she quickly threw a hand up to her mouth to stifle the noise.

"I'm not crazy," she said, "if that's what you mean."

"I didn't imagine that."

"I get—how shall I say it?—overly immersed. That's the way my dad puts it. I could get by without the medicine, do sometimes, but it's better when I'm on it. Hey, everybody's got her little crutch." She looked in at my dad. "Don't be too hard on him."

"I'm not. . . . I don't even talk to him."

Sandy looked at me, all hint of humor gone now from her voice.

"You're living in his house and you don't talk to him?"

"It was a joke."

"Was it?"

"Well, I ask him where the hell the remote control is sometimes." I tried to laugh, but it had come out flat.

"Thing is," I said, "I love him. I do. He's a good person. I've admired the guy my whole life. But what he is now, I just don't know that."

"You don't think he's the same?"

"No."

"That's a mistake."

"It's sad. He worked his ass off his entire life, and things are coming to a bad end for him. He knows it and he's just, well, I don't know what he's doing. It's not just a crutch. It's different. It's self-destructive. It's killing my mom. We don't know how to handle it."

"So you don't handle it at all?"

"I clean him up."

"People make mistakes. Sometimes they need help getting through it. Get him some help. Talk to him."

I didn't say anything.

"Yeah."

Two days later, my father died of an aneurysm. Fell down the back steps—sober, actually, at the time. He was gone, they say, before he hit the bottom. I tell myself I never got the chance to talk to him, as Sandy suggested. But the truth is I just never took advantage of the chance I had. Sandy and Haley came together to the wake, and stood in line. Haley was first. She kissed me and told me how sorry she was. Then came Sandy. She said nothing. But as Haley moved away across the room, I held her tight. And I did not let her go.

16.

There is nothing quite like cleaning out the closets of the dead, nothing quite so sad and guilt-affixing as examining all the accoutrements of a bygone life and wondering if someone—someone else—would want them now. Sandy still breathed and blinked, but I found it no different for her. She did not wear much perfume, but her clothes carried a distinctively sweet and subtle scent that I suddenly realized I had already forgotten. Her basic metabolism had so fundamentally altered, I realized, that even her body now smelled differently, as though it belonged to someone else. I had planned to pack some old blouses and sweaters, perhaps some of the coats and dresses, but found the task too onerous, myself too harried, and took what I had collected—a few pairs of jeans and some plain, casual shirts—to the back door. For my purposes, it would be enough.

Stone Soup was just as I remembered it, a large brick bungalow with tasteful forest-green shutters and a well-groomed yard in the 800 block of Phillips Avenue, a well-kept, quiet little street of tidy bungalows on the east side of town. In the winter, Christmas lights festooned the outside of the house and the bushes regardless of how long it had been since Christmas had passed. In the summer, bushes and bushes of roses bloomed in gardens along the front and one side.

The location of the shelter was not meant for public dissemination and was not even formally registered with the state. It was not designed to be like other, more conventional shelters, those that placed themselves in the most conspicuous places and opened their doors to virtually anyone who walked in off the street. It was for women and children most seriously in need of help, those who were not only down on their luck and in need of a meal and a shower, but who feared for their very lives, and needed protection. It was for those who had been so beaten and battered by abusive husbands or boyfriends that they had no choice but to run and hide.

The women who were referred there by the social service agencies usually arrived at night and, after staying for varying amounts of time, left without ever seeing or being seen by any of the neighbors in the surrounding houses. Some who had money stayed only a day or two, long enough to get their bearings, hide their tracks, and move into an apartment or hotel. Others, the less fortunate and those more in need, stayed longer, then moved into other transitional homes.

Sandy did a lot of legal work there, and other work, too, and she had allowed me on a few occasions, against all the rules, to drop her off. I was actually a little bit apprehensive, as I pulled up, that I would, by showing up and now tacitly acknowledging the fact, get her in some sort of trouble.

Gretchen Lane was the director of the house, a large woman with short gray hair and a hearing aid who was given to wearing shawls and woolen sweaters. I found her in the backyard, sweeping off the walk, and I shouted out a greeting, making sure that she could see the bag I held in my arms. Looking slightly haggard, she turned around and, peering at me as if her glasses were too weak, at first said nothing. We'd met, but she didn't recognize me.

"What do you want?" she finally said in a dull monotone just as I was about to ask her if she had heard me. There was no hint of friendliness in her voice.

"I have a few things here I wanted to drop off," I said. I could hear irritation in my own voice stemming from the way she had talked to me, and I knew that she heard it as well.

Without saying anything more, and without taking her eyes off of me, she trudged across the well-manicured yard to the other side of the house and disappeared. I was left standing alone on the empty walk, bewildered. I walked back to the door on the side from which I had approached and began to knock, half afraid that she had called the police. By the time I had finished, the old harridan was already peering through a nearby window.

"Who are you?" she said loudly.

I was sure that she pictured some sort of wife abuser come to exact revenge for whatever real or imagined transgressions. It was common enough: crazy men forcing their estranged wives to strip naked and locking them in little rooms while they pointed phallic guns. This was where the women went.

"Will Dunby," I answered, "Sandy Cross's husband. I have a few things here that I thought you might need—"

"Who?" she said a little louder.

"Sandy Cross!" I yelled. "I'm her husband!"

That registered.

"*Ohhh*, Sandy," I could hear the woman murmur as she moved toward the door.

Within seconds, she was opening it.

"Good Lord!" she said. "Sandy's husband! Come in here. I would have thought you'd be at the courthouse."

"I'm skipping the pretrial stuff."

Opening arguments were scheduled to start the next day. They'd already selected the jury and Nevers was handling last-minute pretrial motions, including one by Phinney arguing against admissability of some tape recordings Moylan had made of conversations with Billi Stroud while she was staying at his house. Thorpe wanted to play some of them because, he said, they went to motive. Phinney claimed that they were unduly prejudicial because they unfairly portrayed his client as "mentally unstable."

Some of the conversations, according to the briefs, focused

upon what Phinney called Stroud's "unique childhood," one that apparently included severe abuse that led to a variety of other problems that led, eventually, to Stone Soup.

The inside of the shelter had not been finished when I'd walked through years before, and it was much nicer than I had ever imagined. I was in a very spacious, well-equipped, and airy kitchen. Shiny copper kettles and pots hung from the ceiling, glistening with the shimmer of light that streamed in through a skylight in the roof. The stove, with eight burners, was similar to what one would see in a busy and successful restaurant. Everything else seemed to be built of an expensive oak. Even the refrigerator was paneled and looked like it weighed as much as the truck it must have taken to get it there.

Sandy did everything from tend to the roses to tend to the books. She never talked about it much. It was, she always said, something she did just for the sake of doing. Where her interest came from I had no firm idea, but suspected it stemmed from the same compassion and compulsion that made her dedicate her life to defending criminals. Sandy would stand up to anyone she thought was bullying her, and never backed down from a fight, but she was soft-hearted and generous and, if she believed in someone, would do anything in her power to help. She was an uncommon blend of pragmatic determination and a heart so soft that at times it overwhelmed her.

"Sandy . . . ," lamented Gretchen.

It was as if she were addressing Sandy herself, and I sensed the questions she was asking. What compelled her to try to kill herself, and why? How was it possible? Those were the questions that were too plainly evident to need articulation, the backdrop of everything that took place in those months.

"How is she?" said the woman, taking the bag, placing it on a counter and peering inside as a child does with an old pillowcase on Halloween. "These are her things?"

"A few of them. A start."

Gretchen grunted recognition.

"This place," I said, "meant a good deal to her."

She jutted her chin toward the door of the kitchen.

"Would you like to see it?"

This was, I knew, a gesture of considerable proportion, and when I accepted she herded me into the dining room. It was, really, very much like any home, only nicer.

"Sandy wanted these girls to know they were worth it," said Gretchen.

From the ceiling of the dining room hung a large, crystal chandelier. Underneath was a table surrounded by at least twelve chairs. The windows in this room were made of leaded glass. Beautiful built-ins lined an entire wall.

"Sometimes," she said, "Sandy was *too* generous. Sometimes they think we're running a Hilton."

The living room and a large den were not in any way ostentatious. But they looked exceedingly comfortable and tasteful, not opulent but expensively done. One of the rugs was identical to one Sandy had purchased for our living room, and I knew that it alone cost close to a thousand dollars.

"I can't imagine what she's spent, tens of thousands I suppose when you add it all up," said Gretchen.

"She raised that kind of money?" I said.

"Sandy? Donated, I thought," said Gretchen, looking at me as if to say, "Don't you know anything about your wife?"

Gretchen opened a door just off the living room that led to a small study. An old library desk with a green banker's lamp sat in the middle of the room facing the door and, just as there would be in any office, there were filing cabinets set up along one wall. In one corner, surrounding a small coffee table, were two mauve, Queen Anne–style chairs, a matching set, I realized, to the one that was in Sandy's office at work. On the table, like everywhere else in the room, were pictures. On top of the desk. Sitting on top of a filing cabinet. Hung up on the walls.

"This is her office," said Gretchen.

"Hers?"

"She didn't call it that, but it was. Where she did all the books, paid the bills, did the legal work. Pro bono, of course."

The pictures on the walls were mostly of two women. Sometimes Sandy was one of them. Sometimes she was not. Occasionally, there would be a group shot, eight or ten women in a group, often standing in the backyard in the spring or summer, but occasionally gathered in the living room that we had just passed through. All of them had captions underneath, names of everyone in the group.

"Most of these gals stayed for a few weeks or months," said Gretchen. "Some moved on quicker, mostly just the wealthier ones though."

I must have looked surprised.

"There are plenty of those," she said. "You don't gotta be poor to hit your wife. Or kill 'em, either."

For a few minutes, I perused the collection, looking for those that included Sandy. There were dozens. In some, she was hugging someone. In others they simply stood side by side, arms intertwined, out by the clothesline or near a Christmas tree in the living room. In a few, she appeared to be engaging in a joyful pas de deux. They were, in many instances, quite exuberant. I recognized neither the names nor the faces of any of them, but for each picture Gretchen had a story. This one, she would say, lived on the streets for a month before being found beaten up behind a garage. This one left after her husband shot her in the arm. Each tale seemed worse than the one before. This one, she said, pointing to another, "had a baby kicked out of her by her husband. Lived though."

"A lot of pain," said Gretchen. "Some feel it more than others, ones who are salvageable mostly."

Sandy was in many of the group pictures as well. Usually, she stood front and center with both of her arms around women on either side of her. Some of those women were in other pictures on the walls. Some were not. But none—other than Sandy—looked even vaguely familiar to me. It took about five minutes to move across one wall to the other, and as I did I could feel a vague uneasiness rise up in my throat. Everywhere I looked was evidence of a life I had never known about, a woman I suddenly wondered if I had understood. When I moved toward the door, I picked up a framed picture that was sitting on the coffee table and, as I had with all the others, looked for Sandy. There she was again, with her arm around someone I finally thought I recognized. She looked much different, younger, heavier, even more forlorn, but it was Billi Stroud.

"Wilhelmina," said Gretchen.

Gretchen was standing by my side, already looking down at the picture and my eyes followed her finger to its destination. For what seemed like an eternity she didn't say anything more. Then, softly, she murmured, "Billi."

She'd said it quietly, pulling the picture out of my hand and holding it down in front of her.

"Sandy treated that one like a princess," she whispered. "Loved her like her own."

"How long was she here?" I asked.

Gretchen was still looking down at the picture, studying it.

"Oh, I don't know. She was here on and off. Came several years ago the first time, trying to get out of an abusive relationship. Young kid—good kid—break your heart."

"This abuse—her stepfather?"

Gretchen studied me a little longer than she had previously, soaking up the fact I had not come over simply to drop off some old clothes.

"Well," she said softly, "initially. A lot of these girls are just kids, babies, even when they look like and act like something else. They get out of Mommy's house finally, it's a sad thing. . . . They have a hard time making a break, Billi in particular. She needed to come to peace with some old issues. It was a two-steps-forward-one-step-back sort of thing, a project, Sandy said. In a strict sense of the word, she didn't really even qualify to be here after that first time a few years ago. But we let her in anyway—Sandy did really—promised to try to help."

"How?"

"Initially by trying to get prosecutors interested in the stepfather."

"For what exactly?"

She bobbed her head slightly from side to side, and spoke in a monotone.

"She became pregnant for the first time when she was thirteen—"

"Was paternity established?"

"She told a school counselor it was his."

"But he wasn't prosecuted?"

"She later retracted it."

"Was he ever charged?"

"No. You have to remember this is years ago now. She lived in a small town and people were not adequately trained in this stuff. Pretty apparent though in retrospect."

"In what way?"

"All ways. Improper sexual contact with other children; withdrawn and antisocial; prone to fits of violence when she was young; refused to bathe. The whole deal. At one point, tried to mutilate her—"

I cut her off.

"What about the mother?"

"Not sympathetic," said Gretchen.

"Didn't believe her?"

"The mother sided with the stepfather," said Gretchen. "Billi ran away for the first time before she was even old enough to drive. She's been on her own since then for the most part."

"What happened when they tracked down the stepfather?"

"Sandy found out he was dead—at that point for almost two years."

"How did Billi react to that?"

"Confused. She'd spent a lot of years, probably, wishing for just that; and then a lot of psychic energy, I guess, finally getting ready to confront him. And then it was just over before it'd ever started. I think it threw her for a loop."

"How so?"

"I don't know if it was just coincidence, but she lost her job, lost her focus really. There wasn't money for an apartment. She needed a place to stay. I think Sandy would have just taken her into her own home if she could."

This caught me.

"If she could?"

"Oh-h-h—," said Gretchen. "Dr. Moylan was sort of—he was just better equipped for it."

"What?"

"He already acted as an unofficial consultant on some of the cases around here. It was all pro bono, including Billi's," said Gretchen, "so she asked him."

"If Billi could live there?"

She nodded.

"He was, well, he was a very compassionate person. Sandy asked him to get more involved and it just ended up, I think, that he had some room for her at his home. Temporarily, of course. Billi was quite appreciative."

"Till she got caught with the marijuana?"

"Well, things sort of soured before that, actually."

"What do you mean?"

"Treating someone and living with her are two different kinds of things. He came to feel Billi was being a little, well, lazy. That was the reason the pot was such a big deal. He was trying to help her move on from her dependencies and she wasn't really trying. He'd never say that, but I think that's what it was."

"Dependencies? Was she an addict or something?"

"No."

"Alcoholic?"

"I don't think she drank at all, far as I know. The biggest dependency was actually on Sandy."

"Sandy?"

"Sandy bent over backward for her. She would just listen and listen and listen and hold their hands, with all the girls, but especially Billi. Doctor Moylan was trying to wean Billi from that, and Billi didn't appreciate it."

"What do you mean?"

"Sandy was like her mother," said Gretchen. "They were that close. Closer in some ways."

"And Tommy Moylan was trying to end that?"

"Maybe that's the way Billi looked at it. 'Course, she'd already more or less lost her real mother. She was pretty reliant, and I think she maybe resented him getting in the middle of it. Maybe somehow saw something playing out again—"

"So if she was angry with him, it wasn't just over him asking her to leave the house?"

"I don't think there was anything sexual, if that's what you mean. But it was more complicated than someone losing her temper for no reason—if she did it. In fact, I didn't see that she was mad at Dr. Moylan at all, the night before she left."

"You were there?"

"We all were. Sandy got all her friends, all of us, to help Billi pack."

"Out at the Moylan place?"

She nodded.

"Me and the girls. Night before she moved out. Wasn't much really. Just put some things together and moved all her things down to the barn."

"Was Sandy there?"

"She and a whole bunch of us."

“And you all helped her load up the van?”

“She put it in the van herself later.”

Now she turned toward me, sensing my interest.

“Originally, Billi was going to use her own car. But Dr. Moylan insisted that she use the van.”

“Was she having problems with the car?”

“Not that I know of. He’d actually fixed it for her a few times. But, no, he just said the van was bigger and it would just make sense, and that way she could make fewer trips over to the new apartment and then come back and pick up her own car. He wanted to do something for her, I guess. You know? Show her that he was still there for her, even if he was asking her to move out.”

“So, she said she would use it?”

“Well, she told him she thought that she could probably do it with her car but that would have taken forever and he was very insistent. Very insistent. Wouldn’t take no for an answer. I thought maybe he felt a little bad about what had happened, about making her leave in the first place, and was trying to make amends with her before she left. I actually think, by then, they’d reconciled what had happened. They were still going their opposite ways but I think they’d both just accepted it. . . .”

Her words trailed off.

“So she said she would use the van?”

“Well, as I said, he wouldn’t really take no for an answer. But he was going somewhere overnight and wouldn’t be back until early the next afternoon. She was going to be gone before he returned so I think just to end the conversation she said she’d think about it, about using his van, if she ended up having less space than she thought in her car. So she asked us to move some of the bigger stuff down there to the barn from the house, and we did. She was gonna be using her car that night anyway, just going out somewhere for a little while, and said she’d decide which one to use in the morning—the car or the van, depending on how much stuff she had down there—and load up then. That was how we left it."

"And Sandy knew all that?"

"Sure. Sandy knew everything."

17.

By the time opening arguments took place that next day, the temperatures had reached into the upper nineties and the grass around the courthouse had lost all color. It started out lush and green in the early days of July and gradually faded to yellow and brown and, by the time the trial started in the last week of August, was almost white.

Half of the courtroom was reserved for the public and, because it was first come, first serve, there was already a line of about fifty people snaking down the steps toward the sidewalk. It was early morning, but the men already had sweat stains under their arms and down the backs of their shirts and most of the women wore sundresses or short skirts.

The courtroom itself was relatively small and, of the dozen or so reporters allowed, the local press was given preference. I simply flashed my press card even though I was not working, then went in and sat next to Haley. She had walked in as if she had some special entitlement, and none of the bailiffs—who all knew her—had attempted to stop her. They probably assumed she had some work-related reason for being there.

There was an air of unreality about it all, brought on, perhaps, by the bright lights and histrionics of the television reporters. Court clerks who had never worn anything but khakis to work came in their Sunday best. The bailiffs all had fresh haircuts. Those who did get a seat in the courtroom jostled and bumped one another as if it were the opening night of a play. The two lawyers milled around the front, exchanging perfunctory pleasantries, picking up papers and notebooks and barely glancing at them before putting them down again—all part of a superficial attempt to mask their nervousness.

A whole row of seats had been set aside for family and friends of the victim—it was standard courthouse protocol—but only Moylan's mother and father and a brother came through the crowd to sit in them.

The brother came first. He looked slightly younger than Tommy, had moderately long, stylishly cut hair and wore an olive-green business suit and horn-rimmed glasses. His face was tight and somber and he spoke for a brief moment with one of the bailiffs before retrieving his parents from the crowded hallway and leading them to their seats. The mother, probably around seventy, looked confused and cowered into her son's shoulder as she limped along, squinting in the bright lights, her face in a pucker. The father, slender, with an ashen complexion, a headful of white hair, and a hearing aid, shuffled along with the help of a walker. He was the more defiant. It had been more than five months by then since they'd found out about their son's death and still he looked as if he were just trying to digest it, trying to nibble away even just a piece of the shock and horror and absurdity of it all.

They moved within inches of each other, seeking solace against the crowd, and spoke not a word until they got to their seats, where it took them what seemed like several minutes to remove their suit jackets and get situated. It was a long bench they sat on and completely empty, but the brother kept the jackets and his mother's purse on his lap in a kind attempt, somehow heartrending, to make room for anyone else.

The proceedings were supposed to start at nine, and within a few minutes of the hour the courtroom was jammed with spectators sitting shoulder to shoulder, straining for a look at Billi Stroud, stealing a glance now and again at Tommy Moylan's parents. One of the television reporters walked up, sat next to

Tommy Moylan's father, and whispered something in his ear. Putting his hand to his ear, the old man strained to understand, and failed repeatedly as the reporter came back at him, before one of the bailiffs realized what was happening and quickly intervened. At least a dozen other courtroom spectators gave the reporter dirty looks as he strutted back to his seat.

When Billi Stroud walked into the courtroom, both of the parents clasped their hands together in tight fists as if they were fervently praying.

Stroud was still in handcuffs and was noticeably nervous, but looked, otherwise, for all the world like what, at her age, she could have been: a somewhat anemic college student about to go out on a date. She wore a stylish but demure black skirt that came up no more than an inch above the knee, black tights and high-heeled black pumps. Her blouse was ecru and pressed, with narrow lapels that matched a swath of ribbon pulling her hair back and away from her forehead. She wore a small amount of makeup, a subtle shade of reddish-brown lipstick, and a simple gold chain around her neck with a small cross on it.

"Nice touch," murmured Haley.

Phinney stood up as Stroud entered and reassuringly directed her toward the defense table, where she paused and turned, waiting for one of the guards to remove her handcuffs.

"Phinney going to do her justice, you think?"

I said it with a hint of sarcasm in my voice.

"Not like I would."

I suspected she was serious. She would have had no compunction at all, I thought, about defending someone who may have wreaked havoc on us all. She would have seen it as a job, divorced it—unlike Sandy—from any other considerations.

Haley was a defense attorney, but she and Sandy practiced in very different ways. Their partnership was, as a result, an odd arrangement. More than once, Sandy turned down a wealthy potential client because she simply didn't want to work for him or her or bear responsibility. It drove Haley nuts.

"That's so hypocritical!" Haley would argue. "You can't choose who's entitled to a defense and who isn't!"

"Yeah, but I can choose who's entitled to a defense by me," Sandy retorted.

"Using what criteria?"

"My criteria."

Most lawyers go into law because if you are a lawyer and you are marginally smart and work hard you have a fair chance of becoming wealthy. Most simply want to be comfortable and somewhat respected and, when faced with all the uncertainties of otherwise accomplishing the vague objective, settle on law as the easiest and surest course. For Sandy, it was different.

"What, you're only gonna defend the innocent?" said Haley. "You're gonna decide who's evil and who isn't? Who's deserving and who isn't? You're gonna decide which transgressions you approve of and which you don't?"

"Yeah," said Sandy. "Yeah, I am."

Haley told her to grow up. "They're almost all guilty one way or another, Sandy, nine out of ten of them, hell, ninety-nine out of a hundred," she said. "They're entitled to a defense. That's the system."

Haley was much more the pragmatist. She savored her job and, having grown up poor, admitted liking the financial security it afforded her. She also, as much as anyone, hated to lose, hated to back away from a confrontation. Would employ what it took to win.

Haley's position, I always thought, was much better suited to her profession. To be sure, she was subject to the same questions that most defense attorneys face. How can you defend a murderer? Or a rapist? Or a pedophile? There were cold stares from the victims or their families, and sometimes outright resentment, suggestions of immorality. Most defense attorneys hear that more than once, and if they don't, they know that a lot of people think it.

But to pick and choose like Sandy did, to say no in one instance but yes in another, that was something rare and altogether different. That entailed either never accepting a client—a practical impossibility if one wanted to be a defense attorney at all—or at least occasionally to take responsibility not just for a client's defense, but for his or her deeds and morality. That, I suppose, is what kept Sandy up at night, or what awoke her so swiftly and fully when the phone rang in the middle of it. Those were the nights one of her clients had been pulled over for trying to drive home drunk, or for firing off a gun in a fit of anger, or for any other more serious yet, to her, forgivable offense.

It was personal. She would save them.

"Yes," she would say crisply, fully awake, sitting upright, after the first ring. "Yes. This is she."

I would rise up on my side, on an elbow perhaps, try to watch the facial expressions through dreary eyes, attempt to gauge the seriousness before I'd fade back to sleep. Sandy was warm, empathetic, committed. These were fallible but fundamentally good people, she believed, and if they weren't she would not represent them. She would say no.

"Everything okay?" I would sputter.

It was a silly exercise for me, one of etiquette as much as anything, for Sandy rarely could tell me anything of who was on the other end. This was a given. Those who called in the middle of the night were in the midst of, for them, terrific and embarrassing crises. She heard on those nights the cry of the heart and she honored the sanctity of it because she was a lawyer and it was part of the guarantee, but also because I was more than just her husband. She knew my job, when it came down to it, sometimes entailed deciphering just those kinds of conversations—and, indeed, sometimes those very conversations—that transpired beside me in the whispers and assurances of the dark.

"It's nothing," she would say to me, knowing that I didn't really expect an answer. Or, at times, at her most revealing, still not using names, "Really ought to learn to keep his pecker in his pants." Or, "God, I wonder how the legal profession ever survived Prohibition."

I would smile groggily, never ask who he or she was as Sandy got up and pulled on her jeans. I would just roll over and doze until she returned and, if there was enough darkness left, climb in beside me. The next morning she would be exhausted, and for years I thought it was because of the lack of sleep. But that, I eventually concluded, was only a small part of it. When Sandy really wanted to, she could stay up for days with, unlike me, few physical manifestations of sleeplessness. No, the exhaustion those mornings came from what she carried with her, proxies and confessions, unknown burdens and wild secrets, some of which I suspected even then, as Nevers entered and a bailiff called the courtroom to order, she would keep with her forever.

18.

All told, there were ten women and four men, twelve regulars and two alternates, most white, two black, on the jury. Haley, who had attended the jury selection, pointed at a woman in her midforties wearing a neatly ironed button-down shirt and some fashionable culottes. Her hair was cut short and she wore little half-glasses that she was already taking off. She had a tan that suggested she had just returned from a vacation with, I imagined, her husband and kids.

"Small-business owner. Jewelry store," said Haley. "Ten-to-one she's the foreman."

Phinney decided to save his opening for later and, perhaps because of that, Thorpe's was unusually short and perfunctory. Nevers, without pause, told him to call his first witness.

Dr. Hiram Rebich had moved to Droughton from somewhere in the east, leaving behind a teaching post at a small university to take a job that paid relatively little and required him to spend much of his life hovering over the disemboweled corpses of the recently deceased. And yet there was something altogether right about the decision.

Rebich was in his midforties, but he had an air about him that seemed ancient. He was dark and large and hirsute, one of those men whose beard is unclipped and carries directly down into his shirt collar unabated. He was not unclean, or uncouth, but instead of a suit, he wore, even in the heat, a heavy, pilling sweater and had a certain mustiness that hovered over him like smell of a dank closet in the basement of an old home.

Thorpe used Rebich to lay the groundwork and tell the jury how and where the body was discovered.

"When there's a homicide, we're called to the scene for two reasons," Rebich said, placing his mouth so close to the microphone as he spoke that I was glad I wouldn't have to testify after him. "One of which is to officially confirm the death."

His voice was deep and, when he spoke, slow enough to creak like a rusty gate. He evinced no emotion and, but for a slight wavering as he leaned forward toward the microphone, stayed almost perfectly still, as if there was a hinge at his waist but no other mobility.

"And when did you do that?" asked Thorpe, pacing the courtroom now, taking two or three steps toward the jury box, then doubling back again as he talked.

"We confirmed it immediately upon arrival at the Moylan property, shortly after the body was come upon," replied Rebich. "The death itself happened sometime earlier, apparently the previous Monday."

"Could you give me times?"

Rebich leaned forward.

"We confirmed it on Thursday in early evening. Around seven," said the coroner, not referring to any notes.

"But the time of confirmation is, of course, not the time of death, right?"

Thorpe would look up at the coroner as he paced, then back down at his feet after the question had been articulated.

"No."

"Any indication when Dr. Moylan died exactly?"

"We couldn't deduce that with any precision from the state of the body because it was frozen. It was found in a creek below the doctor's house, and the water temperature was close to freezing. There was none of the customary deterioration that would occur with a corpse in normal temperature. So I can't respond to that question with any sort of biological specificity."

"Okay," said Thorpe. "Were there any other indications of time of death?"

"Not physical, no."

"But otherwise?"

"The deceased did have a watch—an old-fashioned pocket watch—in his pocket, the sort that wasn't water-resistant. It was stopped at five fifty-nine."

"So you believe he died around that time?" said Thorpe.

"Not necessarily. Water certainly could have stopped the watch, but he was dead before he was put in the water. He didn't drown. There was no evidence of that, no swelling of the lungs, no irritation of the mucous membranes, no signs of asphyxia. He died before that, perhaps a number of hours before that. It's hard to say exactly."

"So somebody put him in the water after he was already dead?"

"Yes."

Thorpe went to the prosecution table now and picked up a plastic bag, then carried it back to the coroner.

"This the watch you found in his pocket?"

Rebich took it from him and turned it around a couple times in the palm of his hand.

"That is it," he said.

"And you placed it in that bag?"

"I placed it in that bag. I sealed that bag. And that is my signature."

Thorpe, standing still now, turned to Judge Nevers.

"I'd like to enter this as state's exhibit one," he said.

Nevers pointed to his clerk, an older woman with short gray hair, and Thorpe gave it to her, then turned back to the coroner.

Reporters sometimes sit through days of testimony before finding anything at all that seems to be even vaguely relevant. Thorpe had, using his first witness, quickly moved right to the crux of the case—the time of death—and they scribbled furiously.

"Okay, after disrobing the body you also examined it, of course."

"I performed an autopsy."

Rebich and Thorpe had been through this drill before, so the prosecutor just asked a very general question and trusted the coroner to follow through in the most advantageous way.

"Could you—let's start this way: Just generally describe what you found."

Tommy Moylan's father reached furtively for his wife's hand and, finding it in her lap, held tightly. She looked straight ahead.

"The subject was a male in his late thirties, Caucasian. No abnormalities or oddities. Regular physical development. Appeared that—but for his wounds—he could have lived a relatively long life." Rebich looked directly at Thorpe and spoke in a low monotone. "There was some evidence of very initial stages of coronary artery disease, but even without treatment it would not have affected him in any significant way for some time, especially if he led a relatively active, nonsedentary life and received some medical attention. Cause of death was homicide. Two gunshot wounds."

"How do you know that they were gunshot wounds?"

"Aside from the fact that I've seen hundreds, I recovered the bullets from the body."

Thorpe walked back to the table and picked up a small plastic bag, then walked over and handed it to the coroner.

"Are these the bullets you removed?"

He looked at the bullets and a small label on the plastic bag.

"Yes. The bag is marked with the date and time of the autopsy as well as the name of the subject, Thomas Moylan. It's also sealed with a label and my signature is on it."

"That's your signature?"

"Yes. That's my signature and I did sign it on that label on that bag."

"And do you recognize the bullets in that bag?"

"Those look like the bullets. They're jacketed hollowpoint bullets, which is what I pulled out of the body."

"Jacketed hollowpoint. What's that mean?"

"It's a type of bullet used by police. Has what they call good stopping power."

"And you can tell that just by looking at it?"

"Well, most surgeons and coroners are quite familiar with the type of bullet, actually, because when it impacts it bursts outward into what resembles a jagged-edged star. You have to be very careful looking for them and removing them. It's easy to get cut. So, most of us are quite aware of them. They're very distinctive-looking."

"Your Honor," said Thorpe, "permission to pass these among the jurors?"

Nevers nodded. "Let's mark it state's exhibit two."

"Thank you," said Thorpe, taking the bag back out of the coroner's hand and walking over to the jury box with it.

"Could you describe the wounds these bullets made?" he said, turning back around and looking toward the witness stand.

"The first wound, that is the first one sustained, was in the forehead, right between and above the eyes. Quite unusual actually."

"How so?"

"Shootings, given their nature, are usually from some distance and bullets enter at irregular angles and directions. That was not the case here. In fact, the bullet wound was almost perfectly placed, as if the head had been held still and measured almost."

Thorpe straightened up a little.

"I don't mean that that was the case literally," said Rebich. "Just that the wound couldn't have been better centered if it had been measured. And whoever shot this individual did it from a very close range. The gun was touching the victim's forehead when it was fired." Rebich pulled some pictures out of his folder now, and passed them to the prosecutor, who looked at them briefly and, after getting permission from Nevers, passed them on to the jurors.

"These are quite graphic," Thorpe said to the elderly man to whom he had handed them.

The man took them and, without hesitating, started to study them. An older woman sitting beside him peeked over his shoulder and immediately pulled back and turned her head while Tommy Moylan's father tightened his grip on his wife's hand.

Rebich turned to the jurors.

"You can tell by the nature of the edge of the wound, the ring if you will, that the gun, which turned out to be a ten millimeter, was in contact with the skin when it was fired."

"Objection," said Phinney, rising up. "Caliber has not been proven or stipulated to."

"Withdrawn," said Thorpe. "I'll come back to that."

He turned back to the coroner without missing a beat.

"So the killer was quite literally holding a gun to his head?" said Thorpe.

"Literally," said the doctor.

"Can you tell where the shooter was standing at the time?"

"Directly in front of the victim."

"You can tell that?"

"Contact wounds are usually in the side of the head, for obvious reasons. Killers like to have the advantage of surprise and, often, anonymity. So they typically stand behind their victims, where the victims cannot see what they are doing. This case is different. Here you have a shooter standing directly in front of the victim, looking him in the eye. The bullet was fired directly from the front to rear of the head, not from side to side."

"Is it possible it was self-inflicted?"

"It would be physically awkward if not impossible for a person to hold a gun to his own head in that manner unless he was trying quite deliberately to strike a somewhat unnatural pose, and you have to wonder given the circumstances, frankly, why anyone would."

"Objection," said Phinney, who was looking down at some notes in front of him.

"Sustained," said Nevers. "Skip the speculation, Doctor."

Rebich nodded. "In any case," he said, "if the one wound to the head was self-inflicted, if that were possible, the second one certainly was not."

"And how do you know that?"

"The first shot destroyed considerable brain tissue. He could not have functioned after that."

"How do you know the shot to the head was first?"

Rebich, for the first time, shifted forward in his seat.

"Well . . ." he said, pausing ever so slightly, "it's clear to me that this individual was deceased or at least unconscious when the second shot to the groin was fired."

Thorpe gazed briefly up at the ceiling, letting the jurors soak it in.

"Could you elaborate?"

Rebich again shifted his position, and moved closer to the microphone.

"There were cuts in the area of the second bullet indicating that the gun had been thrust repeatedly up into the genital area."

A low murmur rose up from the gallery and Tommy Moylan's brother placed his arm around his mother and, with his other hand, took his glasses off.

"Almost," said Rebich, "as one might simulate a sex act. It was done five or six times, some landing in and around the testicles, some around the anus. Quite violent. Then, of course, there was the gunshot itself to the groin, which appears by the nature of the wounds to have probably come last." He paused. "Almost like an ejaculation," said the doctor.

The jeweler was transfixed.

"So, let me get this straight: This was essentially an act, this portion of the assault, it seems, of sexual mutilation?"

"Yes."

"Why could that have not happened first? Prior to the head shot?"

"Because if that kind of mutilation were performed on someone who was conscious, there would be a physical struggle. The victim would not remain passive. He would fight back, quite violently, impulsively, couldn't stay still if he wanted to, given the violence to his body, unless he was bound somehow."

"Could he simply have been bound and unable?"

"No. There was no evidence of that. In fact, there were no marks at all on this body other than the two gunshot wounds, and these cuts to the groin from the thrusting of the gun, and none of those cuts was anywhere but in a small defined area on and around the scrotum and anus. None elsewhere. No skin underneath his fingernails, nothing. The wounds around the groin were unquestionably done to an unconscious or immobile body."

"Or to a corpse?"

"Or to a corpse."

Thorpe paused and let the jurors take in all the implications.

"Have you ever encountered anything like that?"

"It occurs occasionally, mutilation of a corpse. It's indicative, I would imagine, of extreme anger or retribution."

Phinney started to rise up to object, but Thorpe was signaling that he was done. The prosecutor was heading back to his seat already, and had only a few more words.

"Yes," Thorpe said, just as he was sitting down, "I would imagine."

Phinney rose up the rest of the way out of his seat and, in an instant, before the jury could digest any more of it, approached Rebich. There was no small talk.

"Doctor," he said. "Doctor, you don't offer any opinion as to who exactly is responsible for this shooting, these wounds?"

"No. That would be beyond my purview."

"Well, you seem to have an unusually broad one."

"Excuse me?"

Rebich was looking up at the judge as Phinney walked back to the defense table and picked up a yellow legal pad. He had gotten a haircut. The ponytail and the mustache were gone. He still wore slip-on loafers on his feet rather than wingtips, but the effect was now one of earnestness.

"Let me get this right," he said. "You called this some sort of bizarre retribution or, what did you say? Simulated sex act? That's something you can tell by simply looking at the wounds themselves?"

"It's common sense. Thrusting a phallic object up into a person's genital area repeatedly is, in my estimation, sexual in nature. It simulates or replicates copulation. And much as copulation ends with the emission of ejaculate, all I'm noting is this act ended with the emission of a bullet. I think it's a very fair analogy, actually."

"And you think that this was an act of, what did you say, retribution?"

"That's a possibility."

"That word suggests retaliation for some prior wrong, does it not?"

"I suppose it does, although I'm hesitant to start hypothesizing on that. We're really getting beyond my area of expertise here."

"Just now?"

Several jurors smiled. Phinney was better at this than I had anticipated.

"You'd agree though," pressed Phinney, "that it does suggest retaliation of some sort, the word itself? The word you used? I mean it's your word, Doctor, is it not? 'Retribution'?"

Thorpe objected.

"He's badgering," said the prosecutor.

"Sit down," said the judge to the prosecutor. Then he turned to Rebich. "Answer the question."

"The word suggests that, yes," said Rebich. "But I should clarify, in that context, I don't know that that's what happened here. Perhaps it was a poor choice of a word."

"Well, poor or not, you would admit there is some suggestion of retaliation when you use that word."

"That's what the word connotes, yes."

"Retaliation for what? Can you say?"

"No. I would not know that."

"But the particular area of the body selected for this retribution—the genitals—that suggests retribution for some sort of sexual act, doesn't it?"

"I couldn't know that."

"Well, isn't the area of the wound itself indicative of that?"

"It's possible."

"Well, more than possible, Doctor. Wouldn't you say?"

Rebich just shrugged. "I don't know," he said.

Phinney moved on.

"Any knowledge," he said, "as to with whom the doctor had recently—or let's make it, say, within the last year or two—had sex?"

Pictures appeared suddenly in my mind, as they had spontaneously and unannounced in the days and weeks after Sandy's confession. She, naked, on top of Moylan, breasts swaying back and forth atop him as she moved, gently at first, then caught in a rhythmic series of convulsions. My mind veered away.

"I object!" said Thorpe. "That question is clearly outside the area of Dr. Rebich's expertise."

Thorpe was shaking his head, almost laughing at the preposterousness of the question.

"Sustained," said Nevers. "I'm going to assume, counselor, it's ignorance that compelled you to ask that and not some more nefarious motive."

"Nothing nefarious," murmured Phinney. "Just something I'd like to know."

19.

I did not stay to hear the testimony that afternoon. Thorpe, late in the day, put on an expert, a woman named Leticia Hendrickson from the state crime laboratory, who testified about samples of blood found in Tommy Moylan's barn and opined that someone had shot him there before dumping the body in the creek. Most of the testimony was about how blood is typed and matched, and it had the dry tones of a lecture. I went home and waited for the darkness and then got in my car and drove out to the Moylan property.

I had driven by the previous night after talking to Gretchen Lane, but there had been a surprising amount of traffic and I did not have a chance even to slow down. All I had seen was the vague outline of the house and the barn and, glimmering in the moonlight, the yellow, plastic cordon that police had still not removed.

This time, I would stop.

There are no ditches along that highway. It is as if someone came along and, without having to use a grader first, just dumped and rolled asphalt atop the flat earth. I didn't bother to use the driveway, just pulled off the shoulder after barely slowing down. I drove straight off the edge of the road, across perhaps thirty yards of compacted soil, and cut behind the far side of Moylan's barn. Then, my heart racing, I quickly shut off my lights. No one was driving behind me, but if they had been they would have wondered where I went as they passed by. My car could not be seen from the road.

In my mind, I had parsed my deed into segments, and I sat for a moment to work up some fortitude for the next step. The truth was, however, there would have been no logic at that point, given where I found myself and what it would have meant to anyone else who discovered me there, in turning back. I picked up my toolbox off the passenger seat, put on some gloves, and got out of the car.

No one had bothered to mow the grass since Moylan's body had been found, and it was half a foot high in spots. It gave the entire place a worn and fading aura, the same one that surrounded so many properties in rural Droughton. After making sure no cars were coming down the road, I walked back around to the door that led inside the barn. It was locked. The whole area had been secured and, without a key, there would have been no way to get in without leaving evidence of a break-in. I pulled the keys that had been given to me at the hospital the night of the accident out of my pocket, and slipped one of them into the lock.

It fit.

Inside, there were now two vehicles. Tommy Moylan's van had been moved back into the barn by the police. They had removed Billi's belongings—the clothes and books that were hers, plus the tools she claimed were hers—and then left it parked again inside, just as it would have been the day she moved.

Parked next to it, in the same spot I imagined it had been the day Adam peered through the window, was Billi's Saturn—the vehicle she had decided at the last minute not to take. I used another key on the same ring to open the front driver's-side door of the Saturn, then—my pulse rate still unabated—looked inside the cigarette tray.

Inside, just as had been the case with the van that Billi had taken the day of the murder, lay a partially smoked joint. Distracted, perhaps, by the discovery of Tommy Moylan's body the day of their drug search, the cops had apparently not thought to look inside the Saturn. I closed the ashtray without touching anything inside.

There were, of course, no screwdrivers on the workbench. Billi had taken the tools with her. But I opened up the toolbox I had carried with me and, my hands trembling slightly, used a Phillips screwdriver on a small panel or compartment on the inside of the door up near the window on the driver's side. Once the screw was loosened, the whole compartment came off the door quickly and there inside was a small bag. It was about the same size as the bag that had been found by the police in the van the day that Billi had been pulled over and it was full of the same substance: marijuana.

I looked at it for a moment, then, without touching it, without in any way moving it, I placed the door panel back in its original position.

My curiosity satisfied, I screwed it back in place, locked the Saturn, closed up and locked the barn, got back in my own car and, under only the faintest glimmer of the moon, maneuvered it back over onto the highway.

I took a deep breath and, moving down the road into the pitch darkness, hit the lights.

It must have been tempting, I imagined then, for Billi Stroud to wonder if she could have avoided everything that had happened to her simply by declining Tommy Moylan's offer and taking her own car instead of the van the day she was pulled over. But that would be nothing more than a delusional trick of the perpetually screwed, a mental device used to convince oneself that easier times or a better life were perhaps so much closer to attainment than had ever really been the case. If Billi Stroud had taken the Saturn, the fact is, nothing would have been so very different. The anonymous caller would simply have told police to look for that car instead.

20.

Phinney's cross-examination of Leticia Hendrickson had to wait until the next morning, and there was some surprise, initially, that he even bothered.

She had told jurors that the barn was a "virtual repository" of Moylan's blood. It had been found on some drywall that was cut from the area of the wall above the workbench. It was found in small cracks where the plaster that connects the drywall had separated. It was found soaked into bits of paper towel that had gotten stuck in a floor drain. It was even found in a sponge discarded in the trash out back.

"Yet who would have thought the old man to have had so much blood in him?" I whispered to Haley.

"Thank you, Lady Macbeth," she said, correctly identifying the quote.

"Very good."

We think about the killing, the act itself, pulling the trigger, and the horror and self-loathing—or, worse yet, the pleasure—of seeing the victim crumple, perhaps, upon himself. It is the aftermath that no one really considers, when the moment of horror—or, worse yet, the pleasure—of what one has done comingles with, or is overcome by, the realization that it must be mopped up. Water that, instead of turning dark brown with each rinsing of the mop head, takes on the tint of red. Patterns of scarlet, like colored soap on a windshield, wiped in random fresco, upon a wall or a floor. Evidence not so much eliminated as spread, until it is no longer readily visible in any one spot but instead permeates everything that is around it. This is where evil suffuses the mundane.

Phinney rose up and greeted Leticia Hendrickson that morning, and as he did the sun was just peeking over the lip of the windows that lined the top of the courtroom. She was a slight woman of about fifty with a bouffant hairdo, large glasses, and a quiet, efficient demeanor that matched the creases on her well-ironed pants. She was a law enforcement officer in a nominal sort of way. But what Leticia Hendrickson really considered herself to be was a scientist who happened to work in a state crime laboratory. Because Droughton was not large enough to have its own forensic evidence technician, she was called upon to analyze evidence found in the area where Tommy Moylan was killed.

"Okay," Phinney said to her, after she had been sworn in. "You testified yesterday that there is no doubt in your mind that Dr. Moylan was shot in the barn, and that an attempt was made to clean up the blood there, and that the body was moved to the creek, where it was later found?"

"Yes," she said, straightening up and, after adjusting the microphone, clasping her hands and placing them in her lap.

"Blood was taken from walls, the floor, floor drains—a variety of places. You have samples that were entered into evidence and absolutely all of it was Dr. Moylan's. Correct?"

"Yes."

"All your samples were taken from the scene of the shooting, from the barn?"

"Yes. I was asked to test any samples that could be taken from the barn—and, of course, one from the body of Dr. Moylan."

"And you were asked to examine some clothes, as well, were you not?"

"Yes. I was asked to examine clothes taken from the defendant, from Ms. Stroud."

"And what did that tell you?"

"Nothing. There was no trace of blood on her clothes—she may have changed."

"Objection," said Thorpe.

"Sustained," said Nevers, turning to the witness. "Let's avoid the speculation."

Leticia Hendrickson nodded.

"Okay," said Phinney. "But as far as you know, nobody ever found any clothes anywhere that she might have changed out of."

"As far as I know."

"What about shoes?"

"No."

Phinney returned to the defense table and picked up a bag. From inside he pulled another bag, a plastic one, that had something inside. Then he walked back up to the witness.

"Ever see this shoe?"

Thorpe, head tilted to one side, trying to focus on the bag, stood up.

Phinney, seeing him, said, "I think you'll recall that our possession of this was disclosed to you, Mr. Thorpe." He held the shoe up so Thorpe could get a better look, and the prosecutor seemed satisfied. He sat down.

"Ever see this shoe?" Phinney said again to Leticia Hendrickson.

"No, I don't believe so. Ms. Stroud was wearing tennis shoes that day."

"You've never seen this shoe, have you?" he asked.

"No."

Thorpe had, apparently, never passed it on to her.

"Would it surprise you to know there is blood on it?"

"I have never seen it before. I wouldn't know."

"Dr. Moylan's blood actually, according to the defense's own tests."

"I have no way to know that."

“Nor would you know, therefore,” said Phinney, “whose shoe it is?”

I get migraines, and they are debilitating. I can tell when they are coming and I can’t explain how. Immediately beforehand, there is an aura, a physical manifestation, but even before that, usually a minute or so before, I know one is coming. It is just a feeling that, I think, rises up from my center and seems such an elemental change that it must be chemical and it begins to overwhelm me for I know then that I will lose control. My view of things will distort, infused by little ragged flits of light, like rain on a windshield on a partly sunny day. What I felt in that moment—a foreboding so elemental it seemed physical—was similar. But what came next was not a migraine. It was a revelation that made—and at the time, I swear, I felt this to be literal—my head spin.

That was Sandy’s shoe. She’d bought it during a shopping spree in Minneapolis. Phinney’s investigator had apparently found it at the base of the cliff.

Sandy had worn that shoe the day Tommy Moylan was killed.

21.

Adam Dougherty's mother was a young woman in her early thirties, wearing a business suit, looking like she had just arrived home from work. The trunk of her car was open when I pulled into the driveway, and half full of groceries. She was just coming back out the door to retrieve them as I got out of my car.

"Mrs. Dougherty?"

"Yes."

"I'm Will Dunby."

"Oh."

She knew who I was.

"I wonder if it would be okay if I talked to Adam for a moment. I ran into him at the Moylan barn some time ago when I was trying to find out what happened with my wife."

"I know," she said, using a tone that made it clear she was not pleased with my visit. It did not help, I imagine, that there was probably a hint of desperation in my voice.

"He told you?"

She nodded.

"The police interviewed him, interrogated him, really. Your name came up. He's very nervous about having to testify."

"He's going to testify?"

She nodded her head.

"When?" I had left in the middle of the court proceedings and feared for a brief moment that I was missing it.

"They said just to be ready."

"What's he going to say?"

"Same thing he has already—he doesn't know anything. When he was there after dinner that night everything seemed fine."

"But what about earlier? Did he tell you about that? About seeing Tommy lying in the barn?"

She nodded.

"Do you know what time he was there?"

"I know he skipped his last class," she said, her voice tightening.

"Do you know what time that would have been?"

"You'd have to ask him, I guess. I know last period starts at two-thirty—so sometime not long after that."

"Not long after two-thirty? Are you sure?"

"Yes. You could ask him yourself, but he's not here."

"Where is he?"

She raised her chin a little bit.

"I don't know," she said. "But I've told him to stay away from the Moylan property—so you might want to try there."

Sure enough, when I drove by Moylan's propety, there was someone, plainly visible, standing alone out behind the barn overlooking the creek. Only, I could tell right away, it was not a boy.

I do not believe in ghosts, or specters of the past reappearing, seeking redemption, or revenge. But I reconsidered in that moment, for the man looked strangely familiar, like someone I should know. He was of average height, and looked like many of the professionals one sees in the bigger cities, well dressed and tan. As I got closer, though, I could see he was somewhat disheveled, as if it had been a long day.

He hardly reacted when he saw me approaching, just stood there with his hands in his pockets, his tie loosened.

"You're Tommy's brother," I said.

Tentatively, after a moment, he extended his hand.

"Yes. And you," he said, "are Sandy's husband."

There was an awkward silence I did not know how to fill. But he did it for me.

"Bit of a surprise today, eh?" he said.

I, too, looked out at the creek. "One of many," I finally said.

We stood there for a long moment.

"Were you close to him?" I asked finally. "Your brother?"

"We were very close in age," he said. "Other ways as well."

"You have other siblings?"

"No. No, just the two of us. Just me and Tommy and my parents."

"Grew up on this property, didn't you?"

"I did. Lived here, too, for a time last summer when I was building a house in the area."

There was another pause. I was surprised, given the circumstances, at how readily he accepted my presence.

"Did you meet Sandy?" I asked. It had come out softly, so softly I wondered if I had said it loud enough for him to hear.

"I knew Sandy, actually," he said in a whisper.

He was still looking out at the creek, not at me.

"How?"

"I'm a lawyer, so I knew her that way. But, you know . . ." He paused. "I knew what was going on."

I thought maybe, the way he said it, that he was going to apologize. But he didn't.

"As I said, we stayed in Tommy's house last summer while we were having a house built of our own, so I talked to Tommy every day during that period of time. We spent a lot of time together and I think I probably knew most of what was going on with his life, if not everything."

"He talked about Sandy?"

Bobby Moylan took a deep breath.

"He liked to talk. He was a very open and just sort of unguarded person. There was almost a certain vulnerability to him, you might say."

I regretted, for the first time, stopping.

"What did he say about her? May I ask?"

"I don't know that you want to hear this."

"I think that I do."

He didn't say anything for several moments.

"He knew Sandy, basically through a women's shelter in town," Bobby Moylan said. "She did some volunteer work there, as I understood it, and he did some as well. They became friends."

I nodded.

"Sandy was, he thought, really quite an exceptional person. Smart. Funny. Compassionate. He just enjoyed her company."

"He knew she was married?"

"Yes, it was a concern to him, a huge concern. But he felt that . . ." Here Bobby Moylan paused. "He was very ambivalent about it, the whole thing, for that reason. And he wasn't proud of it."

I felt my chest compress, as if someone were sitting on it and when I looked at him he seemed much farther away, as if I were watching a small bird sit on a twig outside a window.

"How long do you think it lasted?"

"I don't know exactly. My impression was that it lasted for a very brief period of time. It was my understanding that it was over."

"With all due respect, how do you know he was telling you the truth?"

"Because he was a truthful person," he said somewhat tersely. "But also because, after his death, there was a letter that we found."

"What kind of letter?"

"Just a note really. From your wife."

"Really? What did it say?"

He looked down at the creek where his brother's body had been found. Then, for the first time, at me.

"Just said it was over. Said something to the effect that whatever happened happened, but couldn't happen again. She asked him to please realize that, and I think he did."

I myself was not so sure. I once found a letter, found it actually some time before Sandy's accident. It was in a drawer in our bedroom, and I put it back because I did not want her to know I was snooping. It wounded me, then and always, I can tell you, that she had kept it. But for some reason, the same reason we force blood from a wound, so we can see it, I kept it as well—and occasionally read it.

"Dear Sandy," it read:

> *When you are young, you expect that one day love will happen and you do not hold the expectation out in front of you or even think about it so much, I suppose, as simply know she will be there one day . . . with little need to coax. Only when you get older, that is when the doubts creep in and you wonder if she passed you by already one late afternoon while you immersed yourself in papers upon a bench; or one weekend maybe when, at the end of it, all you had left was an empty closet, hangers dangling under a bare bulb. Now, at least, Sandy, I know the truth, my own truth. Love did not pass me by, at least not while I looked elsewhere. I saw it come, and I knew it when it happened. I embraced it. Held it tight until it left me clutching at its vapors. That, I suppose, is the true curse. Knowing love came. Showing me all your secrets, then passing as I watched. Is it really gone?*

I did not mention that letter, oversentimentalized treacle, to Bobby Moylan.

"What happened to their relationship?" I asked him.

"Tommy said she—Sandy—just felt it was wrong and, you know, he did also. She was married, and really had no intention of leaving you. They came to see it, I think, as something that just happened between adults, and shouldn't have."

"And how about him?"

"Tommy? He was very deeply disappointed. But he was a grown man. . . ."

"So there was no animosity?"'

He shook his head slowly. "Animosity?" he said quietly. "Quite the opposite. He certainly wasn't angry with her. He understood. And as for her—I don't get it. I know this probably doesn't mean anything coming from me, but she loved you. She, as I think the letter indicates, certainly had no reason to be angry at him and, again, I know that they remained friends right up to the end."

"So he had no reason to fear her?"

Bobby Moylan grinned slightly.

"No."

The smile extended now slowly across his face, and metamorphosed into a wince, and when Bobby Moylan spoke again a moment later it was with a softness that was barely audible. Tears now were running down his face, and he let them.

"You know . . . ," he said.

His voice broke.

"I know it sounds bad, what happened. Having an affair, or a tryst, or whatever it was. Believe me, Tommy was a good person and felt bad about it. It was a mistake. But Tommy was—and I know I'm his brother here—he was my best friend and he was one of the most moral people I ever knew. He just always was. . . ."

I let this pass in silence.

He sniffled again. Red-eyed, he looked out at the creek. And when Bobby Moylan spoke again, his voice was almost a falsetto.

"You know, he didn't have to work at Stone Soup, and neither did Sandy," said Bobby Moylan. "God knows they had plenty of other things to do. That's what kind of gets forgotten here in all this. These were good, generous people who were giving of themselves in ways most of us never do. They weren't getting paid for it. They didn't expect anything in return. They didn't get anything in return. . . . Except this."

He looked out at the creek, cascading over the little dam, and that was all he said.

That night, on the way home, I bought Sandy earrings. They were diamond, and I purchased them at a local jewelry store. Had them wrapped in colored paper and white ribbons and attached a small card, brought all of it to her in the living room and placed it beside her bed with some faded orange lilies. I opened it and read it to her and watched her breathe her slow breaths, one after another, silent and steady until, I imagined, she had slipped off into a state of silent meditation instead of having been there or someplace as good all along. I tried to put the earrings in for her, but found that I was unable. Frail and thin but still metamorphosing in its own way, her body, it seemed, would no longer countenance any unnecessary accoutrements.

I sat next to her and leaned down close, sputtering and jabbering and hoping that a word or two would register or stick, knowing full well the improbability but continuing on because not to is to condemn with silence, to give up all hope and aspiration for a future. I leaned down close and spoke my mind, spoke it in a way that even when she lived and slept next to me I had rarely been able, openly and freely in a stream of consciousness that encompassed all the complexity and puzzlement and frustration that had come to envelop us.

It is an odd thing when there is nothing left but the body, nothing but the corporeal evidence of a life. And there we are, left imbuing mere skin and blood and cartilage and flesh with the human attributes we want—or don't want—to linger upon.

Did she feel that, in her own time, as well? Did she clean his wounds, caress them? And could that be—like the tender apology of a lover recoiling in horror, apologizing, for a moment of violence—congruous with having made them?

"Sandy's a universe unto herself," Elizabeth once said to me, and it was true. She lived by her own rules, and through her own conventions. She used her own benchmarks, her own compass. Ascribing conventional motive to any one of her single acts was fraught with intellectual peril.

"God, what the hell?" I whispered. "Sandy . . . what the hell?"

22.

When I returned to the courtroom the next morning, there was an easel set up with a blown-up photo of Sandy's car after the accident. It depicted a clump of charred metal with a door sticking out that on one end vaguely resembled the back of a car without tires. Another one showed the area atop the cliff.

I recognized the second one as the picture from a report that Mozzy was planning to use as the news peg for a long story she had been working on about Sandy's accident. She and one of the paper's photographers, an older woman by the name of Hildy Spanner, whom I called Hildegard and had never gotten along with, sat in the gallery right behind me. Mozzy had even assembled a packet of clips and offered, as we sat in the gallery that day before the testimony began, to let me peruse them. With nothing better to do as we waited, I took her up on it.

Most of the stories were from the days following the accident, conjecture about what might have happened and references to Sandy in stories done about Billi Stroud and Tommy Moylan. But there were other, older clips as well. Being from a prominent family, even in a fairly large city like Droughton, Sandy's life was well chronicled. The stories stretched back over thirty years.

DR. AND MRS. JAMES CROSS HAVE BABY GIRL, it read in a headline above an old picture. The photographer had captured perfectly that gentle, almost feral, wide-eyed wonderment of a newborn, and I made a mental note to get a copy. Elizabeth, I thought, would appreciate it.

From early on, there were myriad other mentions of Sandy as well. As a toddler, photographed accompanying her family somewhere, as an eight- or nine-year-old riding in a local parade. There was one piece written when she was about ten and had placed second in a citywide spelling bee. Asked to spell racial, she spelled out ratio instead. Raised in an unintegrated town, she said she had never heard of the word.

Later, there were half a dozen weddings mentioned in which she had served as a bridesmaid. And before we began dating, several mentions of her and various men in the gossip column Mozzy had once written.

“Got around, didn’t she?” I quipped as I looked at that one.

Mozzy chuckled.

Hildegard just gave me a dirty look, which I ignored.

“Sandy practically got her name in the paper for having her first period,” I said, a comment that elicited about the same response from the geriatric photographer.

The trial was starting again, and before even calling a witness, Thorpe picked up a document off the prosecutor’s table and presented it to the court.

“This is a letter,” he said, “and it is addressed to Ms. Stroud’s former attorney, Sandy Cross.” He handed it to Nevers, who looked at it and gave it to his clerk. “I’d like to enter this as state’s exhibit seven.”

The clerk put a sticker on the letter and handed it back to Thorpe.

“The state,” Thorpe said, “would like to call Detective Horace Deiter.”

Deiter, who had been standing in the back of the courtroom, strode up the center aisle in a charcoal-gray, well-tailored suit. He lumbered up to the stand with the gait of a former athlete who has been hit one too many times, raised his hand, swore to tell the truth, and, totally at ease, sat down in the witness stand and subtly surveyed the jury.

After a few pro forma questions, Thorpe handed him the exhibit and asked him to read it.

" 'Dear Officer Stroud,' " read Deiter, " 'This is to inform you that your resignation effective today is hereby accepted. Per conversations with your attorney, Sandra Cross, charges related to Section 34.1(a) shall be excised from the record. Please submit your shield and service revolver, Glock 10mm EE516US. Thank you for your service.' "

"And what is Section 34.1(a)?"

"That's just a section of our policy manual that says an officer shall not, separate and apart from customary law enforcement practices, associate with any person known to be or suspected of having been engaged in criminal activity," said Deiter.

"This letter indicates she was disciplined for a violation of that section, does it not?" said Thorpe.

"Yes."

"So we can assume that Ms. Stroud became too friendly with some of the individuals, or at least one individual, who had a criminal history."

"Not exactly."

"What do you mean?"

"The letter," said Deiter, settling into the witness seat, "is a reference to a youth by the name of Chucky Ware, with whom Ms. Stroud had some contact."

Deiter glanced at me briefly.

"Who is Chucky Ware?"

"A drug dealer, one we'd had a hard time nailing. She, former Officer Stroud, was supposed to be working a sting on the kid. Problem was, she wasn't really keeping in touch with her supervisor—me—the way she was supposed to on it."

"And that's what she was disciplined for?"

"Yes, basically. She wasn't called to the mat for having contact with the kid. That was her job. She just wasn't keeping me adequately informed."

"And that upset you?"

"Well, it just wasn't procedure. There's a reason for the procedure. We can't have people out there freelancing it. There has to be some order about things."

"But she wasn't fired for that?"

"She wasn't fired. That's the other inaccuracy that's been reported. She was on a probationary period and just wasn't hired at the end of it. See, everybody's reviewed at the end of the probationary period. It's all considered probation basically up till then, and she just—well, her review didn't go very well."

"Because of this Chucky Ware thing?"

"That was part of it. She had other problems, too."

"So, by the time Dr. Moylan was killed, Ms. Stroud was no longer a member of the department," he said.

"That's right," responded Deiter, all business. "Probably never should have been. You ask me, in the name of 'diversity' "—here he raised his hands and made quotations marks in the air—"we've lowered our standards to the point there aren't any."

A couple of reporters scribbled in their notepads. It was a tangent, but a newsworthy one, a black detective taking a swipe at affirmative action.

"But she still had her gun?"

"She never gave it back."

"How is that possible?"

"Officers in the department purchase their own weapons at a discounted rate. They actually get a weapon stipend, but the gun is considered theirs. It's part of the DPA—Droughton Police Association—contract. Billi Stroud owned hers like anyone else and took it with her when she left. People can sell them back, and we encourage that because it's easier than having to go out and buy new guns. But no one has to."

"And that was the gun—her gun—used to kill Dr. Moylan, is that correct?"

"Yes. Rifling impressions from Glocks are unique. The barrels of most handguns have square grooves. Glocks are made differently. They have a hexagonal rifling with what gun experts call a right-hand twist. The bullets removed from Dr. Moylan came from a forty-caliber Glock, and in this case they match the bullet we know to have been fired at an earlier point in time from the same Glock. It was her gun. That's been stipulated."

Nevers interrupted.

"That means," he said, turning toward the jury, "that the defense does not contest that fact. It was her gun that was used. That doesn't necessarily mean she was the one to use it."

The jeweler opened up the notebook she had been given and wrote something in it. Several others followed suit.

"Okay, let's switch gears here," said Thorpe. "Any doubt Ms. Stroud had been at the home of Dr. Moylan that day?"

The prosecutor had taken off his suit coat and was wearing bright yellow suspenders.

"No. She lived there until that morning. She told the officer who pulled her over as much, and I don't think that's ever been challenged. She was there."

"And she was there until what time?"

"Well, she was pulled over at, according to the ticket, around two-thirty-five or so that afternoon and she told the officer she had come directly from the Moylan house, and that's about six miles away. Based on Ms. Stroud's own statements, she would have left the house—let's be generous—sometime no later than, say, two-twenty."

"Now let's assume just for the sake of argument that Ms. Stroud did not kill Dr. Moylan. Let's just imagine that to be the case."

"I'm not sure I have that creative an imagination."

There were snickers in the courtroom, but Nevers was not amused.

"Oh, boy," said the judge, not cracking a smile. "Let's at least get some new material, guys."

"An oldie but a goodie," Phinney said in an audible voice of sarcasm to Stroud.

"Okay, now we're even," said the judge, glaring at Phinney. "Let's move on."

Thorpe redirected himself to Deiter.

"Let's put it this way," said Thorpe. "If she didn't kill him, then someone else did. Could that other person have killed Dr. Moylan after she left?"

"Theoretically, although we have a witness—a boy—we believe saw the body around two-forty-five."

"Objection, Your Honor," interrupted Phinney. "No foundation."

"Sustained," said Nevers.

But it was too late. Thorpe had accomplished his goal and would call the boy later.

"Lemme ask you this," said Thorpe. "Was Sandy Cross there that day?"

"Yes,"

"What time do you think she showed up?" asked Thorpe.

"Well, Billi Stroud had been pulled over and was in jail. She called Sandy to come and see her."

"What time was she at the jail?" asked Thorpe.

"She signed in at four-fifty-nine and talked to Ms. Stroud, according to the log."

"And then what?"

"She talked to Billi Stroud for twenty-five minutes, according to the jail log, then checked out, and we believe drove directly to the Moylan residence at that point, presumably arriving sometime around five-forty-five."

"Now, why would she do that in your estimation?"

"Perhaps her client told her what she had done to Dr. Moylan."

"Objection," said Phinney.

"It's a hypothetical," said Thorpe.

"Overruled."

"Another possibility," said Deiter, without missing a beat, "is that I imagine it would only make sense to go out there and try to talk to Dr. Moylan to try to piece things together regarding the marijuana that had been found in his van with Ms. Stroud here. Either way, she drove out there."

"Any indication she did talk to him, to Dr. Moylan?"

"No. But it appears certain from both the evidence, that shoe, and her reaction—what I would call her reaction—that she came upon the body."

"So, you are aware of Ms. Stroud's shoe having blood on it?"

"Yes," said Deiter. "Mr. Phinney's investigator did find the shoe and Mr. Phinney, of course, disclosed to us before the trial that he was prepared to put an expert on the stand indicating the shoe had Tommy Moylan's blood on it. That in no way runs counter to our theory of the case."

"What do you mean 'her reaction'?" said Thorpe.

"This is somewhat speculative, obviously," said Deiter, "but, given the blood evidence, I figure she finds the doctor and, one possibility is, she goes to help him, perhaps checks for a heartbeat. It's a completely natural reaction, the most natural. Very expected. Maybe it's just instinct and she doesn't realize till then that he's already dead. But in the process she contaminates the body—and herself. She gets blood on her shoes."

"Then what?"

"The million-dollar question," said Deiter. "She would have realized he was dead, and once she realizes that, then she's probably thinking there's nothing more she can do for him. Maybe she starts thinking about her client instead, about Billi Stroud."

"Sounds callous."

"Well," said Deiter, looking now directly at the jury, "you have to understand she was a defense attorney. It would have been a problematic situation for her. She presumably would have felt legally obligated to Billi Stroud, whether she wanted to be or not; and at the same time she was obligated to report the crime—and I would imagine felt concerned, or maybe horrified, about the victim himself. That's the reaction any human being would have and it would be greatly complicated by the fact she was a lawyer with an interest in the case. No doubt, there were a lot of competing emotions and obligations."

"Obligations?"

Nevers stared at Phinney, who, through all the heresy and conjecture about motive, didn't object. Someone behind me whispered, "He doin' a crossword or something?"

Haley chuckled.

"See," said Deiter, "there would have been an obligation to report it since she came upon the body, but no obligation to report it right away—no legal obligation anyway. The first obligation really is to the client, who may or may not have already confessed to her. That's how the system works."

"Not a choice," said Thorpe.

"Not a choice—"

"Judge," said Phinney, interrupting, "the prosecutor is supposed to be asking questions I believe, not making statements."

"You're objecting?" said Nevers.

Phinney nodded.

"Make it inquisitive next time," said Nevers to the prosecutor, who barely acknowledged the admonition.

"You believe she cleaned up after the murder?" Thorpe said to Deiter.

"I believe she cleaned up after the murderer, yes. All indications are that she cleaned up after Billi Stroud. There was, after all, blood on her shoes, and she definitely was aware of the body."

"So she either found the body in the barn and dumped it in the creek and cleaned up or she found the body down on the ice or in the river already, and then cleaned up?" said Thorpe.

Incredibly, there was no objection to the leading question.

"That's what happened," said Deiter. "Either way, she cleaned up."

"Why would she do that?"

"She panicked. She was very, very close to Billi Stroud on a personal basis aside from being her attorney."

"What did she do then?"

"Then she got in her car and left."

"She just left?"

"Yes. And had an accident."

Until now the jurors had heard nothing during the trial of Sandy's accident.

"She actually drove her car off a nearby highway into an area—some park land—above the river, and eventually over the cliff," said Deiter.

"You said it was an accident?"

"Poor choice of words. It's unlikely that she drove it over accidentally, based on the tracks up above and the circumstances and physics of the incident. They all indicate otherwise. Common sense as well as science dictate that she willingly drove that car over that cliff. She tried to kill herself."

Several jurors reacted visibly, sitting up and leaning forward.

Deiter now pointed to the pictures on the easel.

"These are photographs taken at the scene," he said. "As you can see, there is a dense growth of trees between the road and the cliff that would have made it impossible that she could have simply lost control of her car on the highway," Deiter said. "The car could not move unimpeded over the bluff without her steering it around various trees. It had to be a conscious decision that entailed significant maneuvering of the car off the highway, then through the woods between the road and the cliff, to get out there in the first place. At one point, I believe, she would have had to turn the car about sixty degrees to the left even to get out there. It had to be deliberate."

"Any idea why she did it?" said Thorpe.

Deiter shook his head.

"No."

"Any conjecture even?"

"Sure I have conjecture," he said, in a way that evoked a small swell of laughter.

"C'mon," chided Thorpe. "You've had months to look into this. Give us an opinion."

"I object," said Phinney.

"He's the investigator, Mr. Phinney," said the judge. "He's entitled to an opinion. Whether it's backed up or substantiated by the facts is up to the jury to decide. You'll be given a chance to cross-examine."

Phinney sat down.

"I think," said Deiter, "it was a combination of guilt and perhaps grief, a lack in some ways of other options."

"Guilt over . . . ?"

"Guilt, maybe, over covering up what had happened. Maybe a little fear, too. Aside from whatever moral regret she might have felt, what she did—cleaning up like that—was also a felony. But she may also have felt guilt in a larger sense over making it possible for it to happen. Ms. Cross was the one who arranged for Billi Stroud to stay with the doctor in the first place."

"And why grief?"

Deiter did not hesitate.

"Because," he said, looking at the jury, "Sandy Cross had a very close relationship with the doctor."

"Was it romantic?"

The jurors were transfixed.

"Yes," Deiter said. "We have corroborating testimony that will be introduced."

Deiter had quite purposely given out the information in order to steal some of Phinney's thunder, hedge the bet. But it still reverberated with the jurors.

"I can't articulate or rationalize what, whatever the reason, was an irrational act by Ms. Cross, driving over that cliff," added Deiter, moving forward, not letting the jury dwell on it. "But she did attempt to kill herself. That's just a reality. So is the fact that she arranged for Ms. Stroud to stay with Dr. Moylan—whom by all accounts she still considered, at the very least, a close friend. They had been lovers at one point. That's uncontroverted. And being or feeling responsible for the death of a good friend, let alone a lover, that could be enough to push somebody to attempt to kill herself, I believe."

Phinney did not object.

"There's no doubt in your mind that she was not the killer?"

"She could not have been the killer."

"Why not?"

"Well," he said, "for one, she tried to report the murder."

It was as though Deiter, without altering the tone or volume of his voice, had dropped a grenade in the middle of the courtroom, so dramatically was the landscape, the very feeling in the air, altered.

"You have proof of this?"

"We have phone records," he said in the practiced voice of someone who was used to testifying, used to wringing as much effect out of a revelation as possible, even while making it seem an ineluctable, unchallengeable, unemotional fact.

Thorpe now walked back to the prosecution table and picked up a packet of paper.

"State's exhibit eight," he said, handing the packet to the clerk.

So much in a courtroom is scripted that it sometimes seems like bad television. But this was one of those rare moments of surprise that landed with a jolt. In my peripheral vision, I could see several heads swivel toward the front of the room. "She called the police," he said, "twenty minutes before the crash."

I could feel Haley leaning forward next to me and straining a little, as if to make sure she had heard correctly. She blew out a long stream of air, as if she were about to whistle but didn't have quite the energy.

"Sandy called the police?" I whispered in her ear.

Haley looked incredulous. This was news to all of us. There was rustling in the back of the courtroom as reporters walked hurriedly in and out and Nevers banged the gavel. Deiter leaned forward to receive something that Thorpe had retrieved from a table.

"She had a cell phone," Deiter said, "and she apparently tried to call us on it shortly before seven."

"What do you mean apparently?"

"She did call, according to the telephone company, but we have no record of it."

"She called police that night and the telephone company has a record of it, but the police don't?"

"Yes, after she found the body of the doctor, she left the scene, but sometime shortly thereafter she called the police."

"How could there be no record of it at the police department? Don't you guys record everything?"

"If a dispatcher gets to it, we do. But not until then. Until then, it's just a machine telling the person to hang on and it's not recorded. The person presumably isn't even talking and there would be no reason to record someone just waiting to talk to an officer, so we don't."

"In other words, she was put on hold," said Thorpe, "and that's not recorded."

Deiter nodded. "Unfortunately," he repeated, "she was put on hold—by a machine."

The reporters scribbled furiously. This would not be good publicity for the Droughton Police Department.

"For how long?" said Thorpe.

"According to the phone company records, not long. She was on the phone less than twenty seconds. That's about the maximum we make anyone wait so it couldn't have been much more anyway. But she didn't stay on the line. She hung up. She didn't wait."

"Why not?"

"I can't answer that question. Maybe she intended to call back. Maybe she wasn't thinking straight. She was overwhelmed, I suppose, by what she had found, and it was clearly something that would have been overwhelming. Horrifying, really, if you've ever seen someone who's been murdered. Especially a friend, someone you know. It makes you think. It makes you think about a lot of things, including your own mortality."

"And that's what Sandy Cross was apparently thinking?"

Deiter answered before Phinney could utter an objection.

"Apparently."

Phinney was already on his way to the stand and Thorpe moved toward him. It looked for a moment as if they were about to collide.

"Just a second, Detective," he said to Deiter as he reached the lectern.

"Wasn't going anywhere," said Deiter.

"When was that picture taken?" Phinney was pointing to the blown-up photo of Sandy's car.

"I'd say," mused Deiter, "after the accident."

There was a wave of restrained laughter.

"Good," Phinney said, smiling. "But how long after the accident?"

"I don't know exactly. Shortly. Shortly after the accident."

"But that same night?"

Czubak, the detective I had exchanged words with when they found Sandy, was standing in the back of the courtroom, and Dieter glanced at him. Then he turned back to Phinney.

"Yeah," he said. "That same night."

"Okay. Let me ask you something," said Phinney. "Do you

think Ms. Cross drove that car straight over? O
first?"

Deiter paused and tilted his head slightly–
almost see him think that, perhaps, he had
Phinney.

"Actually," said Deiter, "it appears the driv
tially stopped the vehicle some distance from the
That's not inconsistent at all with what I said ea

"No, I suppose not. But how do you know that it stopped?"

"The tire tracks indicated that she stopped some twenty yards from the edge. You can tell by the tire imprints."

"Any idea why she would have stopped?"

"I wouldn't speculate."

"Not about this, huh?"

Deiter shook his head slightly from side to side, but didn't answer. He was not amused.

"Lemme ask you this," said Phinney. "After that car did go over, was Ms. Cross thrown from it before it landed?"

"Yes."

"So she was already out of the car—thrown from it—by the time the rescue team and police arrived?"

"Yes," said Deiter.

"Well," said Phinney. "I don't get it then."

"Get what?"

"If she was already out of the car, why would the rescue team possibly have to crank open the door?"

"I don't know," said Deiter, looking at the picture now.

"The fact is," said Phinney, "they wouldn't have. Right?"

"I don't know why they would have."

"Then why is the door on the passenger side open?"

Deiter did not answer.

"It must have been open," said Phinney, "before the car hit the ground."

Deiter did not argue.

u can see,” Phinney said, pressing his point, “that the enger-side door, wide open, is virtually unscathed. Quite unike the other one on the driver’s side, which was squashed by the impact.”

“I see that,” said Deiter.

“So, it was open prior to the time the car hit. I mean, it had to have been. Correct?”

Deiter paused.

“Perhaps,” he said.

“Perhaps?” said Phinney. “What other explanation is there? Could she have opened it in midair?”

“Doubtful,” said Deiter. “We think,” he added in a way that made it clear he had considered the issue before, “that she had to have been the driver. She would not have been on the passenger side.”

“But it was the passenger-side door that was open?”

“Yes,” said Deiter. “We thought about all that, and it’s pretty clear that door was open before the car went over. It’s a bit of a mystery, actually. But we think she probably got out of the car for some reason before getting back in and driving over.”

“But she would have presumably gotten out of the driver’s-side door.”

“You’d think. It appears for some reason, obviously, that she also opened the passenger-side door.”

“Why?”

“Well, it’s conjecture.”

“Could she have wanted to get something out of that side of the car?”

“It’s possible.”

“Did you find anything she might have removed?”

“No.”

“Okay,” said Phinney, “Could it have been possible that someone else got out of that side of the car just prior to the time it was driven over?”

Deiter did not answer this one for at least ten seconds.

"Well," he said finally, "anything, at least theoretically, is possible. But we could find no other evidence of footprints up there and there would have been footprints, other footprints."

"Could they have been obscured?"

"Maybe . . ."

"Did you find some of Ms. Cross's footprints on that side of the car?"

"The prints that we found were all partially covered up, and in some instances obscured by the footprints of police officers, so it was hard to tell. This has been an inexact science."

"So, it's at least theoretically possible that someone else had been in that car and got out shortly before Ms. Cross drove it over."

Deiter looked directly at Phinney and in a level voice, with no hint of sarcasm, responded.

"Based on the totality of the evidence we don't think that was the case. But, theoretically? Theoretically, I suppose. I suppose someone else could have been there."

"So, yes?"

Deiter mulled this over before answering.

"Your answer," he said, "is yes."

23.

Thorpe put Adam Dougherty on the stand that day to support his theory that Moylan was dead by two-forty-five. But he still needed an alibi for Sandy and it came in the form of Kathleen O'Connor.

Kathleen O'Connor was a thirty-something nurse with reddish, shoulder-length hair and a freckled complexion. She worked at the clinic in Minneapolis where Sandy received her treatments. She wore a thin, almost diaphanous, silk top, the sort you see on the young women carrying Coach purses through upscale suburban malls.

Occasionally, O'Connor would brush her hair back off her shoulder, and glance at the jury, although not in a coquettish sort of way. She looked very young and earnest and wholly without artifice.

"How long had you been seeing Sandy?" asked Thorpe.

"Sandy came to the clinic first, I would think, about a year ago. She was concerned about possible infertility and the fact she and her husband were not conceiving."

"And how did you help her?"

"Well, there's quite a bit of groundwork that has to be laid before we accept somebody into the program, physical examinations, histories, psychological profiles even. Sandy went through all that and we were really just making decisions about the specific treatment itself when she backed out."

"Backed out? Why?"

"Well, it was pretty sudden. Sometimes happens, though. You know, people have a change of heart, I guess you would call it."

"A change of heart about having a baby?"

"Sometimes, although usually people are pretty motivated about that by the time they get to us."

"A change of heart about what then?"

"Sometimes it's hard to tell. But we track sexual intercourse rates and timing. As you can imagine, it's part of what we need to know, to gauge what's happening. And all of a sudden a few months into the process the first time around, Sandy said she just saw no reason to continue."

"Why not?"

"She was quite blunt about it, actually. She said she and her husband had stopped having intercourse."

I felt my face redden.

"Did you ask why?"

"I gathered at least for a time they were not living together."

I'd not only moved out, I'd tried to make a point. In an embarrassing fit of pique—and what I had devised as a pointed display of symbolism—I had hauled our mattress away with me when I left, thrown it on the floor of my nearly empty apartment. I didn't want her using it. Then, although they allowed thirty-day leases, I'd paid four months' rent in advance. The apartment sat vacant with the mattress in it long after I'd come back home and joined Sandy in the guest room.

"I could have helped," Sandy said, when I finally brought the mattress back.

I shook my head, as if the thought of her witnessing my well-staged asceticism in that apartment had never occurred to me. That, at least, is one thing I can say now I never required her to see.

Later, she confessed that while I was gone a realtor called her.

"It was kind of weird," Sandy said, sitting in the living room after I'd come back. "She said she'd heard that I might want to sell the house."

"How?"

"I still don't know. Word gets around, I guess. I didn't even know her, but she says to me, 'Oh, I understand you're living there all alone now and might be interested in wanting to sell.' I told her she was mistaken but instead of hanging up on her I start thinking to myself—you know, seriously thinking—hey, maybe I *should* sell. What the hell am I going to want to live in this huge place for all by myself? So, she asks if she can come by and bring her clients—she's got clients—and I say, 'Sure,' figuring it doesn't cost me anything.

"She says, 'Yeah, you know, they're this great little family. Young, and they've got a bunch of kids, and they've just always driven by the house and said to each other, if that house is ever for sale we're gonna buy it. You wouldn't believe,' she says, 'how much they say they want the house, and they have the money, too. Family money,' she says, like it's an illicit secret. Says, 'Yeah, they're going to put a swing set in the backyard.' Like they had it all planned out or had even already done it. . . . Like it was theirs already."

"You didn't tell me this," I said.

Sandy was on the couch, holding a glass of wine by the stem, slowly turning it. Examining it.

"I was at the office," she said. "You were living at the apartment and I'd been talking to this realtor for like fifteen minutes probably at that point and suddenly, I think, What the hell am I doing? I mean, I think I may have even said it out loud. 'What the hell am I doing?' "

She took a long sip of wine, then poured herself some more out of the bottle. My glass was still full and she did not offer me any.

"You know there's still an old swing set, disassembled, stored up above the garage," she said. "My dad took it down years ago, and put it up there. Still there. I always just thought one day we'd haul it out of there and put it up. Just always thought we'd have a reason."

"Let's go put it up," I said, and Sandy, turning back toward me, laughed.

"In the morning," she said.

But in the morning, of course, we went to work.

"I only inquired about the change of heart," said Kathleen O'Connor now from the stand, "to the extent I thought I should. Our services can be expensive, and a lot of times they aren't covered by insurance so we don't just want to give up on somebody, or let them think they have to give up when a problem might be solvable. Intercourse isn't even technically necessary in a lot of instances."

"Did you explain that to her?"

"As much as I felt I needed to. Sandy knew all that. She was a smart person. She just said she still wanted to have a baby but it wasn't the time and it wasn't an issue that could be rectified easily. It wasn't a physical problem in other words. She was just very definite about it, and the money—frankly—didn't really seem to be a concern of hers."

"Were you able to conclude anything about what had happened?"

"Other than that they weren't having sex? No. Not really."

"So you discontinued seeing her?"

"Yes, for a time. For quite a while, actually, and then she came back. Whatever the problems had been, they had been worked out, and she said she wanted to start over, so we did. But that necessitated doing a lot of the initial work all over again. It's just the way we do things. She had to go through the consultation a second time and that took time. She had just recently come back prior to her accident. In fact, that day was only her second appointment after the decision to return."

"The day of the accident, you mean?"

"Yes."

Kathleen O'Connor was about as good a witness as any prosecutor could ask for. She was likable and poised. She had an honest face and a direct manner. And she had no stake in the proceedings, no reason whatsoever to lie or shade the truth.

"She was there that day until at least four," said O'Connor. "I know because I was with her almost the entire time."

About a dozen reporters in the courtroom, including Mozzy, scribbled away furiously.

"And what time did she get there?" asked Thorpe.

"Her appointment was at two."

"Was she on time?"

"She was always on time, and she was on time that day. I know because I wrote it down. I was there when she got there, and, as is the practice with all patients, I wrote down when I first saw her."

"Before two?"

"Yes."

"Okay, so she was there between, conservatively, two and shortly before four. How long, may I ask, did it take you to get here today?"

"Today?"

"Yes, did you drive here from Minneapolis?"

"Yes. I live near the clinic and I'd say it took me slightly over an hour today."

"Unusual traffic?"

"I don't know what usual is for that highway, but today it was light."

"Safe to say, then, that given driving time, she was out of Droughton that day between at least one and five?"

"I don't see how she could possibly have been anywhere near here during those hours."

"Thank you."

Having earlier seen the door opened up to the possibility that

Sandy could have been considered a suspect, Thorpe had, it seemed, just as quickly slammed it. He sat down with a look of satisfaction on his face and, just before he settled into his seat, stole a glance at the jury. I wondered if Phinney would even try to respond.

"Just one or two questions," Phinney said, rising.

Nurse O'Connor nodded.

"You said that Sandy had stopped coming initially, and that happened because Sandy and her husband were not having intercourse. Something with them had gone wrong."

"You know, if folks are no longer having intercourse, that's usually a sign of something in the marriage. That's just common sense, unless there's some sort of health problem. And beyond that, she indicated that she just wasn't sure they could handle a baby."

" 'They' being she and her husband?"

"Yes."

"Did she elaborate?"

"No. But she indicated that she wasn't sure they'd be together long-term."

"She said that?"

"Not exactly."

"Well, exactly what did she say?"

"She said she didn't think she could handle a baby alone."

"And later when she came back and wanted to start over again? Did she indicate that she and her husband were back on good terms?"

"She did, actually. Not directly, again. But she said things had been worked out and she . . . What she said exactly was, and I can quote it almost verbatim, she said, 'I'm . . .' Then she paused. She corrected herself and used the plural. She said, 'We—We are ready to try again.' And she smiled. I took it to mean she was back with her husband, that things had been resolved."

"Okay, thank you."

Phinney turned to head to the defense table and O'Connor started down from the stand. But suddenly he turned and faced her again.

"Oh," he said. "Just one more thing. Could I ask what Sandy's specific problem was in terms of not being able to conceive?"

"Sandy had a fairly typical problem, a case of endometriosis, which is basically sort of an overabundance or inflammation of the tissue that lines the uterus," she said.

"Was it a treatable condition?"

"Yes. In fact, what she had wouldn't normally cause infertility. In more serious cases, surgery is an option and we were trying to decide if it would be appropriate for her. If she'd want it. There are also hormone treatments that sometimes, basically, can help lead to pregnancy."

"Was there any chance there was some other problem?"

"What do you mean?"

"Well," said Phinney, "could the problem have been her partner's?"

She shook her head. "No."

"You know that for a fact?"

"The problem was not her husband's."

"Had your clinic tested him?"

"Yes, eventually."

I looked toward Thorpe, but he showed no inclination at all to object.

"Eventually?" said Phinney.

"Yes. It was actually somewhat pro forma, but we test everybody."

"Pro forma? What do you mean?"

"Just that it was quite certain he was capable of fathering children."

"You knew that without testing?"

"Yes."

"He'd been tested elsewhere before?"

"No, not that I know of."

"Then how do you know he was capable of fathering children?"

She paused, but only for the briefest of moments. Not once did she look at me, or in my direction. Several jurors did though. They looked somewhat discreetly, but they looked. And after they heard what Nurse O'Connor had to say, they stared.

"He knew," said the nurse, "because he had."

24.

Haley lived close to the courthouse in a modernistic condo made of glass and brick and concrete that she had been saying for years she was going to sell.

She wanted a house, a big, old house, she would say, like mine and Sandy's, one that had lots of wood and leaded glass and a big lawn that would lead to some water and whatever else—stature, comfort, respect—it is so often presumed a big lawn leads to. She just hadn't yet gotten around to making it happen.

It was a ten-minute walk to the condo, but it was August and it was hot and we drove it. In silence.

Haley's windows stretched across the front wall, and she had drawn curtains across their entirety. Inside, the living room was almost completely unpartitioned. The kitchen opened up into the dining area, which led into the sunken living room, which was bordered by a wide-open foyer. Down the hall were a few bedrooms, a study and the bathroom. All the floors were hardwood, all the walls were white, and largely bare. In fact, except for a few plants, some scattered furniture, and a cat, the condo was largely empty. She had about half a dozen pictures lined up over the mantel of the fireplace. Most were of her skiing someplace out west or lying on a beach. Sandy was in several of them, and I was in a few others. Most were taken by strangers, people she'd stopped and asked to take a shot of us.

She walked to the kitchen and opened the refrigerator door.

"Want something?" she said.

On one shelf, I could see over her shoulder, was a Diet Coke and a bag of bagels, some cream cheese, and a few doggie bags from local restaurants. On another was a six-pack of beer, a few bottles of wine, and a carton of orange juice. I muttered something in the affirmative and, although it was the middle of the day, she took two of the beers and came into the living room. She handed me an open one, took a sizable gulp of hers, and put it down; then she glanced at me.

"What?" I said.

She glanced again, and took another sip.

"What, Haley?"

"Something I've always wanted to ask you, actually. How come you never told her? How come you never told Sandy?"

"I could ask the same thing of you."

"It wasn't ever my place," she said.

"No? Since when do you mind your place?"

Haley closed her eyes and shook her head.

"Look," I said. "As we both know, it was a long time ago." I leaned back into the sofa and put a hand over my forehead. "A long, long time ago."

"You should have told her," she said.

"Well, I didn't."

"How could she not find out at the clinic?"

"I was tested, even though they knew the result. All that stuff's confidential. Sandy assumed they just knew from the test—which was technically true."

"You should have told her," she said again.

"I know I should have! I'm not proud of this, okay?"

"You mean the not-telling part?"

She took another swig of beer.

"It didn't really have anything to do with her," I said. "That was a long time ago. I didn't even know her then. Not really. It just . . . It's part of the past, Haley. And, anyway, it wasn't like we had a child somewhere."

"Yeah, lucky for you."

She had turned her back on me and taken another swig. The tone of her voice had changed.

"What's that supposed to mean?" I said.

"It means whatever you want it to mean."

"Haley, you had a miscarriage! And I barely even knew you were pregnant. I'm sorry! But we've been over this! A long, long time ago! For Christ's sake, we were . . . what? Nineteen?"

"Twenty-one!" she said.

"So, twenty-one! Whatever!"

"Whatever?" There were tears in her eyes. "It wasn't whatever."

"Look," I said. "I never told her because I didn't want to hurt her. That's the reason. I didn't want to hurt her."

"Oh," said Haley, rising. "Oh! Now I get it! It doesn't have anything to do with self-preservation. You keep all your little secrets to yourself because you're so goddamned concerned about the rest of us."

"What?" I said, standing up. "Haley, I wasn't the one screwing around on my spouse. That was my wife, in case you forgot! Sandy wasn't in the picture when you got pregnant. Anyway, why didn't you tell Sandy about the pregnancy if it was so damn important?"

"What? That I carried her husband's child?"

There was a pronounced silence.

"I wasn't her husband at the time," I said, trying to control my voice. "Look, I should have said something to her about it a long time ago. Years ago! Right in the beginning. I wanted to. I thought about it. A lot. She deserved to know. But I never did, and after a while it became harder. Not only would I have to tell her, I would have had to explain why I hadn't told her earlier. Anyway, I didn't want to know all the details of her sexual exploits before we met and I don't think she would have wanted to know the details of mine. I mean, if honesty is always the best policy, why didn't you tell me about Moylan?"

"Because," said Haley, "I'm not your wife."

"Yeah," I said, "I think we've already established that."

25.

We did not speak the whole way back, but Haley would not be one to let harsh words come permanently between us. She was blunt and outspoken and I was used to it. Sandy had been as well.

When we got back to the courtroom, Thorpe was telling Nevers that he wanted to close with a tape recording of one of the conversations between Billi Stroud and Tommy Moylan. He needed to bring the focus back to the defendant.

"Motive time," said Haley.

Phinney immediately objected, but Nevers, who had a transcript in front of him, cut the attorney off.

"Yes," he said, "these might be prejudicial, but lots of things are. If nothing was prejudicial, there would never be any verdicts, verdicts of any sort. If those notes go to motive, that fact far outweighs any rights the defendant has to confidentiality in this case. The law is clear on that."

The judge looked at the prosecutor while Phinney, who knew he had lost the fight, sat down.

"Call the jury," said Nevers, "and play the tape."

Thorpe waited for the jury to file in, then got up and walked to the front of the courtroom with a tape recorder, placing it on the ledge of the witness box. He bent the microphone down so that it was next to the tape recorder. Then he turned toward the jury.

"This is a conversation that took place in Dr. Moylan's home while Billi Stround was staying there," he said. "Dr. Moylan taped their sessions. He took notes, too, but mostly he just taped them."

"All of them?" asked Nevers.

"At least most," said Thorpe. "I had twelve tapes transcribed, each an hour long. This is just a small portion of one of them."

Nevers nodded and the prosecutor hit the play button.

"This first voice that you will hear," he said, "will be Dr. Moylan's."

There was a sound as if someone was moving a microphone, a crinkling that lasted until Thorpe had made it all the way back to the defense table. Then came Tommy Moylan's voice, clear as a bell, as present as a person sitting across a small room.

"Let's talk about your earlier therapy," he said.

It was eerie hearing that voice, as if an apparition suddenly appeared back from the other side, and you realized immediately why Phinney had not wanted the tape to be played. It brought the victim to life, made him real in a way that words on a page or secondhand recollection never could. Made him real, the truth is, in a more vivid and effective way than putting him on the stand—if he'd still been alive—ever could.

I didn't know Tommy Moylan when he lived, and neither did the jury. They learned of him only after he died—and that, really, is the worst of all times to learn anything about anybody. When one dies, the eulogies are always bright and shiny. The deceased are saints, and if they are not they would have been—if there had only been more time. Billi Stroud would have a hard time competing with a dead man. The dead, in our minds, must always be either punished or redeemed. And everyone knew that, however deserving he might have been for the punishment given him, what remained for Tommy Moylan was only to be redeemed.

"What's to talk about?" said a female voice.

"That's the defendant," said Thorpe.

This was the first time, ironically, that the jury had heard her voice. She was sitting no more than ten feet from them and had not made an utterance the entire trial. You could imagine what she must have looked like, sitting there in Moylan's study, perhaps in a chair beside a table, with the same look of guarded vulnerability and defiance you could, if you looked closely, occasionally catch in the courtroom.

"Well, when did the therapy start?" said Moylan.

I envisioned him sitting there, with his legs crossed effeminately one over the other, a pad of paper in his lap.

"Three or four years ago," responded Billi.

"Yeah, how'd that go?"

"Pretty much a waste."

"How come a waste?"

"I don't know."

"What'd you talk about?"

"Stuff. . . . My mom mostly. Her husband."

"Not your dad?" said Moylan.

"I don't really have a dad."

She was speaking in a monotone.

"Well, your mom remarried, right? So you had a stepfather."

"Yeah."

"How'd he treat you?"

"Great."

"You wanna talk about it?"

"Not particularly."

"Why not?"

"Been there."

"Why don't you humor me a little?" said Moylan, with a bit of a laugh in his voice.

Billi saw no humor. *"Why? So you can get some jollies?"*

"Jollies?"

If he was taken aback, it was hard to tell. You would imagine that, in his line of work, he was used to recalcitrance and defense mechanisms.

"You heard me."

"Why don't you want to talk about it?"

"I have talked about it."

"With whom?"

"Look, I appreciate what you're doing here and all," said Billi, sighing, *"but all I wanted was a place to stay. I need a landlord. I don't need a therapist. I've had therapists and, no offense, but you're all the same. You sit there and ask me to tell you all about how some dirty old man came into my room at night like it gives you some kind of whacking material or something. . . ."*

One of the female jurors visibly blanched, and looked over at Billi Stroud. Her head was bowed, almost down to the level of the table. Her forehead practically touched the surface. She had folded into herself. She looked pained.

"You're clever, you know," said Moylan.

"Thank you. They tell me it's a self-defense mechanism when you don't want to tell some Peeping Tom about your sex life."

"Peeping Tom?"

"Yeah, that's your name isn't it? Tom?"

"I guess it is," he said, the first hint of exasperation coming into his voice. This was an odd conversation, not so much professional, one sensed already, as personal.

"Maybe we should hang this up," said Moylan.

"That's fine with me," she said, more defiant now. *"Neither one of us wants to be here. You're just a place for me to stay, and I'm just a chit for you to trade."*

"A chit?"

"That's what I said."

"To do what with?"

"To get whatever it is you get from Sandy."

"Sandy?"

There was an incredulousness in his voice now, but not one tinged with sincerity. There was a hint of mockery, actually.

"Yeah, Sandy. Your girlfriend," she said.

"Is that what you think?" said Moylan. *"Well, go ahead and think it then."*

There was a rustling on the tape. It sounded as if he was getting up.

"What does Sandy have to do with this?" he said.

Billi laughed at that. *"You're not trying to tell me you're doin' this for me?"* she said. *"C'mon."*

"C'mon what?"

"You're sleeping with her!" said Billi. *"Or trying to."*

He did not deny it. He was, I imagined, secretly proud of it. Sandy was a beautiful, intelligent woman—stunningly beautiful, some would say. And it wasn't as if he'd dragged her off into the woods, after all, or slipped roofies into her gin and tonic. Hell, maybe she was the one who slipped them into his.

"This isn't about me," Moylan said.

"How convenient," she responded.

"I think you need to start worrying about yourself instead of others," he said.

"Oh, thanks, Dad."

"I think you need to start resolving some of this stuff on your own, Billi. And Sandy needs to realize that, too. I'll say that much about her."

"Oh, you will?"

"You know," said Moylan, *"you think because you've had some problems you can do whatever the hell you want; treat people any way you feel; break whatever laws there are; do what you did."* This was no longer a therapy session. *"Smoke pot in my house."*

"Oh, here we go."

"Yeah, that's right," he said.

"I thought we dealt with that."

"Not entirely we didn't."

"What's it matter to you?"

"It matters a lot when it's my house," he said, raising his voice. *"I'm not going to be your little conspirator or abettor or whatever."*

"I'm not asking you to be."

"You don't have to ask. In fact, you wouldn't have the courtesy. But when you come in here with that stuff and when I'm aware of it and when you don't stop that's a problem—my problem. Okay? Aside from everything else."

"What else?"

"Look, why don't you ask Sandy to find you somewhere else to stay. I think it would be best for both of us."

"Thanks to you, I can hardly even get her to return my phone calls," said Billi.

"Yeah? Why is that?"

"I don't know. Why don't you tell me?"

"I think Sandy wants what's best for you."

"No, I think you want what's best for you."

"Oh, that's right. It's never about you, Billi. It's about everyone else. It's about what everyone else is doing to you, or did to you, or is going to do to you, and that makes whatever you do okay, no matter who you hurt. At some point, the past is past."

"What the hell do you know about who I hurt?"

"Quite a bit, actually, as you may recall."

"Yeah? Well, there ain't much you can do about it, is there?" she said.

"I don't know. I'm still thinking about that. In the meantime, I think this is over."

"Yeah, it's way over."

"And not just our little therapy sessions. I can't help you. I don't know if anyone can. I'm not going to worry about you anymore."

"Yeah, well, maybe you should worry about yourself," said Billi.

"Is that a threat?"

"Take it," Billi said, *"however you want."*

There was a long pause now that turned into an even longer one, and slowly the courtroom, mesmerized, came to realize that was the end of the conversation. That was as much as Thorpe was going to give us. He got up, after a few more moments, walked over, and hit the stop button.

"The prosecution," he said slowly and with some affect, "rests."

Billi Stroud just sat there, rocking slowly forward and backward, never once looking up.

26.

Being a reporter doesn't work the way it is portrayed in the movies, or even the way you sometimes see it done on television. You don't stand on the sidewalk as a man in a suit rushes past with his lawyer and yell your question from the back of the crowd.

"Is it true, sir, you killed him? Sir? Is it true?"

Wouldn't it be hilarious if, just once, the guy stopped and turned toward the camera and said, "Why, yes, yes, actually, I did—thank you for asking"?

In real life, you sit across from the guy or call on the phone. Start with the innocuous. Be firm, but polite. Ingratiate yourself a little, if possible. It is okay, sometimes, to fake it. Insist that you are going to be "forced to write it" when you haven't the foggiest idea what "it" really is. Pretend that you know much, much more—or less—than you really do.

Ask the easy questions first, the ones they have no reason not to answer, then build. When you get to the tough ones, ask forthrightly and without altering the tone of your voice. Never, ever apologize. Act as if you are the judge and the jury and the cleric all rolled into one, and not just the executioner.

"Did you lie?" you say. "Are you guilty?" "How in the world do you live with yourself?"

And—oh—one more thing: Do your best to never, ever end up on the opposite side of the query.

"Your Honor," said Phinney that afternoon, "I'd like to present my opening."

Nevers motioned to the lectern, as if to say, "Go ahead," and Phinney got up, briefly pausing to make eye contact with the jurors as he moved forward. They were rapt before he even started.

"I saved my opening until now," he said, moving out from behind the lectern immediately and standing four or five feet in front of the jurors, "for a reason."

He had note cards in his hand, but did not look at them.

"I saved it because I think now that you know the players a little better, you'll understand what I am about to tell you."

He stopped and turned away from the jury, surveyed the crowd in the gallery, pausing ever so slightly when his eyes passed over me. Then he looked back at the jurors.

"Mr. Thorpe is right about a few things," he said. "Sandy Cross didn't kill anybody. Sandy Cross was there, however, and she did panic and cover up for someone. Why, ask yourself, why would she have done that for Billi Stroud? What would the motive be for her to cover up a murder? Think about it. Not only was she putting herself in danger of being a suspect, she was actually committing a crime, a felony. She was. Detective Deiter, you may recall, has said as much. She was aiding and abetting a murderer after the fact, and under the law that makes her a felon herself.

"Let me tell you something you may have thought of," said Phinney, moving his eyes from one juror to the next. "This is not the way a case like this usually proceeds."

Thorpe was almost up off his chair now, leaning forward. But he didn't say anything. Not yet.

"Mr. Thorpe, over there . . ."—he didn't bother looking at his adversary—"Mr. Thorpe, given what he believes, could easily have charged Sandy Cross with any number of crimes—at the very least obstruction of justice. There's no doubt she obstructed justice. The only reason he hasn't is that she is in a coma and it would do no one any real good. Such a charge would probably help induce her to talk—if she could talk. She can't, of course.

But what if she could? How would she explain her actions? How could she possibly explain her actions in any way that would make sense? What motive, what bond, what history, could possibly have been sufficient enough to induce her to become an accessory to murder? What—or who—could possibly induce her to risk not only her license to practice law, not only her reputation, but jail time? She was throwing her life away.

"Who would she do that for?"

He paused.

"The prosecution," he said, "wants you to believe she did all that for a client. That's what Ms. Stroud was, after all: a client. Sandy Cross may have liked Billi—she's easy to like," he said, smiling at her. "I can tell you that, despite whatever else you may have heard here. Or she may have felt sorry for her." He was serious now, again. "But, you know what? When it came right down to it, she was just a client. Never been to the Cross House. Never just went out with Sandy to have a glass of wine or a beer. Never did any of that.

"No. Sandy Cross would not have risked all that for Billi Stroud. No way. That's common sense. But she did—quite obviously—risk it for someone.

"Lemme tell you something," said Phinney, moving now back behind the lectern and looking down, for the first time, at his note cards. "Lemme tell you something," he repeated. And then he looked at the jurors. "Whoever murdered Tommy Moylan knew exactly what he was doing."

The use of the masculine pronoun reverberated. I thought it the loudest word that Phinney had ever said.

"See, he was smart," said Phinney. "He didn't lose it in the sense that passion or anger just overwhelmed him and he marched over and got into a confrontation and did something he would regret. He didn't lose it that way. I guess if that had been the way, you could almost empathize with him. No, he waited for the right moment and planned out what was, setting aside for just a minute the vileness of the act itself, a pretty ingenious little murder. He left Billi Stroud—and Sandy Cross—holding the bag.

"See, I think the person who did this wanted Sandy Cross to witness the aftermath, wanted her to see her lover—you've already heard that's what Tommy Moylan was—lying there. I think that was part of the plan. Sandy Cross had indeed had an affair with Tommy Moylan. And I don't think they were the only two who knew it. Somebody else knew it as well. Somebody who knew where Billi and Sandy had put Billi's service revolver some time before; somebody who, because he's friends with the police maybe got a pass here on really being investigated; somebody, I think, who was at the cliff that night when Sandy Cross drove over. I'm going to tell you how he got there."

The jeweler was transfixed. Her mouth was actually agape.

"I don't have all the answers right now," said Phinney. "But I have most of them. And I'd certainly appreciate it if you'd listen closely while I ask a few questions of my first—and most important—witness."

There was in that room, then, as we waited for his next words, an almost eerie stillness, an uncomfortable sensation that made me feel alone and oddly vulnerable. The room was bathed in competing lights of the television cameras, and I could sense the rustle of coats and bags as people turned almost imperceptibly toward me in the brightness. It reminded me somehow of the rustle of leaves, brown and brittle and foreboding, and I froze, and stared ahead, and when they came, those words, when I heard them, there was no surprise or anger. There was just a powerlessness and self-recrimination and, I think now, something else, something more amorphous. Fear.

"If it pleases the court," Phinney said, turning toward Nevers. "I'd like to call Will Dunby."

Haley was on her feet in a flash.

"Judge," she shouted. "Judge, I represent Mr. Dunby here

and I'd like a word with him. Could I have a minute with my client?"

"After his testimony," said Nevers.

"But, Your Honor—" she began.

"He's here and he's been called. And he's on the witness list."

"Not for this!" she said.

"Sit down!" Nevers barked. "He's on the list."

Behind me, it was as close to bedlam as I have ever witnessed in a courtroom. The babble of voices was rivaled only by the clicking of camera shutters, and one photographer, for some unknown reason, emitted a barely concealed epithet.

"Your Honor—" I started to say, rising.

Haley pushed me back into my seat, disdainfully, and I pulled my arm away.

"Sit down, Will," she said, loudly. Then, "Judge?"

Nevers was pounding his gavel, demanding that the courtroom quiet down.

Haley waited a few moments, looking down at her hands, which, because she was clenching the back of the bench in front of us so firmly, were turning white.

"Judge," Haley said again when the crowd had quieted. "Judge," she said the third time in a lower voice.

Finally, Nevers acknowledged her.

"Your Honor, may I have a moment with my client? Please."

"Ms. Arnold," said the judge, calmly now but without taking his gaze off her, "sit down."

Haley looked at me helplessly. And, after pausing for a minute, I stood up and moved out into the center aisle, looking Phinney in the eye as camera shutters clicked from all angles. Then, after I'd made it to the aisle, I turned to my right and, as several voices erupted into shouts of protest, walked out of that courtroom.

I simply walked out.

"Will!" Haley was shouting. "Will!"

"Mr. Dunby," Nevers said in a low but threatening voice. "Mr. Dunby. There is plenty of room in the county jail."

I ignored him.

"Ms. Arnold?" I heard him say. "Your client is now in contempt."

Several reporters and photographers I didn't recognize got up and followed me and almost immediately the rest of the pack did as well, emptying out of the courtroom and calling my name. It had started pouring that afternoon and I didn't have an umbrella, but I kept going anyway—and so did the reporters. I remembered after I was already outside and in the parking lot that I didn't have my car either—but it was too late to turn back. On the other side of the parking lot, between it and the street I needed to reach, was a culvert full of dirty water and mud.

I was upon it before I realized it was there, halfway through almost before I knew how deep it would become. The current was fast enough that I actually feared it would push my feet out from underneath me. I could not stop. I could not turn around. Soaking wet, filthy, sinking into the muck, cursing Phinney, fearful I would soon be arrested, I kept going—wondering if I would be able to extricate myself, noticing only then how steep a climb it would be up the other side.

27.

It took me some time to find a cab willing to let me inside. As it was, the cabbie who did stop got a towel out of the trunk and made me sit on it. Then, I was sure, he charged me roughly double the normal fare. I didn't want to go home, where people could find me, so I went to Haley's place instead—and sat outside her back patio door until, an hour or so later, she finally showed up.

She said nothing when she found me back there, just shook her head and pointed to her bathroom.

"You can mop the place up," she said, "after you take a shower."

Inside, I turned the water up as hot as I could stand it. Ten or fifteen minutes later the door opened.

"You okay in there?" she said.

I sensed real concern in her voice.

"Yeah," I said. "I'm fine. Just gimme a second here."

"What are you doing in there?"

I expected her to wait outside, but she didn't. She came in and stood close on the other side of the curtain. Haley never stood on formality.

"I'm okay," I said softly, the water beating down onto my back. "And in case you're wondering, I didn't kill him."

I heard her move over to the other wall of the bathroom and sit on the toilet. For several long moments, there was no response.

"I wasn't wondering," she finally said.

"But I did find the gun."

The water beat down onto my neck and shoulders. It was the only sound, for what seemed like forever, in that room.

"Where?" she asked after several more moments.

The hot water was starting to run out, and I felt the first chill.

"Sandy hid it in the garage before she tried to kill herself," I said. "She must have come back just for a moment while I was in the shower that night. I saw her tire tracks later when I ran out the back door. They hadn't been there when I got home. I found the gun up in the garage a few days later. I wasn't looking for it. I was getting some baskets to move some leaves, and there it was."

"Why didn't you just turn it in?"

"I thought at the time they might charge her. And it was before they charged Stroud. Later on, I didn't want to have to explain it."

"Where is it?"

"It's still back at the house. I rehid it."

"Will—"

"I was trying to protect her."

She said nothing for what seemed like a minute. The water was almost freezing now. I was starting to shiver.

"Will," Haley finally murmured. "How much does Phinney know?"

I didn't answer. I didn't know. I turned the water off and reached out for a towel.

"Could you just give me a minute here?" I said, looking around the curtain.

She stared at me, silent, and I paused for a moment to give her another chance to leave.

"Oh, forget that bullshit," she said. "What do you mean, protect her? From prosecution?"

When I came to the realization Haley was not going to leave I stepped out of the shower, and began to dry myself off. The hot water and the steam had driven the temperature up in the bathroom and she was sweating. She unbuttoned her top button.

I wrapped the towel around myself.

There was no judgment in her voice now, and not the slightest affectation, just persistence. It was one of the qualities, Sandy had thought, that made Haley a spectacular defense attorney, the ability to hold in abeyance the normal inclinations and reactions—surprise, shock, outrage, disapproval—sometimes suspend them altogether in order to do her job.

"Yeah, I guess. From prosecution."

She pondered this.

"You'd forgiven her, I take it," she said.

I stared at her.

That was the question.

"For Moylan, you mean?"

She nodded.

I looked toward the mirror, used a towel to wipe the steam off the glass.

"Look, Haley," I said, "you don't just wake up one morning and decide that's the day you're going to forget everything. I wanted to forget it, move on. I tried to, a million times. Tried to stop dwelling on it. Tried to stop rationalizing what Sandy claimed was irrational. Because you can't. But it's a hard thing to forget. There are things . . . I don't know. It just sort of crops up. I mean, shit, she was my wife! She's still my wife. Even if it doesn't feel like it. And, anyway, I wasn't sure it was over."

"Sure what was over?"

"It," I said. "Whatever it was."

"The affair?"

I nodded. "I had thought it was," I said. "Then I find out that she's got Billi Stroud living over there."

"You mean you found out after the murder, right?"

"Yeah, after. And you know what? It still pissed me off. She promised not to see this guy at all—at all! I *thought* the affair was over, I don't know."

"Shit," murmured Haley.

The simple act of enunciation evoked images I tried to suppress: the physical part, her breasts laid across his chest, her legs splayed, him on her or in her or under her. Kissing her. Whatever. I turned around and faced Haley.

"I need an attorney, don't I?" I asked.

Haley was sitting on the toilet with her face buried in her hands, and all she did when she looked up at me, as serious as I have ever seen her, was nod.

All she did was nod.

28.

Haley, an hour or so later, gave me a ride home and we found several cop cars parked in the front yard when we arrived. Deiter was standing on the front porch, and I could see through the windows that at least two officers were inside.

"What the hell's going on here?" shouted Haley, before she was even out of the car. It was getting dark and she had left the headlights on. Deiter had to squint to see us.

"Is he with you?" Deiter said.

"Yeah. What are you guys doing?"

"Nevers is pissed. Told us to find him and arrest him for contempt—now."

"What the hell is up his ass?"

"Just guessing, but I'd say the answer is Will. You don't just walk out on a judge."

"Shit," whispered Haley.

Deiter called to the cops inside the house, told them he'd found me. I could see Elizabeth, summoned apparently by the night nurse, inside as well. Standing near Sandy, she had a look of sad resignation on her face.

"Let's get those cops out of here," I said to Haley as we approached the house. "I'll just go with them."

"Oh, that's big of you," she scoffed. "Will, you're under arrest."

It took just moments for the cops to come out of the house and turn me around. One pulled out a pair of handcuffs but

Haley objected. The uniformed officer looked at Deiter, who waved his hand to indicate they weren't necessary.

"Just get him downtown," said Deiter to the other cop, who—with obvious reluctance—put the cuffs back on his belt.

Haley told me she would follow behind in her own car, meet me down there. Just as they were about to put me in one of the squads, however, a voice rose out from the woods. It was not a scream and there was no sense of urgency. It was simply the voice of a man who was very loudly, but very calmly, calling out for someone, anyone, to come to him.

Suddenly, I realized that some of the cops had been searching the grounds for me while others had gone inside. They'd walked from the house all the way down to the river, and from the clearing to the old fence that marked the boundary between the Cross land and what, closer to the bluff, was public.

"Hey!" yelled the voice now. "Hey! Over here!"

One of the officers had already been working his way out of the woods, it would turn out, climbing in the shadows along one of the steep paths, pulling himself up with his hands. And when he came upon it, it was not at all what he might have imagined. If he could have imagined it at all, I guess, it would have been something less quotidian, less commonplace, something more grotesque perhaps, emitting a sort of green iridescence.

"Over here!" he yelled again, matter-of-factly, in a voice that, when it broke the evening, was like a man standing on a street corner hailing a taxi. And then, as the others began to catch up with him, moved closer and shone their lights upon it, it sank in.

"Holy shit!" someone said.

It was not the gun.

The officers who were about to put me in the squad car wanted to see what was going on, and did not dare leave me behind so it was not much longer before we all walked over there ourselves. When we got there, the one that had discovered it stared alternately at the ground and then back up at the rest of us, but mostly at me, entering my presence and the likelihood I had walked those lands sometime before, into the equation being formulated in that ever-narrowing, crepuscular light.

And then I saw the reason.

He was, by then, a surprisingly tiny assemblage of skin and bones inside a football jersey stamped with a 22. And above that at one end, tilted back at a grotesque angle so that the chin pointed almost straight up to the heavens and the eye sockets pointed back toward the dark earth, what remained of the very first part of Chucky Ware's body to have come into this world from his mother's womb. Only now, in his forehead, or what remained of it, in the middle, exactly as had been the case with Tommy Moylan, was a small bullet-size hole.

I don't know how long we were there, looking, but after the cops hauled me back to the driveway I sat in the backseat of the squad car for innumerable long minutes while they talked on their radios and among themselves and with Haley. Reporters who'd heard the commotion on their scanners showed up and clamored for attention but Haley said we would have no comment and kept them away. I sat there so long that, by the time we were finally about to leave, a car pulled into the driveway and a woman got out.

They tried to forestall her, keep her at a distance, protect her from what she insisted she could not believe unless she saw it. For it was, I finally realized, Chucky Ware's sister. And after she was taken to the place where her brother lay, unrecognizable and covered by a thin layer of dirt, she stared as well.

It was sheer misfortune, I suppose, that he had not been found sooner, that he had remained covered that way there on the Cross grounds through all the days and nights that had come and gone since his demise—either that or an ill-fatedness so dark and absurd that when he was finally found, when on that night what remained of his body finally came to light, his sister knelt slowly down on that soft bed of earth and wondered how it could possibly be so.

"Oh, my God," she wailed in shock and surprise. Then, in a monotone, already hardening, so loud that I could hear it from where I sat.

"My God."

29.

They placed me in a large holding cell that night where there were two cots, each affixed to a wall with brackets. In the middle was a sink with a scratched piece of metal above it that was apparently supposed to serve as a mirror. The toilet was at the other end, at the foot of one of the cots, and there was no seat on it—just a large piece of excrement floating on top. I flushed the toilet, and a man sitting on one of the cots looked at me, expressionless. He was more a boy, really, hairless and corpulent, out of shape. His belly hung down over his pants, which were held up by a drawstring and looked to be jail-issue.

The next morning, one of the deputies brought the paper in and—in what I first mistook as generosity—handed it to me through the bars. I thanked him, then realized why he had brought it.

Although I had been arrested for contempt of court, a picture of me in the paper ran right next to the story that focused on the discovery of Chucky's body. People who did not read the story closely, I knew, would immediately assume that I had been arrested for his murder. People who did read it closely, on the other hand, probably thought I was lucky not to have been.

"Son of a bitch!" I sputtered to myself. "Shit!"

I was reading the article for the third or fourth time when Haley showed up.

"You're getting out in exchange for a promise to take the stand," she said.

"Thanks for consulting me."

"Thanks for paying me."

"I'll pay."

She shook her head the way a mother does at a child in whom she is sorely disappointed.

"I don't want your money. I want you to exercise your Fifth Amendment rights. But you have to take the stand in order to do it."

"Whatever."

"No, not whatever. Not unless you want to spend the rest of your life with that cellmate buddy of yours. Will, grow up. We need to figure out what you should do here."

"Well," I said when we got outside, "I know exactly what I should do here."

I ran to the *Courier*, a copy of the paper still in my hand.

There was no byline on the article, which was extremely unusual. That meant it was a collaboration, perhaps with Hemper heavily involved. It also suggested that Mozzy, who'd obviously had a hand in it, didn't want her name on it in the end.

CROSS/DUNBY TIED TO MURDERS read the headline.

Underneath was a long story that focused not only on Chucky and where he had been found but, in no particular order, the fact that someone else had apparently been with Sandy shortly before she tried to kill herself the night of the Moylan murder, and the relationship between Sandy and Tommy Moylan. The eighth or ninth paragraph was a quote from me.

"Got around, didn't she?"

I gasped when I saw it.

They had quoted most of Phinney's opening, including the accusations about me; then they had segued to the discovery of Chucky Ware in my backyard. Mozzy, or whoever had written it, had been careful to use innuendo rather than libel after that. But the story, to anyone who could read between the lines, clearly pointed a finger at me. They were insinuating that I might have been involved in both the murders.

And they noted at least three times that I had refused to comment.

When I first picked up the paper that morning, I wondered if my insomnia had caused me to hallucinate. Nothing looked the same, or sounded quite as it once had, and I had to look at everything two and three times before it registered. I was, I had already found in those days, plagued by aphasia, and actually worried that I was developing an extremely premature form of Alzheimer's or dementia. The simplest words—plow, hose, bracket—were eluding me. When I looked at the picture of me next to the article, I was struck by how old I appeared, gaunt and sallow, with pronounced bags under my eyes.

My insomnia had worsened, and I craved unconsciousness.

I ran into the *Courier*, barely acknowledging the guard, a middle-aged, slightly built man with a growing paunch by the name of Gene who made you flash your identification card every time you entered the building. If you didn't have one, if you forgot it or lost it or left it in your desk when you went to lunch, you were out of luck. Gene, even if he knew your name and had greeted you with it a thousand times, still insisted on calling your supervisor, and your supervisor had to come all the way downstairs, flash his or her own identification card, and then sign you in. Many mornings, this meant you would find someone who had worked at the *Courier* for ten or twenty years standing at the front desk, staring at Gene and silently fuming as his or her boss got pulled out of a meeting or the cafeteria to come downstairs and grouse. But rules were rules, and Gene made no exceptions.

I pulled out my wallet, showed him my card, and pressed the elevator button. Gene invariably greeted me by name—but not this time. As I pushed the buttons a second time, he said only, "Hold on, I need to call your supervisor."

I flashed my card at him a second time.

"There it is," I said, turning toward the elevator.

"I know," said Gene, picking up the telephone. "I need to call your supervisor."

The door to the elevator had already opened, and I stepped on. "I've got the card," I said as the door closed.

"Hey! You can't—" I heard him begin to yell as the elevator moved upward to the fourth floor. I pulled a copy of the morning paper out from under my arm and looked again at the front page.

Mozzy was not there when I got to her desk. It was empty except for a folder and on top of it the letter I had given her regarding Stroud's resignation.

"What are you doing?" I heard a voice yell, booming across the room.

It was Hemper.

"What am I doing?" I screeched. "What the fuck are you doing?" I held up the paper. "What the hell is this?"

I was out of control, and most of the newsroom were on their feet, staring. I started to move toward Hemper, but he came at me and put a hand on my shoulder.

"Let's move out in the hall," he said quietly.

"No."

I pushed his hand off my shoulder and thought, for a moment, we might come to blows.

"C'mon, Will."

There was a tone in his voice that he had never used with me before, a paternalistic, no-nonsense authoritativeness, but I ignored it.

"No!" I held up the article. "Just what the fuck is this?"

"Out in the hall!" he said. "Now!"

But I would not go.

"Look, Will," he said, right in my face, "if you know what's good for you, you'll turn around and go. I've been a little uncomfortable with this all along, and now it's . . . Well, it just can't be ignored."

"What can't be ignored?" I said. "What are you talking about?"

Beads of sweat were forming on my brow. I felt the anger and the heat seep from my face.

Hemper was shaking his head. "Don't make this harder than it is," he was saying, trying to keep his voice down. "We've been pretty damn fair about this whole thing, you gotta admit."

"Fair? Is that what you call this?" I started to hold up the paper again, and I laughed. "About what exactly have you been so goddamned fair?"

I was frustrated and raised my voice, but Hemper was much angrier than I thought.

"Will!" he said. "Put yourself in my position! Our position! Just once! This thing is all of a sudden much more complicated than any of us knew."

"How?"

"Look, like it or not, people connect you with this paper. You know that. We have to be fair to everyone, unbiased. You know that better than anyone! And now with this stuff . . ."

"What stuff?"

"You tell me," he said.

"Tell you what?"

He was incredulous.

"Oh, c'mon! She was having an affair with him! Have you lost your fucking marbles? Now they find a body in your backyard! Phinney pointed the finger at you. He blamed you! He says you're a murderer!"

"You didn't even get my comment!"

"You wouldn't let us! We tried. You know the rules! What'd you want? A pass? You, of all people!"

Just then, another voice yelled out from across the newsroom in an incomprehensible croak. I turned around and saw Gene, bounding at me. Behind him were two city police officers.

"I told him to stop," he said, explaining to Hemper. "He just kept going."

"Why would I stop?" I yelled.

"Because I told you to!"

The volume of Gene's voice surprised me. I didn't know he had it in him. One of the cops said loudly from ten feet away, "Okay, buddy, you need to go now."

I raised my hands up in front of my chest and said, "I'm not your buddy."

He gently put a hand on my arm in the condescending way that only cops can, and the two of them exchanged glances, purposely looking amused.

"Oh, sorry," said one. Then in a lower voice, almost whispering: *"Bud-dy."*

He nudged the cop standing next to him and that one stifled a laugh.

"C'mon, pretty boy," whispered the second one.

I pushed his hand off my arm, but he grabbed it again, this time harder.

"Would you mind," I said, not raising my voice, "not doing that?"

I was trying to keep from losing my temper, trying to get him to hear a little bit of resignation so he would back off. But he didn't.

"Settle yourself, Willy!" said the cop. "It's gonna be okay."

He was the kind of cop who could look right through you, as though you weren't really worth taking the time to focus. Like no one else in the world, cops know how to be assholes. In a thousand subtle, ineffable ways, they know how to make you feel insignificant and criminal. They are masters at it, either by never really looking at you, or by wearing a particularly irritated look, or maybe just by the inflection in a voice. They are not the playground bullies, not the kids who are too dull-witted to disguise their proclivities and end up in the penitentiaries. They are just a hair smarter. They are the ones who'd keep bumping into you on the playground, then apologizing, then bumping into you again;

the ones who would sit behind you and whisper "*pussssy*" in your ear until you wanted to kill them.

"I wanna talk to your boss," I said.

"I don't think he's in today," said one of them, pulling me now toward the hall. "But we'll have him call ya if he comes in. First thing. Right away, okay, buddy? In the meantime, why don't you answer something for me?"

"Like what?"

"Like what the fuck?"

Hemper stayed behind and we were out in the hall now, out of eyeshot of the newsroom. Suddenly things got rougher.

"Hey!" I stammered.

"You got balls, you know, you little smartass," said one.

The cops' faces looked different now, sharper, harder, as if the air had gone out of them.

"So lemme ask you something, Willis," said the other one under his breath now. "How long was your wife fucking that Moylan character?"

I felt it like a punch in the chest.

"What?"

He chuckled. "You heard me."

I tried to pull away.

"How often you think he used to slip it to her, anyway?"

I took the bait.

"Fuck you," I murmured.

"No, fuck you, asshole."

I exploded up at them, but they were quick and as one pushed me from behind the other raised an elbow. It was almost effortless and before I fully understood what was happening I was on the floor back in the corner by the door, sprawled out. I tried to open my eyes but was too dizzy and it took a moment for me to understand that he had hit me in the face with his elbow, hard. A pain seared through my temple and I felt a warm liquid run into my mouth. I was bleeding. I tried to sit up and I felt a couple of arms lift me up. It was a piercing pain, like I'd been hit by a ball-peen hammer above my left eye, and I pulled down a blood-stained hand. When I brought it up, then down again, there was more blood, and it ran down toward my elbow and through my shirt. I felt like I was going to throw up.

"You fucking imbecile," I said.

I saw it coming this time, even before it landed, a fist with a ring in the middle pounding into my forehead like a center punch, drilling deep. Then darkness—absolute, perfect darkness.

30.

"What the hell happened to you?" said Haley, sliding in next to me in Nevers's gallery.

"We can talk about it when you put the civil suit together."

"Against whom?"

"Let's talk about it later."

She shook her head, but let it go.

"What," I asked, "did they find out about Chucky?"

After they found him that night, I learned, it rained in torrents and they built a little tent around him, or what was left of him, and there was room inside for two or three, or maybe four if you counted the boy himself. And when the tent was up and illuminated on that little patch of ground, and after the dwindling light had turned pitch dark, it shone through the woods like a beacon suspended in the trees over the riverbank. And from it, for a long time after they found him, came flashes from the cameras, as they documented just how he had come there and ascertained what had happened to him.

"They finished the autopsy," she said.

"And?"

"He was shot twice. Once in the head and once elsewhere. . . . In the crotch."

"Exact same as Moylan," I said.

"Exact same."

"Have they compared the bullets?" I asked.

"They're from the same gun: Stroud's Glock. Two rounds of jacketed hollowpoint. Looks like he was shot, then dragged to the cliff and pushed over. Dragged some more after that."

"Man."

"He was dead by then . . . ," she said, staring at the cuts on my face.

Thorpe walked out of Nevers's chambers and approached us. Haley's voice trailed off.

"He gonna testify?" said Thorpe to Haley, as if I were not even there. He did not look at me.

"He'll take the stand," she said. "After that, it depends what's asked."

To her, it was an opening gambit, the first position in what she expected to be a negotiation. But Thorpe was apparently not in the mood. He raised his eyebrows, stood up straight and, without saying anything more, without looking at me once, retreated back toward the judge's chambers.

"Carney," said Haley, when he started to walk away, but he did not answer.

When Thorpe got back to Nevers's chambers, he had to knock on the door, and I could see Nevers himself waiting expectantly for the response when it opened. Both Haley and I could also see Tommy Moylan's parents and brother inside and realized for the first time they were not in the courtroom gallery.

"What are they doing in there?" I asked Haley.

"At least he knows you'll get up there," said Haley, not answering the question. "That should get you out of the contempt issue anyway."

"But why's everybody else in there?"

"I don't know."

It was another half hour before the door opened again and first the court reporter, then the attorneys, then Stroud and the bailiffs came walking out. Just in front of Nevers, as if the judge were ushering them to a table in a restaurant, was Moylan's family, eyes downcast, moving slowly back toward their seats. Not one of them said a word, or smiled. There was not a murmur in the courtroom as Nevers took the bench, placed his hand over the microphone, waited for everyone to get settled, and then turned to the jurors.

"I'm sorry about the lengthy in camera proceedings," he said finally, pausing. "But there were a few things that needed to be hashed out in this case, and, frankly, to satisfy me more than anything else. To be honest with you, I'm still not sure I'm fully satisfied with everything I'm hearing. But I'm just the judge and in the end everyone has to make their own decisions around here, attorneys and defendants and prosecutors alike."

He was making eye contact with individual jurors now.

"The long and the short of it is that—for reasons you may come to understand more fully at a later point—your service is no longer required at this juncture."

Several of the jurors were visibly surprised as they tried to decipher what had happened in chambers. Haley put a reassuring hand on my leg.

"You have all been excellent and attentive jurors," he said, "and I and the rest of the court thank you for your service. If you'll follow the bailiff out of the courtroom, he'll make sure that you are properly discharged and, again, thank you for your time. It's greatly appreciated."

That was it. The jurors, looking sideways at each other, rose up and slowly moved out of the courtroom as Nevers watched them go. You could hear the ones in front begin to talk to each other and, as they moved through the door, the jeweler looked at me one last time.

I smiled, but she turned away.

"Okay," said Nevers, after they had filed out. "Let's get on with this."

He addressed himself to the middle distance now between the attorneys and the gallery, a sign that he was making a record of what had been agreed upon. Occasionally, as if to confirm this, he glanced at the court reporter taking the transcript.

"For those of you who are wondering," he said, "a plea bargain has been reached between the state and the defense, and for reasons that will soon become apparent the state has agreed, in exchange for some testimony, to dismiss the charges against Billi Stroud as relate to the Tommy Moylan case."

Several spectators in the gallery murmured to themselves acknowledgments of surprise.

"What's going on?" I whispered to Haley.

She looked at me for a full five seconds before answering, as if pondering how to put it.

"I would imagine," she said, speaking slowly, and very softly as she leaned toward me, "that the location of Chucky's body is a big problem for the prosecution."

It was true, she said, that the wounds provided a nexus between the two crimes. Whoever killed Tommy Moylan either killed or knew all about the killing of Chucky Ware. Bringing Chucky's murder into the Moylan trial, however, would have been a delicate problem for the prosecution. It would only make sense for Thorpe if he could directly link Billi to both murders. He'd be able to make some connections, to be sure, but they'd only just discovered Chucky's body, and he'd had no time to contemplate or investigate things. He'd be feeling his way blindly along. The problem for him was that even if he could link Billi to Chucky, he would have to be careful not to link other "suspects," as Haley put it, as well.

"Suspects," I decided, was under the circumstances a kind euphemism.

The location of the body, the fact that it was found on our property, and the inference that we, either Sandy or I, could by the jurors reasonably be assumed to have known it was there, would raise all sorts of questions that would complicate Thorpe's case.

His best argument to Moylan's parents, Haley guessed, was that it was appearing increasingly unlikely that Billi Stroud was going to be convicted in the murder of their son. At least, with the plea bargain, they could gain a little knowledge about what she had been up to in the case of Chucky Ware, perhaps make some inferences about what happened to Tommy, and get her off the street.

Billi, of course, got something as well. She got a pass on the Moylan case.

"The court," said Nevers, "calls Billi Stroud."

Most of the courtroom, hushed now and utterly surprised, turned and looked toward the rear doors, where witnesses usually entered. Billi Stroud, however, was ushered in from the front through the doors that led to the judge's chambers. She had been in on the conference, too. For the first time since the trial had started she was wearing her standard blaze orange jumpsuit and some ridiculous-looking flip-flops, as if it no longer mattered. The bailiffs led her up to the witness stand and then retreated, one to each of the doors that led into the courtroom. She sat down and nervously wrapped her hands around each other.

"Ms. Stroud," said Nevers, as several cameras flashed. "That's enough of that!" he snapped. "Get them out of here!" The picture taking stopped, but it was too late. The bailiffs ushered the photographers, who complained but complied, out into the hall. "Okay," said Nevers, calming himself, "let's get this on the record. Ms. Stroud, you're prepared to testify this morning about your knowledge of what happened to Chucky Ware?"

There was a collective gasp in the courtroom as she nodded.

"Has to be yes or no, Ms. Stroud. Let's get that straight first."

"Yes," said Billi.

Stroud was enveloped by the creases and folds of the prison jumpsuit, and it made her look even smaller than she was. She looked pale and nervous and her eyes flitted about from Nevers to her lap to Phinney.

"Okay," said Nevers. "And it is your understanding that, in exchange for that testimony and a subsequent plea, which is all going to be on the record and can be used against you in what may be a manslaughter charge as regards Chucky Ware, that this proceeding before us, this charge in regard to the Moylan murder, will be dropped."

Again, a wave of whispers spread across the room.

Nevers picked up his gavel, and the crowd immediately went silent. Without using it, he put it down.

"Ms. Stroud?" he said.

"Yes," she said. "That is my understanding."

"And in addition, there is one stipulation, is there not? One requirement you must meet in order for that agreement to remain in force."

She looked at him, nonplussed, as if to say, "What?"

"You have to tell the truth," said the judge.

"I understand that."

"And if you don't, if you are found at some future point to have lied here today, then the deal is off."

She nodded.

"So you have some incentive to tell the truth here, do you not?"

"Yes. I do."

"Okay," said the judge, looking out into the gallery. "Now, I want some quiet in here. I want to be able to hear a pin drop. You can yammer all you want later, but not here. Now, Ms. Stroud—"

Nevers was himself apparently going to do the examination.

"Ah, Your Honor," came the voice of one of the attorneys. It was Phinney, sitting behind the defense table. "Your Honor, there is additional agreement, I would just like it to be made part of the record if we could, that none of this testimony today will pertain to the Moylan case. My understanding, our understanding, is that those charges are to be dropped, that this testimony about to be taken may constitute, probably will constitute, evidence about a completely different victim and a separate charge—manslaughter—to which the prosecutor and myself have jointly agreed to recommend a period of incarceration."

"Hmm," whispered Haley. "I wonder what they agreed to."

"That's all correct, Counsel," said Nevers, glancing at Thorpe to make sure there was no objection. When there wasn't one, he turned toward Stroud.

"All right," said the judge, "Let's get a little background here.

"You are currently incarcerated, is that right?" he said to Billi Stroud.

"Yes."

"For homicide?"

"That was the charge."

"Homicide in the case of Dr. Thomas Moylan."

"Yes."

"And that charge is going to be dropped today in exchange for your testimony on this other matter, right?"

She looked at Phinney.

"The matter being the death of Charles Ware," said the judge.

Stroud was nodding.

"Yes," she said.

"Okay," said Nevers. "Now, Ms. Stroud, explain how you knew Mr. Ware."

She looked at the court reporter, whose fingers danced in slow motion across the keys of her machine.

"I knew Chucky from when I was a police officer," said Stroud in a clear though hushed and nervous voice. "He'd been in trouble some and was somebody I was supposed to get to know."

"What do you mean by that?"

She looked toward her attorney, but Nevers wanted her attention. "You can direct yourself to me," he said.

"There were individuals with whom we were supposed to familiarize ourselves. As police officers, I mean. I was new on the force—Detective Deiter decided to try to exploit that."

"Exploit it how?"

Stroud seemed to calm down now a little, as she shifted toward the judge.

"Detective Deiter suspected that Charles Ware was quite heavily into drug dealing and wanted to try to break that up, and I was just supposed to try to form a friendship with him."

"While you were an officer?"

"I was on the force. But he didn't know that."

"Okay. So how did you do this, befriend him?" asked the judge.

"Just gradually. I got to know a friend of his at a party, and waited till I finally met Chucky. We were introduced. It appeared spontaneous, but it was all very planned, very gradual, and it worked. After a while, I sort of befriended him."

"As in boyfriend-girlfriend?"

"No. We were just friends."

"Was it sexual?"

"No."

"But am I to understand in fact that the night he disappeared, you were out with him?"

"Yes. I was."

"Where'd you go?"

"We went to a movie."

"A movie?" said Nevers.

"We'd had a bet about a professional wrestling match and I lost, and I had to take him to a movie."

"And after the movie was over?"

"He was driving, and I thought he was taking me home, but he turned off into Promontory Park, which, you know, is sort of a lovers' lane."

"Did you go there voluntarily?"

"I asked him to take me home but he went in anyway."

"And what time did you get there?"

"Around midnight or so. I don't think the movie got out till eleven-forty-five and it was shortly after that."

"What happened once you were there?"

"At first, nothing much. We sat there and talked a little bit. He had bought some beers, and he was drinking them."

"Were you drinking?"

"Yes. A little. Given the situation, I didn't want to seem a prude. I mean, I was already insinuating to him that I wanted to buy some drugs—"

"You hadn't done that yet?"

"I hadn't actually bought any, no. He'd given me some marijuana but I hadn't actually bought any."

"He'd given it to you?"

"Yes."

"And you took it?"

"Yes, it wouldn't have made sense not to."

"What happened to it, by the way?"

"Nothing at first. I just kept it. Later I smoked some of it."

"Is that the same stuff you smoked at Dr. Moylan's?"

"Yes."

"But not what ended up in his van the night you were pulled over?"

"No. I don't know anything ab—"

"Objection!" said Phinney loudly. "Judge, this is outside the scope of the agreement."

Nevers weighed it for a moment, then agreed.

"Sustained," he said, turning to the court reporter. "Strike that last part."

Then he turned toward Billi.

"Okay," he said. "So, what happened next?"

She was alternating her gaze between her own lap and Nevers's face.

"He was having a beer, several actually, and he'd been smoking a little bit—"

"Smoking what?"

"Pot. And at some point I said I wanted to go. He said he

wasn't finished yet and I said, as a way of getting him out of there, that he could finish them and I would drive."

"How did he respond to that?"

"He said he wasn't gonna let no girl drive his pickup, and he kind of laughed."

"And then what?"

"I didn't make a big deal of it."

"Then what happened?"

"Eventually, he tried to kiss me."

"And was that okay with you?"

"No. No, it wasn't."

"And you told him that?"

"At first I just tried to let it pass. I tried to laugh it off."

"Did that work?"

"No. No, you have to realize," she said, looking intently now at the judge, "I tried not to make a big deal of it. I didn't want to embarrass him. I needed to have some kind of good relationship there. But he was very, sort of, trying to be macho, you know, and he was a little bit drunk. Or high."

"What happened?"

"Well, he stopped for a minute, but then a little bit later he did it again, started doin' more. I told him I didn't want to, but he just kind of ignored that. I finally told him to grow up, and that I wasn't kidding. But he just laughed, kind of like he was teasing, and it kind of escalated."

"So, he didn't stop?"

She was squirming now in her seat, slightly, but noticeably.

"At first, like I said, he kinda laughed and he said—he said, 'Who you holdin' out for? Who you holdin' out for?' Like that. I said I just didn't really feel like I wanted that and I was sorry if—if he felt led on but that I hadn't meant to, that I had been careful not to, and then, well, that went on for a while."

"Okay," said Nevers. "Slow down."

"I was very firm," she said, after taking a deep breath, "and he sort of took it as condescension. He called me a bitch. He was drunk. Then he said he guessed we were going to have to get to know each other anyway."

"What did you say to that?"

"I don't know. He seemed so young, you know, I thought he was just acting macho, his whole act. I thought I could handle it."

"But you couldn't?"

She looked down at her lap.

"No."

"What happened then?"

"I asked him to stop—he had his hands on me—and he wouldn't, so I tried to get out of the pickup."

"And did you?"

She made eye contact again with Nevers.

"He wouldn't let me. He was still kind of laughing, saying I didn't mean it . . . and he was still kissing me, or trying to, and he had grabbed ahold of my shirt. So I slapped him."

"And?" said Nevers.

"He got mad—real mad. And he ripped the front of my blouse open. He was real crude. Just popped the buttons off. It was very sudden. He . . ."

She continued looking at Nevers, but for the moment said nothing, as if she were arranging the words. Then it came out.

"He said, 'Show me those little titties.' Like that," she said. "And I remember he had a half a bottle of beer in one hand still, and when he ripped my shirt he threw it in the back like he didn't care. Just tossed it over his shoulder, half full. It sort of clanked against the window and spilled out, and I remember thinking it was a brand-new pickup that he had, and he wouldn't even let anyone else drive it. And then I got real scared. He climbed over on top of me and I was wearing a skirt and he reached up and pulled my underwear down. Just pulled it down hard before I could even react. It hurt. It was so quick. I was screaming, but he had my arms pinned down and I . . . I really couldn't do anything. . . . So I spit on him."

"You spit?"

"In his face. It was—I didn't think about it. I . . . It was stupid. He completely lost it."

She stopped here. But she was still relatively composed.

"What happened then?" said Nevers.

She said it softly, but with a matter-of-factness that made one realize it was not outside the sad realm of her prior experience.

"He raped me," she said, slowly. "He pulled down his jeans . . . and he started to rape me. . . ."

She stopped, wavered for a moment.

"Take your time," said Nevers.

"Only he couldn't really do it because I was thrashing around and he was trying to pin down my arms. It was very violent. He punched me, several times, hard. I thought he might choke me or something and I knew that I had a gun, my gun, in my purse. He didn't know it. He didn't know I had a gun, didn't know I was a cop. It was right by my side in the purse on the floor of the seat. I was pinned on my back and I reached in and found it. It took me a few tries. . . ."

She paused. Then took a breath. Held it for just a moment.

"And then I shot him," she said, simple and plain, as though it was an exercise in a phonetics book. "I shot him."

"Where?"

"I wasn't sure. I think in the groin. I just shot. My arm was still kinda trapped underneath him. I was afraid, actually, I was going to shoot myself. But I shot him."

"More than once?"

"At first I thought I missed him, because he just kept coming at me for a second, and then—it was almost like a delayed reaction—he just screamed, yelping like a dog. And he looked kinda surprised and sorta lifted up off me and got this look, this shock, about what had happened. And then he just, he went wild. . . ."

Until then, the courtroom had been completely silent. Now, in the back there was movement. Someone was holding on to Chucky Ware's sister, who was pulling away, trying to get out of her seat, moaning gently.

"What happened then?"

"Well, I managed to open the door and I—we both sort of fell out onto the ground and he came at me again and I still had the gun. So I shot him again. I shot him in the head. . . . I thought he was going to take it away from me so I shot him right in the head."

Tears were welling up in her eyes now, and streaming down her face, but she continued to talk without stopping.

"His body was on top on me, bleeding. Most of the blood ended up on me. There wasn't hardly any in the pickup, and there was some outside on the ground. But I was covered with it. I was just covered with blood and it just freaked me out. I was crying, and I panicked. It didn't seem real. I was scared."

"And what did you do then?"

"Nothing."

"You just lay there?"

"No. No, I got up. I don't know how long it took, but I realized he was dead. I had a cell phone and, finally, I—I called Sandy."

"Sandy Cross?"

"Yeah."

"You told Ms. Cross what had happened?"

"Yes," she said, staring down into her lap.

"But nobody else?"

"No."

"You never told anyone else?"

"Well, just Dr. Moylan."

"You told Tommy Moylan?" said Nevers.

"Later, when I lived there."

"Objection!" said Phinney. "Objection!"

Nevers was nodding. But it was too late.

“Sustained,” said the judge. “That’s sustained.” He looked at the court reporter. “Strike that.”

Phinney was vehemently shaking his head back and forth.

“There’s a motive,” whispered Haley. And then she repeated herself, a little more softly: “There’s a motive.”

“Okay,” said Nevers. “So, what did you tell Ms. Cross?”

“I told her where I was, and she said she would be right there. She told me just to wait.”

“Did you?”

“That area, it’s right off the road, and I was worried somebody else would drive in. I was scared. I wasn’t thinking straight. I panicked and I was right by the bluff and I know a lot of cars come in and out of there, and I just panicked.”

“What do you mean?”

“I dragged the body over to the edge of the bluff while I was waiting for Sandy to come and I just rolled it over.”

“You pushed him over?”

“He was dead.”

“But you pushed the body over the edge?”

She looked down again.

“Yes.”

Her chest was heaving now, up and down. “I checked the truck, but it was pretty clean. I mean I wiped up what blood there was and later on—I don’t know how long—Sandy got there . . .”

Nevers paused for a moment and took a deep breath.

“Then what?” he said.

“I was crying, sobbing. I lost it, and Sandy was just sort of shocked, I guess. She wanted to know what I had done. She started crying, too, when I told her, and she kept asking me if I needed to go to the hospital. I was scratched and bruised pretty good, but I said no. And she kept asking me if I was all right. You know, I’d been raped. And I said I thought I was okay, as much as I could be—”

"But you never did go to a hospital?" interrupted Nevers.

"No . . . no."

Nevers, all business now, nodded.

"And then," said Billi, "Sandy, after that, she was really just trying to figure out what happened, and I wasn't communicating it very well. She made me go through everything, like, two or three times. Kept asking me why I'd moved the body and tried to clean the truck. I was scared. I panicked. And she, she sort of held me. And in the end, you know, she said, we had to go to the police."

"What did you say?"

"I begged her not to. I just begged her. I—I wasn't ready for that."

"So you didn't?"

"She tried to insist. I told her that the body had maybe actually landed on her property, or at least close, and that I should at least look to find out where it was now that it had been moved and if it had maybe that would give us a little time to figure out what to do. And she . . ."

"What did she do?"

"She kept saying we had to go to the police, but I wouldn't. So we just sat there and finally she said, you know that you could sort of tell where her property started because there was a fence there, an old, like, wire fence, and on the other side of the fence was private property, her property, and nobody hiked there, or even went there anymore so far as she knew. So I got down there somehow with a flashlight, and I dragged him over onto Sandy's property and just did my best to cover it up. I told her I had already moved the body so moving it again at that point was no big deal. Then I went back up and I told Sandy what I had done and eventually we decided that we should finish cleaning the pickup and that I should drive it down to the bus station and leave it there and we did that and Sandy gave me a ride home. And that was it."

"What do you mean that was it?"

"Well, when the police started asking questions about Chucky and where he was, I said I didn't know and, later, when they asked more questions I told them to talk to Sandy. She was my attorney."

"Did they suspect anything?"

Stroud paused.

"All I know for sure is that I wasn't supposed to talk. Sandy arranged it for me just to resign."

"How did she arrange that?"

"I don't know. It was the end of my probationary period, anyway. They didn't even mention Chucky Ware in the end. It was just over. I think, since whatever happened was going to be embarrassing to the department, they maybe didn't really want to know."

Nevers nodded, digesting what he had just heard, and wrote something on a piece of paper.

"What about the gun?" he said finally, his voice stern, but barely above a whisper.

"I took it with me. I mean, I needed it to work. That's what I thought at first. And when I realized I wouldn't be working, when I got fired or whatever, I just kept it. I had it when I moved to Dr. Moylan's house. It was hidden, and that night that everyone helped me move my stuff, I took it down to the barn and put it in a drawer."

"What drawer?"

"One of the drawers in the barn."

"So you didn't take it with you when you moved out of there?"

"Sandy cautioned me not to. You know, she just didn't want me to have it on me and so we decided I would leave it there, at least initially. I wasn't sure how I'd get it. I might have taken it with me when I returned that second time for my stuff, I guess. I don't know."

"So, Sandy knew it was there in the drawer?"

"Yes. And after I got pulled over and called her and she came to the jail she knew that the police—because they'd already found the drugs in Dr. Moylan's van—would go to his house and the barn to search for more. They'd have an excuse."

"And she also knew they'd find the gun," said the judge.

"Yes," she said, hanging her head. "Yes."

"And," said Nevers, although it wasn't so much a question now as a statement, "you and Ms. Cross did not want that."

There was an edge to Nevers's voice now, and Billi shifted uncomfortably in her seat.

"No," said Billi Stroud. "No . . . we didn't."

31.

Chucky Ware's family did not attend Billi Stroud's sentencing. His sister told Mozzy that whatever justice was being dispensed that day could not possibly extend far enough to assuage the fear and disappointment and outright anger of those who could not get beyond the simple fact that her brother had laid in the dirt, unsought, for almost a year.

Others picked up on the remark, and when that morning dawned not long thereafter, a modest-sized group of Chucky's friends staged a demonstration outside the courthouse. It had been reported that the attorneys agreed to recommend a fifteen-year sentence as part of the deal, and there were many who thought the punishment too light. Several carried signs that read KILLER COP and COP COVER-UP, and one boy, his hair sweeping out from underneath a lime-green bandanna, stomped back and forth on the courthouse steps. He was screaming something largely indecipherable, out of which could occasionally be understood the words "fuckin' cops."

When Billi Stroud's time came to speak that day, she was slouched over, her hands clasped in front of her, looking down at the tile floor of the courtroom. She was wearing civilian clothes, a light-green blouse, and some matching pants. Under her eyes were dark bags of deep purple. There was no makeup.

"I never intended . . . ," she whispered, head down. Then she started to sob. "I'm sorry. . . ."

She tried again, but couldn't get anything out and after a moment Phinney got up and sat her back down in her seat and handed her a Kleenex and that was it. Most of the spectators had just been beginning to lean forward in their chairs, and that was it.

Nevers said much more.

His comments initially were not aimed at Billi Stroud; they were aimed at the police.

"People have every reason to be concerned, even mad," said the judge. "How a boy, whatever the circumstances, can simply disappear without the police so much as issuing either a missing person's alert or apparently asking more than a few questions is beyond me. And I'm gonna get some answers."

"Damn straight!" someone said loudly from the back of the room.

Nevers motioned for quiet, and the spectators closed their mouths.

"But that is not the question at hand today.

"It is true," he said, "that no one can be completely unsympathetic to Ms. Stroud's past. The only reason we didn't have a parade of therapists testifying today was that we have her records from—what?—five, six, seven therapists or doctors regarding the traumas she suffered as a child. And that was all stipulated to. We don't know the veracity of every incident or detail, certainly, but I think based on the history of reporting starting at a pretty young age—the pregnancy, the behavioral problems—that she was a victim and it is hard not to have some sympathy for her on that. She's going to need continued help and I hope she gets it in prison."

Phinney, almost hunched over the defense table now, grasped Stroud's hand at the sound of the word *prison*.

"Certainly, too," said Nevers, "justice is not always as pervasive as we hope it will be, and it is really one of the tragedies of this case that her problems were not addressed somehow in a more direct, legal fashion, and I mean through a criminal inquiry directed at the perpetrator of the abuse, many years ago. But, that being said, that did not happen. And I can't sit here at this time and say why. I can't reach back into the past and alter anything, and neither can anybody else. Much as he might like to.

"The fact is, though, Ms. Stroud," said Nevers, "there is a person dead here." He was staring at her. "Mr. Charles Ware is dead. And the reason we will never know how that happened with any sort of certainty is that you covered it up and destroyed evidence and tried to ignore taking responsibility for even explaining it until you were forced to. Maybe no one was ever, even in the beginning, going to know with absolute one-hundred-percent certainty what transpired that night other than you, but it would have been a whole heck of a lot easier if you had put the gun down after the shooting, and called one of your fellow officers. And gone to the hospital. And laid the whole thing out from the get-go.

"The unfortunate fact, for everyone maybe, now including yourself, is that you did no such thing and that really precludes me at this point in time from giving much, if any, credence to your story. It doesn't mean it's not true. It just means I have no way of knowing. No way of accepting it as true. You were a police officer, or at least a trainee. You of all people knew the law. You must have known that, however hard it was going to be—and, yes, given the circumstances, there was going to be a firestorm—you had an obligation to be honest about what happened, an obligation to yourself and an obligation to the community.

"It was days and weeks and months that the family of Chucky Ware had no idea what had become of him—no idea . . ."—he raised his eyebrows up now—"and that his body lay there decomposing in the dirt. Where you dragged it. That really is what concerns me most of all.

"You are supposed to be a sane person, here. No one claims

otherwise. No one has ever suggested this is a question of non compos mentis. Where do the excuses end . . . ?"

Nevers paused and, if you listened, you could hear the sound of the protestors, those unable to get in the courtroom, out in the commons.

"Ms. Stroud," he said, "please stand up."

She did so, wavering slightly, then looking the judge in the eye.

There is no other power on earth quite like the power of the judge to pass sentence. Rarely is it literally a choice between life and death. But the effect is often almost the same. There is no other moment in a free society in which one person legally has such absolute and utter control over the destiny of another, in which a mere utterance based on the law, but also on feeling and whimsy and emotion and obligation and hope and maybe just ineffable feeling at a given, fleeting moment in time, can give a person so much: Sunday dinner, the possibility of children, a birthday party, a beer, a warm bath, or an open field, mornings, afternoons, and evenings, a whole life, really. Or take it all away. In an instant.

"Ms. Stroud," said Nevers, finally and simply. "The recommendations of the defense and prosecution aside, I believe I have no choice but to sentence you to a long period of incarceration in the state prison system. I hereby sentence you to thirty years in prison for the death of Chucky Ware, a term to commence immediately."

Billi Stroud's head dropped at least six inches, and she turned to Phinney to see if she had heard correctly.

"Thirty?" she asked Phinney.

She was stunned.

Everyone was.

Phinney, himself dumbfounded, was still staring at Nevers.

"You said fifteen," Stroud murmured to Phinney.

Phinney was just as shocked as his client.

"I thought," whispered Billi Stroud, "it was fifteen. . . ."

Nevers was getting up now and Phinney, looking utterly perplexed, turned toward Thorpe, who raised his hands up in the air, as if to say, "What can I do about it?" Billi Stroud herself melted down in the chair behind her, wearing an expression of profound disbelief.

part THREE

Haley would not accept payment for her legal services, but finally agreed early in the fall to let me buy her dinner at a fancy place called Bellomiro, an expensive Italian restaurant on the outskirts of Minneapolis.

Bellomiro was one of those cafés where they left white Christmas lights on the trees year-round, and when it got dark it felt like an ersatz holiday. We were inside, but it was still chilly and by the time we finished the first glass of wine and had started in on the second, goose bumps were already forming on her arms. We moved closer to one of the fireplaces and I offered her my coat. Then we sat there in the glow of a warm fire, drinking without thought of consequence, determined, despite the tragedies of the months previous, to enjoy the respite.

Haley was wearing a white knit dress that left her arms bare from the shoulders down. She wore no jewelry, no rings or necklaces or earrings, just the dress and a little bit of makeup around her clear, blue eyes.

"I feel," I said, "like people are staring."

"At what? Us?"

"More likely me."

"Why?"

"I don't know. I still don't feel exactly exonerated."

"You should," she said. "Phinney was throwing that stuff out there. He was desperate."

"Not," I said, "that he ever apologized."

Haley looked at me as she took a long sip of her wine.

"You sound a little bit like your wife."

"How do you mean?"

"He was just doing his job."

"Calling me a murderer?"

"Nobody thinks that," she said. "And if they do, screw 'em. Whoever killed one had to kill the other. She had the opportunity, the weapon, and the motive for Moylan. Why do you think no one was outraged about Nevers's sentence? Regardless of what happens on appeal."

Billi Stroud's new attorney, a legal gun from Chicago, had successfully filed an appeal arguing that Phinney had provided inadequate representation and, among other things, failed to warn his client of the possibility that Nevers might disregard the negotiated sentence. The Appeals Court agreed, but it was unclear how that could help her. Mozzy reported that she'd simply have to be resentenced.

"Reporters," scoffed Haley, when I alluded to the article.

"Just doing her job," I said.

Haley raised her eyebrows a little.

"You know, Will," she said. "One of the things I like most about you is your capacity to get over the past—in all kinds of ways."

"Yeah, Mr. Adaptability."

She smiled slightly.

"Billi Stroud's got a hell of an attorney," said Haley.

"Yeah, well, it helps to have money."

The rumor was that Gretchen Lane was paying for the appeal, and that meant much of the money probably originally came from Sandy or was raised by her. Sandy, once again, was footing the bill for Billi Stroud.

"Even the fact that he agreed to represent her," Haley said of the attorney, "tells you right there he thinks he can have a big impact."

"What do you mean, a big impact?"

"There's no way he does something like this unless he can make a difference."

It was after dinner already and Haley was getting tired. A few minutes later, she flagged down the waiter and asked for another bottle of wine. When it came, we paid the bill, slipped the bottle in the pocket of my coat, which she was still wearing, and walked to her Jeep. A glass of wine was still in her left hand. In her right hand, she carried the keys.

"You okay driving?" I said, feeling the buzz myself.

"Actually, I was hoping to lie down in the backseat," said Haley.

"Can I join you?"

Haley chuckled and opened up the passenger-side door for me. I got in and she walked around to the driver's side.

"Are you sure you're all right?" I asked, when she got in.

"I'm okay. I've got a mint in there." She pointed to the glove compartment, started the car and cranked up the heat.

Haley smelled faintly of expensive perfume, soap, and wine, and as she leaned across my body toward the glove compartment I felt vaguely expectant. The cold air had made her nipples hard as she brushed against my arm. As I looked, she turned toward me, serious, and I stroked her cheek. She didn't move and, gently, I kissed her. Just for a moment. She was a little inebriated, we both were, but she was serious, too, as she slid across the seat and, throwing her arms around my neck, straddled me. Haley had the slender body of a young girl, thin-waisted and lithe. She was not wearing a bra and I caressed her with the back of my hand as she straightened up a little and the sport coat fell to the floor. When I kissed her again, she met me halfway and there was, this time, a sweetness and, still, a soft hesitation. She ran the back of her hand down my cheek and the front of my shirt, then pulled back a little and looked at me. When I moved to kiss her again, she leaned backward and pressed the button that momentarily rolled down the window, then dumped her wine outside in the snow, a splotch of red in the pure whiteness.

Haley knew how to kiss; I knew she had not forgotten.

One night, long before Sandy's affair, she came down sick with the flu on the night of the Droughton County Press Club banquet. It was rather a formal affair and, rather than have me go alone, Sandy suggested that I take Haley. I shrugged it off and said I would go solo, but Sandy picked up the phone and called Haley anyway.

"Will desperately needs a date," Sandy deadpanned into the phone.

"I'm not going with Haley," I whispered, Sandy ignoring me.

"She was even more adamant about it than you," Sandy laughed when she hung up.

Haley and I garnered quite a few whistles and laughs that night about the blatancy of our "affair." But, of course, it was quite the opposite. Sandy's insistence on my taking her best friend—someone I had, in fact, once dated—to the most public of dinners was the ultimate statement of confidence in both her husband and friend, who made a statement of her own by wearing a tight knit dress, getting unabashedly drunk, and hanging all over me most of the night.

I got a bit drunk myself and played along, but was still surprised when, at the end of the night, Haley insisted I walk her to her door, then gave me a gentle, friendly kiss. Any twinge of guilt was erased a day or two later when, in my presence, Haley bragged to Sandy about "even getting a good night kiss." I somewhat awkwardly upbraided her in mock anger for "telling," and felt better.

Now, Haley, after emptying the wineglass in the snow, brushed her hair back away from her eyes and undid my shirt, letting her hand fall when she got to the last button. Her dress was already pulled down around her waist. Outside, we heard voices coming along the sidewalk. They just as quickly receded into the night as the reflections, splintered and diffused already by the condensation on the window, and perhaps by the three or four glasses of wine I had consumed, faded off into the past.

Sandy and I, I remembered, had once made love in a little Chevy parked in front of what was then her parents' house one Christmas Eve after midnight Mass, back when we attended Mass. It wasn't spontaneous, not exactly. It was the sort of thing that, between two people who know each other well, sometimes builds up throughout the night, through small lingering touches and certain types of conversation. It was crowded at church that night and, although I did not regularly attend, I was asked to help distribute the Eucharist, something I had been trained to do years earlier but had never made a habit of. Unable to say no, I acquiesced and found myself moments later up on the altar. I remember it was cold outside and someone had overcompensated by turning up the heat, which rose even higher when the pews filled with Christmas worshipers in wool coats and dresses. Everything was sort of boiling up and evaporating because it was so hot, and beads of sweat ran down my back and I thought I was going to faint when they started filing up toward the altar.

I know, even now, exactly what Sandy was wearing that day: a blue skirt, a white blouse, and a cashmere sweater that buttoned up the front. She smiled at me briefly, almost smirking at the irony of me, even then a cultural Catholic at best, distributing Communion on one of the holiest of days. But as she got closer, she looked away and became quite solemn. She believed, when it came right down to it, and there was no denying that. She closed her eyes and barely opened her mouth, wide enough only that she could tilt her head back and I could insert the communion tablet. I remember that she held her hands, with a rosary intertwined, right up underneath her chin, only not the way most people hold them, clasped tight. They were sort of turned upward and empty and her eyes were closed and I felt just sucked toward her, even then, transfixed by the look on her face, the peacefulness that was so immense.

Haley pulled back.

"What?" she said.

"Nothing."

But it was too late, and she turned her head to the side, toward the window.

"I'm sorry," I said.

"No . . ."

She left her arm around my shoulder, but slowly moved off to the side.

"I'm sorry," I repeated. "I just . . .

I was silent for what must have been almost a minute.

"What's going on?" she said.

"Nothing."

"Tell me."

We sat silent, Haley staring out the window, me rubbing her neck, for several minutes.

"You know," I said, finally, "I remember, after Sandy and I really started going out, had gotten serious, the first time we were really apart, when she was away at law school . . . Sandy was all I thought about, day and night . . . all the time."

Haley said nothing, just pulled the dress up over her chest and I felt a slight stab.

"I'm sorry," I said.

"No, this isn't right."

"It isn't wrong either," I said. "I just—I mean, Haley . . ."

"What?"

"I would actually run to the mailbox at my old house to look for her letters."

"We shouldn't be here."

"I want to be here."

"Do you?"

"Could you just listen?"

She nodded.

"It doesn't seem that long ago," I said.

She was looking away from me, out the window.

"It's funny what comes back to you. . . . I can't forget those letters," I said. "Even when they came, I couldn't read half of them. She had horrible writing. Like a little girl's, almost worse."

Haley was sitting there with her head cocked, listening.

"Yeah," whispered Haley. "I know."

"But, you know what was really strange?" I said.

She didn't answer, just turned back toward me slightly.

"It was like as much as I missed her, I always had trouble seeing her face, envisioning it in my mind. You know what I mean? It was odd, it was like I just wanted to see it too much, and couldn't for some reason. Like I was trying too hard to remember. I mean, I had spent probably a year if you added up all the time we had spent together just looking at her. Probably every minute of a year if you added it all up. I knew everything about her. Not just what she thought. I mean everything, physically, about her whole body—literally."

Haley nodded almost imperceptibly.

"And then she went off to law school and it was like I was trying to keep her with me, but couldn't, you know? It was like I'd try to conjure her up in my mind, lying in bed in the middle of the night, just wanting to see her face. But I couldn't. Sometimes I would get up and turn the light on in the middle of the night to look at one of her pictures. I must have had a dozen of them, and I would stare at the goddamn thing and try and imprint it in my mind. But then I would go back to bed and it would be like I couldn't remember what I had just seen."

Haley took her arm off my shoulder and leaned forward. Her elbows rested on her knees, and her hands were balled up underneath her chin.

"And you know what, Haley?" I said. "It's the same way now. It's exactly the same way. I can't seem to see her the way she was.

It's only been a year, less than a year, and I can't remember how she was. I can't even imagine her. I look at her in that bed. She's not even the same person. I sit there and stare at her and I wonder if I ever even knew her. I don't know . . . maybe I can't leave her behind me before somehow getting her back."

"You know, Will," said Haley, still looking out the window. "Maybe it's the other way around."

33.

My sleeplessness intensified on those nights, left me restless and agitated and wandering the rooms of the Cross House in the darkness. First I'd try the bed, the one we had shared, till the covers and sheets were balled and hot, then the couch, or a living room chair. There was a time when I could not sit in that chair, a leather recliner that seemed to embrace you as you sat, without falling asleep. Suddenly, I could sit there for hours staring at nothing, wide-eyed and awake.

I tried to use the time to read, but found that almost as soon as I picked up a book and tried to concentrate my mind wandered far afield into places long forgotten or repressed. A girl I had once known who, when you kissed her, tasted like spearmint and cigarettes. Inner-tubing on a river. Guzzling beer as it spilled, warm and sticky, down the front of my chest. I dreamed of a boy I once knew in grade school who later died in a hunting accident, shot accidentally by his own father. I saw the faces of my own parents. Non sequiturs came to me, one after another, proceeding seriatim with no apparent link but never leading to the deeper realms of subconsciousness, rarely resulting in sleep. It was as if these things rose up and lived with me, stayed with me even in the waking hours, and became part of my consciousness. They converged upon and exhausted me.

I replayed over and over and over again the conversations I had with Elizabeth about Sandy, the conversations Sandy and I had once had ourselves. Endlessly, I played over in my mind those things we resolved—and those things we hadn't.

After I found out about the affair, and eventually moved out, I returned only during the day when I knew that Sandy would be at work and there was time to pick up my clothes and mail. I was surprised when I got there early one afternoon and saw her on the dock by the river. I could see her from the French doors in the living room as she lifted a diaphanous white sundress up over her head, revealing lace underwear. Sandy had had her braces removed in tenth grade and her teeth were white and straight and glossy. Even from the house, I could see them shine. Her hair was pulled back behind her head.

She moved slowly and deliberately and there was a sadness and a dignity to her ambulation.

I opened the doors for a better view then and watched her remove the underwear as well and jump into the water. She was lithe and graceful, there was no way to deny it. Her head broke the surface of the water about fifteen yards beyond the dock as she began swimming effortlessly out to a sandbar that rose above the surface some twenty or so yards farther. She could swim so far underwater that it was always a relief to me when she actually resurfaced.

I, like Sandy, grew up near the river. But we saw it, reacted to it, felt about it, differently. Sandy was a strong swimmer. She could move effortlessly through the water, first in a breast stroke, then moving to a crawl, and I can still imagine how after each stroke or two she would turn and lift up her head above the surface, pause for a moment to let the water wash off her face and then open her mouth at the last moment before sliding back down under the waterline, her dark hair matted to her brow. She simply opened her mouth and let it fill with air through a sort of osmosis, then closed it again as she went under. It was all so fluid and easy. She did not gulp at the air the way I do. I am not a strong swimmer and each breath is both a panic and a relief.

By the time I got to the edge of the patio, she had already made it to the sandbar and was sitting there above the water.

From a distance it looked as if she were, somehow, miraculously resting upon it, her arms wrapped around her knees, her chin resting almost on her kneecaps. She saw me, managed a plaintive smile and a wave and I nodded, began to move toward the beach and the end of the dock where I slipped my tennis shoes off and sat down, letting my feet dangle in the cold water.

After a moment she slid back in and, this time, did not break the surface once to catch her breath. The water by the dock was no more than four feet deep and, washing the river out of her eyes, she rose up almost directly in front of me. Athletic and in superb shape, Sandy had slim, brown, muscular legs and a thin waist that tapered off from small breasts. Having held her breath for so long underwater, she gasped and sputtered just a few words at the end of each exhalation. Nipples hard from the cold water, her chest heaved up and down as she talked, water cascading off her.

"C'mon," she said, "You're coming . . . in!"

Catching me off balance before I could protest, she easily pulled me from the dock and into the water. Still wearing my T-shirt and khaki pants, I flailed toward the surface and turned to my side, surprised at first, kicking my legs out as I hit the top, protesting. By the time I righted myself, stood up, and opened my eyes in a paroxysm of half-panic, Sandy was most of the way back out to the sandbar.

I took my pants and shirt off, and threw them back on the dock, at first wading and then doing the backstroke until I reached the sandbar. By the time I got there, she was lying on her back with her eyes open, still catching her breath as I climbed up. Frowning, she looked exaggeratedly at an imaginary watch on her wrist and I couldn't help but chuckle. After weeks of silence, it was an acknowledgment.

Using both hands, she reached back and gathered up the dark hair that stretched midway down her back, then wrung it out as though it were a towel. Then she gathered her knees up close to her chest and again folded her arms around them as the water dripped off our bodies.

"What happened to us?" I asked her, finally.

Her eyes were red and narrow and she seemed not to have the words. It seemed like forever till she found them, and when they came, they came slowly at first, sporadic, and with an almost animal anguish. Then in torrents. She talked long enough that she dried almost completely and the sun, a brilliant orange, began to sink like a perfectly shaped balloon toward the peaks of the distant trees.

"You want more details?" I remember her crying out.

"Sometimes," I said, looking off. "Sometimes I wonder what it is that made you need to tell me about him in the first place."

Now it—I—became harder.

"It's like you, you open the box, but you won't let me inside," I said. "I feel like I don't even know you anymore."

She smiled sadly.

"You know all there is to know," she said. Then she gestured at herself, sitting there naked, and chuckled. She was beautiful and, it is true, wealthy, and someone a part of me would never have dreamed of knowing. I sometimes imagined what it would be like to be myself but to know nothing of the life I had, simply to wake up one morning and discover all of it, more than pleasantly surprised I could imagine. There would be this beautiful, intelligent and, yes, wealthy woman, and who wouldn't be intrigued? I still was.

What person, it is true, does not occasionally ask himself, or herself, if he had mistaken that intrigue—for lack of a better term—for the more important and truer thing: love? I concede that. But that is just honesty, and not a confession. I do not think that I was ever an impostor in my own life, not like some people. If you had similarly stripped away all that Sandy had and she was just a woman sitting alone, with nothing but herself, on a sandbar in the middle of an unknown river, I would have loved her. I know that in my heart.

She smelled of soap and sweat and just a hint still of the darkening waters that rippled past, and I made love to her there atop the sand in the middle of that river as the sun set. And when the morning came, the morning that fall so long after, I sat in the living room beside her body and watched that same sun come up as if it had been but one long and everlasting night.

34.

It was a crisp, clear day in late October when Hemper stopped by my desk.

"Now don't get mad at me," he said.

I looked up at him, not smiling. I'd gone back to work and we'd made amends, but there were lots of lingering scars. I still couldn't quite bring myself to talk much to Mozzy.

"What?" I said.

"We're shorthanded—"

"We're always shorthanded."

"I need you to run over to the courthouse."

"For what?"

"Your old friend has some sort of appearance before Nevers. It's no big deal, probably just some kind of scheduling thing. But we need to have somebody there."

"The Stroud appearance? I thought Mozzy would be doing it."

"She's off today. I don't think it's that big a deal."

I bobbed my head from side to side as if to say, "Maybe, maybe not."

"Just get over there," said Hemper. "It's only some kind of preliminary bullshit about the remand hearing. Get the facts. We need to have somebody there. It's just a short."

This meant he knew there was a conflict having me cover it, but that it wouldn't really matter because what I wrote would be so short that my byline would not appear on it. No one who read it would know who covered it and Hemper just hoped that nothing would happen. Those sorts of compromises happen at small papers.

"When's it start?" I asked him.

Hemper looked at his watch. "About five minutes ago."

When I got there, I was surprised to see that there was absolutely no one in the gallery. Thorpe sat at one table. Billi Stroud and the Chicago attorney, wearing an expensive, dark suit, sat at another. His hair was graying and he was tan and looked fit and confident. I had visions of a legal team surrounding him, of portable files and expensive leather satchels. But there was none of that—no crowd. I couldn't stop thinking that it was probably Sandy's money that had brought him there.

Billi Stroud looked tired and nervous and still—months after the original sentencing—rather stunned. I sidled up to the bailiff, a former cop I knew who was standing inside the door to the hallway, and asked what was going on.

"She doesn't want to be sentenced again by Nevers, so Thorpe is trying to get another judge," he said, cupping his hand around his mouth to muffle the sound.

"Never happen," I said.

He glanced at me as he put his hand down.

"Whatever you say, Mr. Smarty-pants Journalist."

I took a seat in the back of the room. Thorpe, standing up, was the one talking.

". . . and essentially the initial defense counsel in this case, Mr. Phinney, conceded he had not informed his client of the possibility that you would exceed the sentencing recommendation in the plea agreement. Basically, Ms. Stroud says she was under the impression that you were bound to give her only fifteen years when in fact you gave her twice that. We all, at least the lawyers among us, know that's within your discretion, of course, but the Appeals Court, as you know, has agreed that her lack of awareness is a reflection upon the performance of her attorney. So as you know, it's remanded."

"Remanded to this court," said Nevers.

"Well, it's remanded to Circuit Court," said Thorpe. "This is the branch where the case was before."

"This," said Nevers, issuing a correction, "is where the case is now. I have no reason to recuse myself, even if I wanted to. And that being the fact, I guess I'm just a little unclear as to what it is you want me to do today, Counselor?"

Thorpe slowly took in about half a liter of oxygen. This was not going well.

"Sooo, basically you're not inclined to reduce or alter the sentence? Or move the case to another judge?"

It was a very direct question for a prosecutor to ask a judge, and Nevers leaned back for a moment before responding.

"I think I've answered that," he said.

"Okay," said Thorpe. He pondered this for a moment. "Frankly, Your Honor, I'm not altogether sure where that leaves us, given the Appeals Court decision."

"Well," said Nevers, turning toward Stroud, "let's find out. Ms. Stroud, you're represented by new counsel here today?"

"Yes," said the attorney, starting to rise. "My name—"

"We all know your name," said Nevers. "And you can stay seated. There are a few options here."

He looked directly at Stroud now.

"Obviously you do have the right to stick with your original plea agreement, Ms. Stroud, which we all know the terms of. And in that case, I would simply resentence you. We can't do that today. You'd have an opportunity to line up character witnesses. I'd order another presentence report drawn up and whatnot. But I could resentence you as soon as next week if that's what you choose."

"To the same term?" said the Chicago attorney.

Nevers smiled. "Well," he said, "let me just say that the problem in this instance was not the sentence."

The attorney raised his hand, almost as if he were in a classroom.

"Feel free to speak," said the judge. "Our local rules are pretty lax in this sort of hearing."

Not usually, I thought.

"I don't see that Ms. Stroud here has gained anything under that particular scenario," said the attorney.

There was no pomposity about him, no bloviating. He said things simply and plainly in a way that, somehow, gave his words more heft. This, I decided, won you over as much as anything: the studious attempt not to give offense.

"Well, what she has gained, you have no doubt long ago deduced, sir, is the choice once again of whether or not she wants to accept the plea bargain that was offered by the district attorney's office. If you do accept that again, Ms. Stroud, I think you can see what will happen—again. If you don't, certainly, I think it's fair to say you'd, perhaps, be subject to prosecution on whatever the district attorney is legally able to charge you with."

Stroud nodded, without responding.

"So you need to make a decision," said the judge, looking at Billi.

"I don't want to be resentenced," she said.

She said it quickly, almost before Nevers had finished speaking.

"Okay, so that means we just start from scratch here. We go back to where we were immediately prior to the plea agreement. And that means there is a reinstatement of the murder charge against you pertaining to the death of Thomas Moylan.

The Chicago attorney was, again, raising his hand.

"Yes?" said Nevers.

He started to stand up in deference to the judge, but then caught himself.

"If now is the appropriate time, Your Honor, I would like to move for dismissal of that charge on the ground of insufficient evidence."

"Well, you're free to do so. That's a motion that can be brought at any time."

The attorney from Chicago took that as an invitation to stand.

"Judge Nevers," he said, "if I may?"

"Go right ahead."

He buttoned the coat of his expensive suit.

"Well, Your Honor, I've taken a long, hard look at the transcript and what transpired in this case—the Moylan case—and I know you know it better than I, but permit me, just for argument's sake, to reiterate to the court what had transpired immediately prior to the plea agreement. There was scant evidence presented by the prosecution—very scant. The only thing linking the defendant to the case in any way really was the gun, which was never found and has only a tenuous link to my client."

Other than, of course, the teeny-tiny fact that it was hers, I thought.

"The motive is manufactured," the attorney argued, "and opportunity does not a murder make, not by a long shot. Combine that with a key witness—Mr. Dunby—who refused to testify and this cries out for dismissal. Judge Nevers, there really is no hard evidence pointing toward my client."

Nevers glanced at me, and I put away my notebook. I decided, no matter what happened, I would tell Hemper I could not write a story, or even a short, about it. Still, I stayed.

"Not only that, Judge. Perhaps more important, there was deficient legal representation here in this case as well, the Moylan case, in many more ways than one. In fact, a motion for dismissal should have been made during the trial, certainly after the prosecution rested and probably at other times as well. I make it now."

He unbuttoned his suit, and positioning himself in front of his chair again, sat down.

"Mr. Thorpe?" said Nevers.

"Well, Your Honor, I disagree, obviously," said Thorpe. "The charge was well founded and I'll let the record stand on that."

"Is that it?"

"That's it."

"Well, then, that is it."

Nevers looked down at some papers on his bench for a moment, and shuffled them. Then took a deep breath.

"I agree," he said, looking directly at Thorpe, "with defense counsel. This case just does not withstand scrutiny—as you well understood when you decided to enter into the plea agreement. It's dismissed."

Thorpe's head tilted back and his eyes, just for a moment, stayed shut.

"Judge—" he said.

But Nevers cut him off.

"You had your chance," said Nevers.

The Chicago attorney now rose again, and Nevers turned toward him.

"Judge," he said, "I would ask then that my client be released."

Thorpe was up instantly. "Well," he said, smiling incredulously. "May I speak?"

"This time," said Nevers. "Yes."

"Well, Your Honor," said Thorpe, "that's all well and good, but we still have the small matter of Chucky Ware."

"Do we?" said the Chicago attorney.

Thorpe visibly sagged.

"Your Honor," he said. "We will very shortly—today, in fact—have a newly drawn complaint charging Billi Stroud with the murder of Mr. Chucky Ware. And we request that she be bound over for a formal arraignment."

The Chicago attorney rose up now, and Nevers acknowledged him.

"I object to this," he said. "This is clearly going to be an insufficient complaint."

Thorpe stared at his opposing counsel. He was aghast.

"Mr. Thorpe, why don't you run through it," said Nevers.

"Well, Judge," said Thorpe, "it's really quite simple. The defendant has publicly conceded her involvement in the death of Mr. Ware and I believe th—"

"When?" said the Chicago attorney, still standing up, but with his hands in his pockets.

Nevers nodded, and directed his attention back toward Thorpe.

"The question is," said the judge, "when did she make that concession?"

Thorpe was staring at the Chicago attorney, mouth slightly agape.

"Here," Thorpe said, softly, looking at Stroud. "In this courtroom."

"She only testified," the attorney said, sounding almost bored, "because of the plea agreement. The plea agreement no longer exists, nor, legally, does the testimony induced by it."

"Well," said Thorpe, "I think what actually induced her to testify was the fact that we discovered Mr. Ware's body. That's the real difference here today, the real inducement. We have the body. That's prior to the plea agreement and that's certainly, without a doubt, admissable."

"So, you're saying the admission in court is not necessary as proof? Or for the charge?" asked Nevers.

"That's right," said Thorpe, shifting back and forth.

"What links her to the body?" said the judge.

"Bullets, which we believe match her service revolver," he said.

"Where's the revolver?" asked Nevers.

"I don't know, Your Honor," said Thorpe.

"Got anything else?"

"Well, just the strong circumstantial element that she was with the boy the night he died or at least knew the boy—"

"Objection," said the attorney. "He's getting that from her testimony again," he added. That's not admissable."

Thorpe was shaking his head now, staring down at the prosecution table, a look of incredulity on his face.

"As they say, the law's an ass," said Nevers. "But it is the law."

Thorpe did not want to engage in repartee.

"Your Honor," he said, using a very subdued, almost solicitous voice now, carefully choosing his words. "Your Honor, I need to ask that the court allow this matter to be laid over for a day, a day maximum, just a day is all, in order that the prosecution be given an opportunity to redraft another complaint in the Ware matter. A day, and no more, Judge, that is all I am asking in all fairness."

"Fairness is all I'm concerned about, Counselor, and the sad fact is that a day will make no difference unless you have something else to offer. And given the history, it's apparent you don't. What, to be blunt, could you possibly add?"

Thorpe opened his mouth, but had nothing to say.

"I'm just asking for a day," he said.

"It wouldn't matter if I gave you a month. Given the inadmissability issues, there's a deficiency of evidence to support the charge. Now this bothers me greatly, to be honest with you. But the law is the law, and the law is going to be the same tomorrow as it is today. We can't circumvent it."

Thorpe opened his mouth, but said nothing more. He had nothing more.

"Okay, then," said the judge, raising up his gavel, "case dismissed. The Ware case is dismissed. Motion denied."

"And the Moylan charge?" said the Chicago attorney. "That is dismissed with prejudice?"

"It's dismissed. Given the complexities, we'll deal with issues of prejudice at some later point if it is ever necessary. In terms of the Ware case, it can certainly be refiled in the event more evidence is gathered, but as it stands right now, that charge is certainly not supportable."

With Billi Stroud looking on, still from one to the other, Nevers banged the gavel and started to rise.

"This proceeding is adjourned."

Thorpe froze. His hands were outstretched and he did not move for several seconds, even as Nevers started to head toward the door to his chambers. When Thorpe did move, it was at first almost imperceptible, a slow-motion about-face. He was stunned. When I looked next at Billi Stroud, after what seemed like an eternity, she was standing up near her chair and, it seemed even then, waiting for one of the guards to approach her and place the handcuffs upon her wrists.

But no one did.

Billi Stroud, it slowly dawned on her, was free to go.

35.

"Terry, she's out!" I sputtered, bursting into Hemper's office. I had run from the courthouse next door.

He was standing up, and on the phone. His top button was unbuttoned and his tie loosened so that the tip, even when he stood up straight, almost dangled into a coffee cup on his desk. His brown hair, shaggy and thick, looked as if he had been in a windstorm.

"What?"

"She's out. Stroud's free!"

He had already hung up the phone. "You're serious?"

"I'm dead serious. Thorpe says he's going to draft another complaint in the Ware case, but Nevers let her go anyway. Said it won't hold water. The Moylan charge was dismissed."

He grabbed my arm. "Okay . . . okay," he said. "Will, I need you to sit down. Give me your notes and sit down."

"Yeah, there's no way I can write it."

"I'm going to give them to somebody else."

"Good."

"But you have to sit down."

"What?"

He raised his hand up and placed it on my shoulder.

"I need to tell you something."

He moved behind me and shut the door.

"What's going on?"

He latched on to my forearm.

"Will," he said. "Sandy's mom called just a few minutes ago."

"What?"

"It's Sandy," he said.

"What about her?"

I was still standing up.

"Will," he said, "Sandy died this morning."

It was that simple. I sank down into the chair behind me, and dropped the notebook on the floor.

"You should go home," he said.

I did not move. It was almost surreal, that moment—even though it was something I'd known would come.

"I don't know when exactly," he said. "Sometime this morning. I just found out. I was about to send someone over to the courthouse to find you when you walked in."

"Okay . . ."

Much of Sandy, the fact is, had died long before; and I knew, of course, that the rest of her would go. But to hear Hemper say it as I sat in his office, to have him actually enunciate it made it feel as if Sandy had been there all along after all and was only suddenly snatched away. It felt to me as if, when she left, when she was gone, she had simply walked across a threshold and disappeared around a corner, without a word of warning, without the courtesy of a wave or a kiss or a nod of the head. Though I had not realized it until then, I had been deceiving myself, fooling myself, doubting that what I knew in my own heart was actually real enough to be known and shared and realized by anyone else. That is what it felt like. Billi Stroud free, and Sandy gone. . . .

"You want me to take you home?" Hemper was saying.

I felt, I suppose, as a parent does when he briefly loses sight of a small child in a large crowd. There is a moment of pause when outwardly, there is no discernible manifestation of emotion, just a furtive darting of the eyes, as if any greater movement would confirm, make real, the fact that the child really is not there where she had been just a moment before, a beautiful child with curly hair and eyes wide open the size of quarters, concerned about other things, smaller things, the stuff of life. There is in that moment an overwhelming sense of anxiety, loss, fear, and utter panic—guilt—that extends beyond that moment and sucks in all the future. You think this is too dramatic when I knew all along this time would come? All I can tell you is that no matter when it happens, or how, all of it is lost in the same confluence of time. All, it seems, at once.

"Will?" said Hemper.

With a lost child, if one is lucky, the moment passes as quickly as it arrived. The child is there, hidden briefly from view behind a pillar or a skirt or an old unshaved man in a sweat-stained shirt who could just as easily have picked her up and whisked her away without even the aid of a shadow. But the other way, when it really happens and you know it has happened, it is the other side of a chasm, and it is hard to make the leap even as you have done it.

We are all made of our past. It is history that forms us, as long as we live and breathe. Sandy drunk sitting in a car, swearing and crying because she said she did not want to love me and yet couldn't help it. Sandy standing in the kitchen on the phone, screaming in laughter as she talked to Haley and ran her fingers through her hair. Sandy yelling at a lawn service that killed a large chunk of our lawn. Making love to me. Rocking back and forth. The veins pulsing.

"I love you, William," she'd say.

"I love you, Sandy."

My notebook was on the floor still, and Hemper reached for it. Placed it on his desk.

"C'mon, Will," he said. "C'mon."

I went with him, allowed him to guide me out of his office and through the newsroom. And then, as I went, I did one more thing.

I felt for the empty bottle of curare in my pocket, just to make sure it was still there.

36.

When I came upon Billi Stroud's service revolver that day in the garage, and after I realized what it was, I simply put it in one of the baskets and carried it to the compost pile and buried it under the first load of leaves I raked from the garden. That is what I did.

Later, there would be a second load of leaves and a third and a fourth until it was buried several feet, probably. I had fully expected them to look there the night they found Chucky Ware but, perhaps distracted by what else they found, they didn't. They would have, I imagine. They just never got that far. So, there it lay, covered by leaves and grass clippings and dirt until I retrieved it during one of those nights after Sandy died.

I started with the spade from the garage, first tossing shovelfuls of damp and surprisingly heavy compost back into the underbrush, then, as I got deeper, moving more slowly and carefully and finally getting down on my hands and knees and reaching deep into the feculence, squishing it between my fingers and letting it seep down underneath my fingernails. It took me some time to find it and when I did I half expected it, too, like all else around it, to be disintegrating, reverting back to some basic and prior form. But, of course, it hadn't. It lay neatly in between two layers of intact leaves, insulated so that when I pulled it out I could hold it up in the moonlight and see it shimmer. It wasn't even dirty.

And then I brought it inside and, wanting to gather everything together in one spot, placed it in a drawer in Sandy's office with all her old legal files.

Sandy was to be buried beside her father on the Cross grounds and we decided to have the wake at the house because it would simplify things, but also because Elizabeth wanted it that way. Elizabeth, for the same reason that some people bury their loved ones under a particular tree or wearing a special tie, liked the idea of Sandy spending one more night in the house. It was once common, she said, waking the deceased in their own homes before the morticians started calling their trade a science and, for largely financial reasons, started holding the ceremonies at mortuaries instead. Elizabeth wanted things done the old way.

So while the grave diggers dug their hole next to Dr. Cross's headstone out in the family cemetery, one set of movers came and hauled the hospital bed away from the house, while another group, from the funeral home, assembled a small dais in its place. It was amazing how quickly that all happened. They festooned it with flowers and ribbons of silk and set up a small kneeler and a dozen or so chairs in the living room.

Sandy's body was gone from the house for less than forty-eight hours, transported to the funeral home, embalmed and readied, and moved back. Elizabeth and Haley decided she would be buried in her black velvet dress with some white pearls I had bought her draped around her neck.

Someone, before the wake, placed a rosary in Sandy's hands. It was intertwined with her fingers in a way that made it seem she was holding it, counting out her prayers. It was part of the illusion that the morticians worked so hard to create, the illusion that life in its most basic temporal way went on, and even as it did Sandy strove to reach beyond the secular with the rituals and rote prayers presumed to be so long ingrained. There was some truth in it, I suppose. Sandy, I always suspected, would eventually have returned to the faith of her youth. I don't know, in fact, if she ever fully lost it.

We did all that we could do, had to do, to prepare, Elizabeth, Haley, and I. We cooked and cleaned, partook of the rituals of mourning. When time got short, Elizabeth suggested that Haley shower at the Cross House instead of running home.

"But I didn't bring a change of clothes."

"There's a whole closet of clothes in there," said Elizabeth.

Haley paused.

"I think I have time still."

"Oh, don't be silly," said Elizabeth.

Sandy's closet was still almost half full with skirts and shoes, sweaters and jeans, and most of the more formal dresses she had owned. Haley came out carrying two outfits—one a formal black number with a modestly cut back, the other an even more demure beige pantsuit.

"Which one?" she said, holding one up and then the other. She had taken a shower and her hair was still wet; her skin glistened pink. She placed the black one in front of her and turned from side to side, tossed it on a wicker chair, then did the same thing with the beige one. It had flared legs and a narrow collar.

"Looks like we're gonna start over in the sixties," she said.

"I guess black's the color of the day," I said, and she, in the end, chose that one.

By the time the hearse arrived, we were looking for ways to occupy ourselves, sipping beer and wine. We busied ourselves with small tasks that we had done a dozen times before while they placed her in the living room.

It was still not winter and, as sometimes happens in this part of the country, there was a warm spell. You could sense the warmer streams of air permeating the cool evening breezes, running through them like deep currents of promise. Fall was Sandy's favorite season, and mine. There was a lingering finality to it, but a prescience at the same time, anticipation of what was to come.

Within an hour, there was already a large crowd assembled, including friends and some of Sandy's old clients and a passel of lawyers. Mozzy showed up, brought a casserole and some flowers, and we made amends. She told me that she never would have done the story, or even had a part in it, if she could have predicted how it would turn out. It started out as a feature, she said, but turned into a news story when the trial took the turn that it did. Hildy had talked about the "Got around, didn't she?" comment and it spread around the newsroom. When Hemper heard about it, he asked if it was true and, from there, it made its way into the story. On the copy desk it was moved up close to the lead and in the end Mozzy, upset and certain she could not be objective, asked that her name not be associated with what appeared in the paper. That is the way things work in a newspaper.

"Nothing personal," she said, and gave me a slight smile.

Gretchen Lane came, too, with several women I did not recognize from Stone Soup. They stood in one corner, off by themselves, and talked in whispers. Others were slightly more ebullient, friends of mine from the paper, neighbors, old school friends. I spent much of the evening drinking, and standing in the cool air on the porch as, one after another, they left their groups and walked toward me, patted me on the back or threw an arm around me. There would be no formal ceremony during the wake, just, from most, words of sympathy, struggles with the thundering triteness of expression. There wasn't only death to try to encompass; there was the manner of it as well, or what they knew of it: the original self-imposition when Sandy drove herself over the cliff. That, now, to me, seemed strangely far past.

"I'm sorry, Will," they would say. Or, "Just wanted to offer our condolences."

My goal was the gin-tinged freedom of a deep-seated exhaustion where thinking has been forgotten, a lull in the emotional storm that, with the funeral so close, was about to come to a head. The house was open, and people filtered in and out without anyone really keeping track. That added to the informality, the blur of comings and goings as thoughts and conversations melded one into another. The casket was still open, and beside her was an old blue blanket with frayed edges and a picture of a bear on it. Elizabeth had placed it there.

"Thank you," said Elizabeth to me softly at one point. She alone—and Haley, whom I told as well—knew I had used the curare on Sandy, and it linked us now in an immutable bond.

A few, those who had drunk as much as I had, hugged me hard and wept, leaving tears and smudges of lipstick on my cheek and shoulder. I wept with them as we moved about, talking, crying, and occasionally laughing, not discourteously, but in a way that ensnares the "survivors" and binds them back into the simple discourses of life.

I was talking to Gretchen Lane when I noticed it, people whispering and pointing. Billi Stroud was standing by the coffin, dabbing at an eye, and people watched as I walked over to her.

I stood a few paces away, silent, until she finally noticed me.

"You come to confess your sins?" I asked.

She didn't for a moment avert her gaze.

"I've acknowledged all my sins," she said.

"Well, then," I said, "perhaps it's a good thing you came."

I moved away before she could respond, first into the office and then outside, out into the darkness of the night. Billi Stroud had gotten her Saturn back. The door to the car was locked but I took her keys out of my pocket—the ones to her car and to Moylan's house that I'd had since the night of the accident, the ones they'd given me at the hospital because they presumed they were Sandy's. And when I was done doing what I did, I moved my own car into the driveway so that hers was blocked. Then, back inside, I called Deiter. He agreed to come.

Deiter arrived in an unmarked squad car, but there was a marked car—and some uniformed officers with him as well. I waited until I saw him walk over to Stroud's car and look in. Then I headed out and across the room toward the front door. As I did I felt a tug on the sleeve, and turned around, ready to make an excuse for continuing on. It was Kathleen O'Connor, the nurse from the infertility clinic whom I did not realize had come. She extended her hand and I shook it.

"I'm sorry," she said. "About everything."

"Thank you," I said, turning slightly to acknowledge her, but continuing on at the same time.

"About what happened in the courtroom, too," she said.

"I know," I said, trying to extricate myself from the conversation.

"I didn't want to," she said.

"I sensed that."

"Thank you for understanding."

"Thank you for coming. And I don't blame you—for anything."

Again, I turned to go. But she had not let go of my sleeve.

"Are you okay?" she said.

I turned toward her, to end it.

"I'd almost forgotten about it, to tell you the truth," I said, "what with everything else; and I know you did your best to protect Sandy, us, throughout all of it. I appreciated it then and I appreciate it now. Don't think any more about it. Please . . ."

I turned again, but she was not done.

"I mean, she was just such a wonderful person and I don't normally let myself develop any sort of connection with our patients, but she was just so hard not to admire."

"I'm sure she'd appreciate that. And I'm glad that you came."

"I considered her, I can't explain it, really, a friend."

"She had that effect on people," I said. "I just wish it could have worked for us. She would have loved to have had kids. Me, too."

"Yes, it had to have been extremely disappointing to her to hear that she'd lost one after waiting all that time."

I was, until then, only half paying attention.

"Excuse me?" I said.

"I said it must have been disappointing."

"What?"

She paused, her mouth twisted. "What do you mean?" she said.

"What must have been disappointing?"

She looked perplexed.

"That she'd lost it," she said, almost whispering.

"Lost what?"

"The baby."

I was now turned fully toward her and actually pulled her back a bit from the crowd and toward a corner.

"What did you say?"

"The baby," she said.

"Are you telling me that Sandy was pregnant?"

"Oh, my God," she said, turning ashen.

"Was she?"

"You knew that," she whispered, putting her hand up to her mouth as if to catch the words and take them back. "You knew that."

"No," I said. "No, I didn't know that. When?"

"She'd only found out about the pregnancy a week or so before."

"Before what?"

"Before the accident. That's why we had her come in again so soon after that other appointment—but by then, of course, she'd already lost it."

"She was pregnant, and she knew it for a week?"

She paused, but there was no turning back now.

"Yes," she whispered. "But she miscarried."

"And you determined that there was a miscarriage the day of the accident?"

She shook her head and gasped. "Yes."

"My God," I said. "How come this never came out?"

"What do you mean?"

"How come you never said anything?"

"I thought you knew."

"But you didn't say anything on the stand."

"They never asked. They told me not to offer information other than what was asked. No one asked."

"So you never said anything?"

"In my business it happens all the . . . I'm sorry. God, I thought you'd have known. . . . I'm sorry. . . . I just assumed that you knew. . . ."

37.

I found Deiter backing his large frame out of the front passenger side of Stroud's car.

"Lookee here," he said, lifting up Billi Stroud's service revolver. "In plain view on the floor."

"Where is she?" I said, looking around.

I'd addressed the question to no one in particular, but Gretchen Lane was, like others who had seen the police arrive and were drawn to the commotion, standing nearby.

"She ran," she said.

One of the officers, then another, flashlights flickering in the trees, rushed off into the dark woods. Within moments, conversations were lost into the blur of red flashes and whining sirens. The police started ushering the mourners away from the wake, encouraging them to get in their cars and leave. Back in the house, I sat in a chair beside my wife.

"Mr. Dunby?" one officer said. "Mr. Dunby—?"

"Please," I said. "Not now."

The police began working their way outward from the house, looking for evidence that Billi had gone in a particular direction. Now that they had the gun, they could charge her again. She couldn't get far.

"You can't just disappear into thin air," I heard one say as I got up and left the house.

Part of their problem was that there was more than one main road. The woods she had run into were not self-contained. In one contiguous stretch, they surrounded almost two sides of the city of Droughton, abutted two highways and a handful of other roads. They also ran up next to the river and, by morning, the truth was, she could be almost anywhere.

A cop walked out of the back patio door and looked around. I was but thirty yards away and looking directly at him, but he could not see me in the blackness and he turned and headed back in. It was like looking at an accident scene, only they were not running or screaming, but evincing a controlled energy and nervousness. No one stayed still, and several moved, always walking, in and out of the house, time and time again, talking into the radios and then heading back inside. One walked directly over to Sandy, and looked at her the way a small child looks on a dead cat, with a morbid fascination devoid of all self-consciousness. Peering at her, bent over, just inches away. He flipped his tie back over his shoulder as he leaned down over the body, then straightened up again. Death absolves one of all etiquette.

I turned as he peered at her, trying unsuccessfully to suppress the lurching movement of my diaphragm. But even after I had emptied my stomach there on the lawn I continued to heave time and time again until there was nothing left inside me, absolutely nothing that I could feel.

"Will?" came a voice from the patio, moving toward me.

It was Haley.

"Are you all right?"

Her voice was wrought with emotion, and I saw in the moonlight glistening tears slide across her cheeks and leap down into the dark, green grass.

"Did they get her?" I asked.

I had seen one of the cars fly down the driveway toward the house and, as it squealed to a halt, an officer got out. He raised his arms in a sign of exasperation—and failure—and another officer nearby shouted something at him. He got back in the car and sped out again.

"Don't think so," said Haley, trying unsuccessfully to compose herself. "Will, why don't you come back in?"

"I'll be there in a moment," I said.

As Haley headed back inside, I turned and walked across the dark yard almost to the dock, where I bent over and felt my stomach heave upward again. I caught myself before I retched, but wished I had allowed the catharsis. A suffocating heaviness enveloped my chest and my esophagus felt about the size of a cocktail straw. When I rose up again, I saw three or four more cars pull into the driveway, and I turned and faced the black waters.

Reaching into my pocket, I pulled out the keys to Moylan's house and barn and Billi Stroud's car and threw my arm back and heaved them out into the darkened waters as far beyond that sandbar as I could. I had already turned around to head back to the house when I heard the splash.

38.

I woke with a start.

"Did you hear that?" Still wearing Sandy's outfit, Haley had fallen asleep on the couch. Now she was standing in the bedroom door, her silhouette framed by the hallway light.

"What?"

"I heard something."

I rolled over and turned on the light.

"You sure?"

"Somebody's in the house," she said.

"What?"

"I heard something."

I sat up.

"What time is it?" I said.

"Late," said Haley.

"Well, it's an old house."

"There's somebody here, Will."

"I don't hear anything."

"I'm not kidding."

I got up and walked over to one of the windows. Deiter was nowhere to be seen.

"See anything out there?" said Haley.

"Just the Saturn."

"What will they do with it?"

"Seize it, I would think."

I was in a T-shirt and some flannel boxer shorts and quickly reached into a drawer and pulled out some sweatpants.

"Where are you going?" she said.

"To take a look around."

"I'll come with you."

She walked out into the hallway with me and down into the living room, where the casket was. I don't know why but I almost expected to see Sandy moving.

"Why don't you stay up there," I said, looking at the clock. "I'll be right back." It was three in the morning, two hours since I'd gone to bed.

"Should I call the police?"

"I don't know."

We walked back up the stairs and Haley went into my bedroom. She climbed into my bed and pulled the covers up while I, for the second time, walked down one step, then another, stopping and starting, listening, my heart pounding, creeping slowly. I walked past the casket again and checked the front door. It was locked, and the front light was still on. I flipped the light on in the study. I thought then I heard something elsewhere in the house, then just as quickly thought I had imagined it. Dismissed it, then wondered if I should have. "Shit," I murmured. My heart was pounding.

"You okay?" I shouted to Haley.

"Yeah," I heard her say in a sort of throaty shout, as if she were too scared to talk any louder. "I'm okay."

I trotted back up the stairs two at a time, and looked in on her one more time. She had the covers pulled up over her shoulders, and gave me a faint smile.

"Why don't you lock this door. Just stay inside. You have a phone, right?"

She picked it up off the bed stand and held it up.

"Good."

"Should I call the police?" she said again.

I paused.

"If you want to, yeah. Yeah, call 'em. Tell 'em I'll meet 'em at the door." I closed the bedroom door behind me and walked back into the hall, then down the back steps that came out next to the mudroom. At the bottom, I flipped on a series of lights in the kitchen, the dining room, and the back hall until, in the dark night, the old house must have looked like a ship at sea, glowing yellow in a sea of deep, black ink. Then too I turned on the lights in the basement, where I'd resolved to go next. The house was old and the foundation several feet thick. It was too sturdily built for much water ever to have seeped in, but condensation was a common problem and it was cold and damp and ill lit, not much good for anything but storage and my workbench. There was too much space elsewhere in the house for anyone ever to have considered renovating it. And, like the basements of most old houses, it was divided up into a series of small, dark rooms. I yanked on a chain at the top of the steps and a dim bulb illuminated about two-thirds of the basement. The corners remained dark.

Piled up in boxes and bags, sitting on shelves up off the floor, were many of Sandy's belongings. I passed by them, peered back under the steps and walked through a succession of rooms, from the back of the house toward the front until I came to a couple of closets. One was open and, getting used to the dim light, I could see now almost to the back, through shelves of canned fruit and vegetables. I stood still, trying not to breathe as I listened, quivering. There was nothing but the sound of myself, and I moved to the other closet. My feet were bare, and freezing.

Quickly I pulled it open and the door, much lighter than I had expected, flung backward against the wall, clapping up against it with a clacking that echoed faintly across the basement and back. This one was larger and darker and, almost hyperventilating, I poked around inside, hitting nothing and quickly, relieved, letting out a breath, backing out, cursing myself for not waiting for the police. There was no place else for anyone to hide, so I turned and walked back to the steps, past Sandy's things. Inside a box, I saw a lacquered copy of an old newspaper article.

There was a picture of Sandy as a little girl, wide-eyed and full of joy, staring up at me. It looked alive. I felt a chill. I could feel my heart beating.

I pulled the light off and walked back up the steps. Tried the back door again. Still locked. Exhaled. Walked back up around the front. As I did, I could see Deiter and another cop standing there by the front door, waiting for me. I opened up the door.

"What's the problem?" said Deiter, a flashlight in his hand.

"Nothing, I don't think." I exhaled, realizing how nervous I was. My voice did not sound to me like my own. "Thought I heard something."

"Where?"

"I don't know."

"Like what?"

"Just a sound."

"Outside? Or in?"

"I'm not sure."

"Anybody else here?"

I realized that he would have seen Haley's car still parked out there—not far from Stroud's Saturn—on the side of the house.

"Haley fell asleep on the couch."

He looked over at the couch, but she was, of course, no longer there. He peered at the sweats I was wearing.

"We'll look around," he said.

"Thanks," I said. "Probably nothing."

"Why don't you go back to bed."

Turning to the cop, he added. "You look around out here."

He followed me upstairs, and Haley unlocked the door.

"You all right?" I asked.

She nodded.

Deiter looked sideways at me, but said nothing.

"Why don't you stay in here," said Deiter. "Lock this door and we'll check the rest of the house. You, too, Will."

"You see me going anywhere?"

He didn't laugh.

Haley was shivering, and we moved back to the bed. I climbed in beside her.

"You all right?" I said again.

She moved down under the covers, and lay her head on one of the pillows.

"I'm fine," she said. "I'm also staying here, if you don't mind."

For I don't know how long we listened to Deiter move through the Cross House, from one room to the next, like a ghost in search of a lost artifact. Finally, he rapped on the door and, without trying to open it, said everything was okay and that he would be outside.

"You sure?"

"I'll be outside."

I reached over and turned off the light, eased down into the covers as Haley curled into me.

"Jesus," I said, realizing the adrenaline was still pumping. "It's eerie down in that basement."

"You were in the basement?"

"There's nothing there."

"God!"

"Scared the shit out of me, actually."

She kissed me on the cheek, gently, and placed her head on my shoulder.

"Let's get some sleep," I said, letting out another breath. But, of course, sleep—"balm of hurt minds," said Macbeth—did not come.

I lay still for several minutes, and my heartbeat finally had begun to slow when I first got the vague feeling we were not alone.

"Haley?" I half whispered.

She was breathing deeply already, and I wondered if I had fallen asleep for a short time. She did not answer. I stared up into the dim light, almost certain there was someone there, convinced the next moment that I had to be wrong. Staring into opacity. Chastising myself for my imagination. Staring again.

"Will!"

Haley was suddenly awake.

"What!"

She bolted upright as I reached for the light.

Then it came.

"What!" I yelled.

There was another voice.

"Leave it off," it said.

"Will!" Haley screamed.

"Who is it?" I cried. "Sandy?"

I lurched, as if the floor had buckled and thrown the bed and me upward. She was standing there at the foot of the bed. I saw her now, a dark shadow punctuated by a glimmer of metal. She had never left the house. Billi Stroud had never left the house.

"Will!" Haley screamed again.

We were clutching each other. Haley was trembling.

"Fucking . . ." The voice trailed off. It was calm, and it sent a chill through me and I grasped Haley's hands tightly in my own.

"Billi?" said Haley.

"Isn't this cute?" said Billi.

She'd been in the bedroom closet.

"Please . . . ," I said.

"You'll do better to keep your mouth shut," said Billi, moving around the side of the bed.

Haley cried out again, and Billi grabbed her by the arm.

"Get over here," Billi said, moving a kitchen knife to her left hand and motioning for her to get out of the bed.

Haley paused, cowering, and Billi said it louder.

"Now!"

Stroud yanked Haley closer and told her to stay. "Get out of there," she ordered me. "And don't even go near that light switch."

I moved for my robe.

"Don't get modest now," she said. "You, too. Out. Now!"

I felt for the first time a fear as real and palpable as a cold hand on the back of my neck.

"What are you going to do?" I asked her.

"Don't do this, Billi!" said Haley.

"Deiter's right outside," I blurted out.

"That's good," said Billi Stroud, placing her forearm around Haley's neck. "Call him. We're all going to move out into the living room now, and you're going to call him. . . . Oh, and tell him to bring my gun."

39.

Teeth clenched, Haley sucked in a series of short staccato breaths that made it seem she was about to hyperventilate. She faltered near the casket and started to collapse, but Billi, with one arm, pulled her up again with startling force and placed the knife against her neck.

"Open the front door," Billi told me.

Deiter had heard the screams and was on the front porch already before my call went through. If he was surprised at the turn of events, he did not manifest it. When he saw her, saw Billi, it was with no more emotion than if he had run into an acquaintance on the street.

"Billi," commented Deiter, moving into the foyer, tucking his chin slightly in toward his neck, and just briefly closing his eyes. "How'd you get in here?"

"Where is it?" she said.

"What?"

"The gun."

He opened his coat and slowly pulled her gun out of an inner pocket. It was inside a plastic evidence bag.

"Let's talk about this for a minute," he started. "It's not too—"

"Give me the gun!" she screeched.

Deiter held it up in front of him.

"Is it loaded?" she said.

He shook his head.

"Slide it over here," she ordered. "Now!"

Deiter crouched down and slowly placed the gun on the floor, then pushed it so that it came to rest near the bottom of the dais that held the casket.

Billi did not pick it up. Instead, with her left hand, she suddenly grabbed Haley's hair and, without warning, yanked her head backward, violently, so that Haley's neck was exposed. It was unadorned, white as cotton, without so much as a necklace to separate it from the knife blade. Haley looked like a doll, a china doll with a toy head, its red mouth open. Eyes bulging. Veins pulsing. A surreal figurine.

"Where'd you find it?" demanded Stroud.

"In your car," said Deiter.

"Not where you put it. Where you found it, smart-ass."

Deiter looked perplexed, and Stroud had had enough. Without changing the expression on her face and without further warning, she pressed ever so slightly the sharp edge of the knife into the soft flesh of Haley's neck, opening a small incision. It was only then, as I saw the blood start to ooze up, that it registered fully. She had been cut. Stroud had cut her. Haley screamed in an abbreviated, breathless gasp and started to raise her hand up.

"I found it! In the garage," I confessed, the words gushing out of me. "It was hidden here."

Billi paused and stared.

"You liar," she said.

"I did."

"How'd it get there?"

"Sandy, I think. She must have driven back here that night and hidden it."

"And then you planted it in my car."

I said nothing, then nodded.

"You little fuck," she said, her voice starting to climb. Billi's eyes were moving back and forth from me to Deiter now. She realized he was surprised to hear my revelations.

"You killed Moylan," she said to me.

"I didn't."

"You're a liar."

"No! The only reason I kept that gun a secret after I found it was to protect Sandy."

"You're so full of shit. You tried to frame me."

"I thought you killed him."

"You planted the pot in the van, too, and then called the police. Told them to pull me over."

"No. Moylan did that."

"Moylan couldn't have done it."

"Why not?"

"Because Phinney looked into it. We thought it was Moylan, too, for a while—till we found out he couldn't have made the phone call. He couldn't have. He was with a group, doing some kind of therapy—something I can still prove."

Billi let that sink in.

"I didn't know that," I said.

Billi gestured toward the knife she was holding to Haley's throat. Began to move it.

"And then you let Sandy kill herself—or goaded her into it."

"That's not true."

"You were there when she drove over the cliff," said Billi to me.

"I wasn't."

She started to move the knife again. Haley looked frozen, petrified.

"It wasn't him," said Deiter slowly, with an almost studious calmness. "It wasn't him, Billi. Not that."

Deiter was looking at Billi, but glancing at me out of the corner of his eye.

"What?" said Billi.

"It was me at the cliff," he said. "I was the one there."

Billi looked stunned.

"She called me," said Deiter. "Sandy did. I thought she wanted to talk about Chucky."

"Why would you think that?"

Deiter took a deep breath now.

"She'd already told me about it."

"When?" said Billi.

"A few weeks after you killed him. I cornered her. She begged me to leave it alone, but I wouldn't. She said you did it and she helped cover it up."

"It was self-defense," said Billi.

"That's what she said," said Deiter.

Billi Stroud stood there for a long moment, digesting it.

"If you knew about Chucky, why didn't you prosecute me?"

"How?" said Deiter, tilting his head now, showing the strain of the moment for the very first time. "How? Sandy was your attorney. She was supposed to be bound by confidentiality. Most of what she told me about what you did was probably never going to be admissible in court, even if we charged her, too. And I didn't want to do that. Plus, you were a cop and that complicated things. Fact is, I was just looking at the angles. Figuring out a way to get you. Save a little face for the department. Maybe find a way to keep Sandy out of it."

He stopped, and shook his head.

"And then I get this call," he said, the words starting to pour out. "That night . . . to meet her at that lovers' lane near the cliff. She's out there soaking wet, her hair half ice, matted to her forehead. Just oblivious to everything. Tears streaming down her face, stuck to her like little icicles. She was completely tapped, just exhausted. Turning herself around and around. It took me a while to get her back into her car. She kept saying that no one would ever understand. I thought she was talking about Chucky Ware. I was saying I'd help her work it out. . . . And then she tells me about Moylan."

"What about him?" whispered Billi.

"She said she was responsible. Then she said she lost her baby. I didn't even know what she meant. I thought she was delusional. She said everything she touched died."

Deiter spoke slowly now. His voice was almost inaudible.

"I just—I got out of the car, went back to use the radio in mine. Left the door open. And . . ."

He started shaking his head.

"As soon as I got out, it was like somewhere inside her this—this switch flips, and she stops crying just for a moment and looks at me, really knowing-like. I swear to Christ it was the saddest face I've seen in my entire life. . . . And then she did it. . . . She drove over."

"You didn't call it in," said Billi, accusingly.

"By the time I got back to my car someone who lives up the bluff had already done that so I sat there; tried to figure out what do to next. I didn't know what to do. So I radioed back and said I was responding."

"You covered it up," said Billi.

"I wasn't sure what had really happened," he said. "I still thought it was you who killed Moylan."

"But she confessed! Sandy confessed!" said Billi.

"She said she felt responsible!" said Deiter. "It couldn't have been her. And I never even thought it could have been Will. He would have had to have known about Chucky to do the same thing to Moylan. I thought it was you!"

"And now?" she asked.

He stared back at her, pondering her words.

"Billi," he said. "You're going to come out of this all right. That gun still can't be linked to you, not with what Will has admitted, with what I have admitted—setting you up, being with Sandy, lying about all of it. There's no way you can be prosecuted for what happened to Tommy Moylan."

He motioned at the bloody knife in her hand.

"As for that," he said, "I'll drive you down to the station myself and we'll explain it."

"And you?"

"My days as a cop are done."

"And Will—he just walks away."

"He's not walking anywhere," said Deiter. "We know right where he is."

"I didn't kill anybody," I said.

Her hand tightened on the knife.

"Worry about yourself here, Billi," said Deiter quickly. "Everything else will shake out."

Billi stared, her hand still clutching the knife, shivering in anger and indecision, saying nothing, looking from Deiter to me, then back again, motionless for an eternity.

Until, finally, she dropped it.

40.

I thought about killing Tommy Moylan. I would not be telling you the truth if I did not tell you that. Thought about it in the fleeting and self-indulgent way any husband might. I also imagined briefly, when I found the gun, that Sandy might have done it—though that was less a realistic possibility then the fantasy of a spouse wronged. No, anyone who knew Sandy knew, from the beginning, she did not have that in her. Sandy was not perfect, but she was good and decent and the most trusting of all of us. That was what made her vulnerable.

When Sandy got to the barn—rattled already by the realization that she had lost the one thing she wanted more than any other, our baby—she found something totally unexpected, and yet totally believable. And her world just erupted. She found Tommy Moylan lying there, the gun next to him, and in a split second she lost everything: faith in the past, faith in Billi Stroud, whom she knew had killed Chucky Ware in the same way, faith in herself and what still could have been. She came to the same logical conclusion Deiter would, that the killer was Billi. And she panicked.

How to reconcile her inclination to help Moylan, for I am sure it existed, and yet also help Billi, I cannot say, except that Sandy was full always of competing impulses. She cleaned up and took the gun and went back to the one place she thought she could go—the Cross House. But she came to realize when she got there, I suspect, that it could not be her refuge. For whatever comforts those walls offered they contained, too, a history of honesty. For Sandy, in the end anyway, it always came down to that.

Of Tommy Moylan's character there is less to say and I will tell you that he was not a victim absolute and pure. He had his sins, though not so many as I once thought. No, somebody else, it became clear, placed the pot in the van and the Saturn and that same somebody called the police; knew that Billi would call Sandy when she was arrested and taken to jail; knew from Sandy where Billi had put the gun and that Sandy would go to retrieve it and stumble upon Moylan's body. Knew exactly what had happened with Chucky Ware and Sandy's part in that. Knew all about Sandy and Tommy Moylan, and no doubt tried to make sure I knew it as well by, so much earlier, sending that anonymous picture in the mail. Knew, finally, that once Sandy found the body and the gun, there were many ways it could have ended, but none that could bring anything but trouble to Sandy, and none that would point easily to the real killer. That much could be predicted.

Some things, however, cannot be predicted, small things, details, and there are always some of those: acts of kindness or generosity that are really sort of surprising given all else. Like Tommy Moylan offering Billi his van when it had been so certain, so logical, that she would simply take the Saturn, her car, and drive off into what she only thought was the unknown.

Or Tommy's unimagined gift, long before, of his old tools, which should really have been there, just sitting there still in the barn in the minutes after Tommy Moylan had been shot. But, of course, they were not, and that was bad luck of the damning sort. And so the pot that had been placed in the Saturn door, in Billi's car, just in case that was the car Billi took, had to be left there because there was no way for the murderer to get it out quickly. The killer planned to remove it, along with the joint in the ashtray, if the opportunity arose at some later time.

It was all there still in that car that last night just waiting for the police to discover it, and look further, wonder about things, piece it all together. If they did not find the proof that Billi had been set up, surely Billi Stroud would find it herself.

After that, the judgments would be easy—though not all of them.

Let me tell you this, and you can judge for yourself. I loved Sandy. And I know in my heart that she loved me. I hated what she did with Tommy Moylan. It hurt me beyond expression. But I loved her even at the end, maybe especially at the end, when I felt that the question was not so much whether I forgave her as whether she forgave me. For what I had become. For what I lacked. For not knowing what love was. That is the realization that came to me. It was a fact and I could almost see it hang there in the dark night air, bright as a star, so bright that I felt as if everyone else could see it as well.

And that's the thing, I guess. Sometimes you just wait and see and things become apparent. The future comes to you, or doesn't. Answers appear, or don't. Sometimes all you have to do—all you can do—is stay awake and try to recognize the evil. Even as it immerses you. Be vigilant when everything is quiet, and the world is asleep.

For that, I tell myself, is where all this begins and ends, really, with love, or what in our minds often passes for it. We are all capable of deluding ourselves for love, are we not? And we are all capable of deluding others for the same.

The truth is I lay awake for several hours that evening after Billi dropped the knife and was taken away—my final waking. And up to that point, when I finally rose up in the darkness and moved to the window, I had my own faith about what had been. For I did not kill Tommy Moylan. And I had, too, my own hopes about what might be. You see, I wanted to believe in coincidences and ironies; I wanted to believe in love. I wanted to believe that the thing for which Haley yearned was someone to love and hold her tight for the truest and best of reasons: for who she was, rather than who she was not. Not someone rich enough to ignore money and billable hours, not someone beautiful and funny and carefree enough to cause two men to profess their everlasting love to her, not someone fortunate enough to realize her greatest dreams of being a mother. For Haley, I believe knew nothing, till that last night, of Sandy's miscarriage.

Yes, I wanted to believe, and maybe did, right up to that moment when Haley, having left the bed and slipped downstairs, emerged from the shadows of the back door, a yellow screwdriver in her hand, and moved quick as a thief, silent and alone underneath all the brightest stars and distant planets, toward Billi Stroud's car parked at the end of that driveway.

And when she returned, having removed the evidence from that car, I did not dream. I simply lay there with Haley next to me, her head on my shoulder until her breathing got deep and steady—until, as had always been the way with Sandy, she rolled onto her back, her hair glistening with the moonlight, the scent of spearmint on her breath.

Haley slept well, and deeply, upon Sandy's pillow, unperturbed by whatever it was—a hint of perfume perhaps, maybe something more immutable and basic—that lingered there. Sandy, I suppose Haley could tell herself, had sealed her own fate. And who could prove, or even suspect, it to be otherwise?

Certainly—Haley might have figured from the first—not the police.

Haley could have surmised from the very beginning that killing Sandy outright and ending up with everything she had would have been far too obvious.

There was, I think, however, much more to it than that.

Maybe, as I look back on it now, what Haley desired was simply all that Sandy did—nothing more or less. If you asked her if she hated Sandy, I am quite sure she would have said she loved her. If you asked her if she admired Sandy, she might have said assuredly so. But there were things she loved and admired more—the possessions, the marriage, the very life that Sandy had.

I sometimes suspect that Haley wanted me to know what she had done, that she needed me to accept it and how she'd gone about it, that if she had turned around and seen me in that window that night it would have scared her—but thrilled her as well. We were, after all, to her way of thinking, much the same. Much of what she'd done, I suspect she told herself, she'd done for me.

As for me, I still can't say for sure where love separates from envy, and where envy turns to malice, only that it seems possible to find yourself passed, if you are not careful, from one to another without being sure, in the end, how you ever got there.

"I love you, Will," Haley whispered as she went.

I lay there silent for a long, long moment, awake as I would ever be—then felt myself move close against her in the cold night air.

acknowledgments

I am truly a novice at this book writing thing, a fact to which everyone involved in this venture can attest. My brother Brian, my mom, and my friends Tom Seymour and Andy Ritten all read early drafts and kept the snickering to a minimum. Each gave good advice and great encouragement. My colleague and buddy Meg Kissinger was unjustifiably enthusiastic and kind enough to hook me up with Mike Ruby. Mike, a busy man who didn't know me from Adam, took the time to read the manuscript and pass it along to two of the best agents and wisest readers in New York, Flip Brophy and Jody Hotchkiss. Carolyn Marino, my editor at HarperCollins, took me under her wing, gave me the benefit of her judgment, and gently coaxed me into making this a far, far better story. Marty Kaiser, the editor of the *Milwaukee Journal Sentinel,* gave me the flexibility and the support to finish what had been started.

To all of them, I am indebted.

Finally, and most important, there is Jane, my wife and my very best friend. Writing a book is a quixotic endeavor—especially when there are diapers to be changed and walls to be painted. It was Jane who, juggling the demands of her own career with everything else, made this book possible.